Mutts Murder and Mayhem

Ellen Gilman

Print ISBN: 979-8-35092-060-4

eBook ISBN: 979-8-35092-061-1

One

Daisy's left hand ached—a lot. A ninety-five-page deposition had taken her all afternoon to mark up. She shook her wrist and tried to loosen up her fingers. Only seventeen pages left. So much for the felt tip pen she was using. Even it was giving out on her.

She leaned back in her desk chair and swiveled around to look out her one small window. It was already dusk. The streetlights flipped on.

That did it for her. She was done. There was always tomorrow. She really needed to get home. Max, the rough collie she was dog sitting for her neighbor, was waiting for her.

She grabbed her crossbody bag off the chair arm just as her cell vibrated, the sound of quacking ducks spewing from the speaker. *Darn.* It was her mother's silly ringtone. She had to answer. She pivoted back around and tapped on the speaker.

"Hi, Mom."

Her mom sounded exasperated. "Daisy, you won't believe what I did. I—"

The door to her office opened. She looked up in surprise as her dad's voice boomed. "Daisy, I need your help."

This was not a good scenario.

Now she'd have to deal with her dad—who was also her boss—and her mom at the same time.

She took a deep breath and let it out slowly.

"Mom, hang on just a minute."

Daisy winced at her error. She shouldn't have let her dad know she was talking to her mom.

Now she'd be lucky if he didn't make some snide comment. Her parents had redefined the term "bitter divorce" when she was eleven.

Oh well. Too late now.

Without saying anything, she patted her dad's forearm and pointed with her index finger to the chair across from her desk. He scowled before he turned his back on her and sat.

Thankfully he kept quiet.

Her office was small with not much room for privacy, so she moved out the door to her assistant's space and spoke softly. "I'm back, Mom, but I only have a minute. Your voice was cutting out before. Start over."

She wanted to be home. Instead, she had to deal with her parents.

Her mom sounded panicked. "I'm trying to tell you. I broke my wrist. The Fur-Baby Gala is this weekend, and I'm the one who's supposed to decorate and do the flowers."

Daisy was trying to process her mom's words while hearing her dad's foot tapping incessantly. He could be demanding.

"There's no way to replace me so close to the event." Sounding wretched, her mom said, "I could use your help."

Daisy let out a sigh. Her mom wanted her to come to Houndsville. How would she ever manage that with her big trial starting Monday? Nothing like pitting her parents against each other. What a mess.

"Mom. I just don't know how to answer you right now. I'm so sorry. I gotta go. I'll call you back as soon as I can." And she would, as soon as she could come up with a solution.

She instantly felt bad about hanging up so abruptly, but when she glanced at her watch, she saw it was even later than she'd realized. Instantly her stomach knotted up. She had an even more pressing matter to think about right now—getting her dad out of the office so she could get home to Max.

Deep breath, Daisy. She walked over and perched on the edge of her desk. "What's up, Dad?"

"Can I see the Forester file? But first, what did your mom want?"

She shrugged, refusing to answer him, and stood up to walk over to the credenza behind her desk. It took her a minute of fumbling around to find the file he'd requested and hand it to him.

Rather than continuing to stand, she sat in her desk chair and watched him go through page by page as if he was looking for something specific.

It was agonizing.

If only she could tell him she had to get home—but he wouldn't understand. She had to restrain herself from tapping her fingers on her desk and telling him to hurry up.

Instead, she stuffed a handful of chocolate buds in her mouth, hopefully surreptitiously, and tried not to fidget. He'd make a negative comment if she did.

Twenty-forever minutes later, he closed the file. "I was looking to see if I could find where the opposing attorney made a mistake on citing a particular case. Could you do some additional research?"

"Sure, Dad. I can work tonight and have the file back to you tomorrow." She happily agreed—anything to leave, to get to Max. She stood up and grabbed her blazer off the back of the chair.

Her dad got the hint and stood up. "The sooner, the better." He left, and she let out a huge sigh of relief.

At least he hadn't asked again about her mom.

She felt like a hot, sweaty mess after the back and forth with her parents and didn't even bother to slip on her jacket, although she suspected the late-fall night might be chilly, the sun gone for the day. All she wanted was to get home. She tossed the Forester file into her tote bag and rushed to the garage to her SUV.

Poor Max. He's stuck waiting for me. She imagined him standing by her door with a forlorn expression in his huge brown eyes, wondering why no one had come to walk him.

The drive home, through D.C. to her apartment in Woodley Park, normally took about seventeen minutes, less time if she lucked out and the five traffic lights were green. Today she spent that time thinking about how she'd be able to satisfy both parents and wondering why they couldn't get along. Why did everything to do with them have to be so traumatic?

There was no way she could go to Houndsville, a small town on the Eastern Shore of Maryland, and help her mom when she had this huge case starting Monday. Clearly her dad, a workaholic and a perfectionist, would expect her to be available over the weekend for any last-minute concerns. Was there any way to persuade him she needed to help her mom?

If she were a gambler, she'd give herself odds of one in a hundred.

On the other side, her mom would be understanding if she was unable to come. But she would like to help, and the prospect of leaving her mom with no help did not make Daisy feel better.

Darn it! She couldn't see any easy way out. There was only one thing she could think to do.

Her best friend, Meghan, would have a good answer for her.

The phone jingled. "Hi, it's Meghan. I can't get to the phone. Leave a message. I'll call you back."

"Meg, it's Daisy. I have a humongous problem. I could use some lifesaving advice." Daisy paused, and then before she ended the call, she decided to catch Meghan off guard and said, "And guess who's dog sitting?" She chuckled.

"You can shut your mouth now. Bye."

A minute later, she could see her building up ahead.

Finally! Home sweet home. Now just let Max be okay.

She pulled into her parking space, grabbed her handbag off the passenger seat, and sprinted into the smallish brick building she called home.

Just another minute, Max, and I'll be there.

She had to wait for the slowpoke elevator when all she wanted was to get to Max. It finally came, and she pressed the button for the second floor and scrambled around in her purse for her key.

When the elevator doors opened, she sprinted down the hallway, stuck her key in the lock, and turned the doorknob. She flung open the door and looked right at Max, sitting perched on her sofa as if he had been waiting for her. He stared at her.

Feeling guilty for having left him so long, she ran over to him, flung her arms around his neck, and nuzzled his fur with her nose. "Max, I am so sorry I'm late. Let's take a nice, long walk."

She ran her hands back and forth over his fur before she stood up and walked to her closet to find her windbreaker. Max jumped down from the sofa and followed behind her to the kitchen where she grabbed his leash and a fistful of peanut M&M's from a bowl on the counter. She could munch on them while they walked. Her dinner would have to wait until she'd taken care of Max.

"Okay, Max. Let's go walk."

That's all he needed to hear. He tugged her toward the door, and the twosome headed out on a walk around the neighborhood.

The wind had picked up, and with it being dark and getting colder, Daisy was glad her windbreaker had a hood. If only she had brought gloves. Her hands and toes always got cold first.

They meandered around the block as Max sniffed and peed on what seemed like every bush. One other person passed by walking their dog, a black lab, but other than that, the street was deserted. Most likely everyone wanted to snuggle inside on this chilly night.

Back inside her apartment, she fed Max and microwaved a small frozen pizza for herself, sharing a piece of crust with him. Usually she'd watch the news while she ate, but she'd arrived home so late tonight the news was over, so she opened her computer to do the research for her dad.

An hour later, the work successfully completed, she ditched her phone on the night table beside her bed, fluffed up her pillows, and plopped down to watch TV. Max jumped up and laid his head on her leg. A stray thought entered her head as she petted him.

I'll miss him when he's gone.

She breathed deeply, her eyes drifting shut until her cell pinged, startling her.

She scrambled to reach it, but it fell on the floor.

Darn. She leaned down to pick it up and looked at the screen. It was Meghan FaceTiming her. Quickly she swiped it to the right to accept the call and sat back on her bed.

"Hi, Meg."

She didn't get to continue.

Meghan hollered, "Flowers, what do you mean you're dog sitting? How is that possible? You always complain you work too many hours to have a dog. And where is he?"

Daisy chuckled softly. She loved Meghan calling her by her last name.

"Hang on, here he is." Daisy held her phone so Meghan could see Max sleeping next to her before she continued. "Yes, I do work seriously long hours, but Lisa couldn't find a dog sitter to come right away. She begged me by playing on my emotions." Daisy stroked Max. "Max is seven and has never been boarded before and might get sick in a strange place. How could I turn her down? Besides, it's only until Friday."

"He's gorgeous."

"Yes, and super sweet too." Daisy pulled her comforter over her legs and scrunched down deeper into her pillows.

"But listen, I really do have a huge problem. We have this huge trial starting Monday and my mom fell and—"

"Stop right there." Meghan held up her hand. "I just got off the phone with Millie. She called to tell me about your mom. She feels responsible."

"Why? Was it Millie's fault?"

"No, but Millie persuaded your mom to foster a dog, and she slipped—"

"Hey. Wait up. What do you mean my mom is fostering a dog? That's why she fell? How come she didn't mention it to me?"

"Come on, Flowers," Meghan said kindly. "She remembers how much you wanted a dog as a kid, and she and your dad never let you have one. Telling you she has a dog now would have been an issue. But what's the problem here? Come help your mom Friday and Saturday and go back to D.C. on Sunday. You'll be back in time for the trial."

"I'm not sure that would work. "Do you remember me talking about a huge pharmaceutical case? Well, the trial starts Monday. We have a dinner meeting on Thursday night, and I'm sure the team will be working all day Friday and through the weekend. My dad has me preparing a key witness."

Daisy could picture Meghan running her fingers through her hair. "Yikes, I can see how that might be a problem. That's a big deal."

"Yup, that's why I don't see how I can make it work to leave." She patted Max. "And I have this big guy to take care of, although Lisa is supposed to be back Friday."

"So what if you come late Friday and leave first thing Sunday morning? I'm sure that would still be a big help to your mom."

Daisy sighed deeply. "I can try talking to my dad. When it comes to my mom, he can be particularly tough."

"You work tirelessly for your dad. Maybe he'll surprise you."

"Doubtful." She frowned. "I'll text you his response. But hey, before we hang up, tell me about my mom's foster."

Meghan lowered her eyes, choosing her words carefully. "Millie said she was walking a new rescue and stopped in your mom's shop to pick up some flowers for a friend. Seems your mom was smitten with Sidney."

"My mom smitten with a dog? That's a switch," Daisy said.

"Be nice. That's Millie's story. He's this tiny sheltie. Weighs about fourteen pounds and has the cutest little face. Millie happened to mention the local sheltie rescue was in dire need of foster parents. Next thing you know, your mom is fostering."

"And you know this, how?" Daisy asked while feeling a twinge of sadness. Now that she was grown, her mom finally got a dog. Why not when she was a kid and begged for one?

"Millie called to tell Samantha, who told me."

Daisy wondered why Samantha had been so quick to tell Meghan but Meghan had not called to tell her, but of course she knew the answer. Meghan was concerned she'd react just like she had—badly.

"Millie loves to tout her successes with finding homes for her group's rescues. Remember I told you Samantha got caught in Millie's crosshairs when Bailey and Berry needed a home, and now she thinks it's amusing when Millie finds a new target. Anyone who doesn't have a dog is on Millie's list as a possible adopter."

Meghan sighed. "Maybe you should move here. Millie will make sure you have a dog of your own in no time."

Daisy laughed.

"I'm serious. I haven't wanted to say anything, but you seem stressed lately. You're on a path to becoming a great lawyer, but something appears to be going wrong. I'm not sure what it is, but if the work environment is not good, you could move here. You can open your own law office or find something else to do if the law is not for you." Meghan paused. "As to your parents never letting you have a dog, that's old news. Get over it. Focus on the issue at hand. Your mom is stuck. With the gala in a few days, there's no way to find another florist—at least not one who is as talented as she is."

"Well, it'd be useless to have my sister help. Her math skills may be phenomenal, but asking her to arrange flowers is a joke."

"So I'll say it again, come," Meghan replied softly.

"Got it. I'll call you when I know what's going on." Daisy waved goodbye and ended the call.

Two

Millie Whitfield sat with her elbows on the kitchen table, her head resting on her clasped hands. The multi-colored fall leaves drifting to the ground outside her patio door went unnoticed. Even the presence of her two beloved shelties, Luke and Annie, sitting under the table didn't divert her.

The third annual Fur-Baby Gala was in three days, and as chairperson, her job was to see that everything went smoothly.

And it had been going perfectly well until last night when Frannie Flowers, the florist, called to report she wouldn't be at the planning committee meeting this morning. She'd fallen and broken her wrist.

Now Millie was too antsy to sit at home. She needed to talk to Samantha, her cochair for the event, whom she knew would already be at work at the Buckshead Inn, the site for the gala and this morning's final planning meeting.

She grabbed her handbag off the counter and went to pick up her notes for the meeting when she realized she'd left them at the bakery. *Darn!* Now she would need to stop there first. She headed out to her garage.

It took about fifteen minutes to drive through tree-lined streets to get to Houndsville Commons, the center of town. She parked in her usual spot near her own business, The Best Doggone Bakery,

"Good morning, everyone." Millie tapped the spoon she'd picked up against her coffee mug, using it to get everyone's attention.

Everyone looked toward her and smiled—everyone, that is, except Annabel, the owner of Annabel's Coffee and Tea Emporium, who sat with her usual pinched expression.

Darn!

She was probably waiting to make trouble. What a miserable person.

The seat next to Annabel was empty. Most likely she planned to have her coconspirator, Betsy Carlson, sit there. The two of them enjoyed creating discord.

Millie looked around the table. "If anyone wants something to eat or drink, please get it now. I'd like to get the meeting started."

Grace and Karen took Millie up on her suggestion. Millie waited for them to take their seats before beginning.

"Okay. Let's get right to business."

Millie rifled through her handbag to find her notes, looking up as Betsy Clarkson pranced in on four-inch stilettos. She was overdressed in a black tailored suit and carried an expensive designer handbag. Her short dark hair was styled in a sophisticated bob, and around her neck was a double strand of huge pearls. She looked ready for the gala, not a committee meeting.

She waved before slipping into the empty seat next to Annabel.

"Glad you could make it," Millie said, gritting her teeth.

Betsy shrugged. "I'm here. That's all that matters."

A few months back, Betsy had approached Millie and Samantha with the promise of a large donation and asked to be on the planning committee for the gala. This was a conundrum for them. They wanted the money, but Betsy had a horrible reputation.

Last year, she'd bred her merle collie to another merle collie, and the results had been understandably catastrophic. Cleo's two puppies had been born blind and deaf. To make matters worse, once Betsy discovered their genetic abnormalities, she'd planned to have them euthanized. Meghan and Nicholas had intervened and saved them.

Even if Betsy had mended her ways, which they doubted, Millie and Samantha had still been hesitant to put her on the committee. They'd told her they were happy to accept her donation but didn't need any more committee members.

Betsy had been resolute. Her money had strings attached. Spread the word that she was a benefactor and put her on the planning committee or forego her gift.

They should have realized that spelled trouble, but the donation was huge and they'd assumed they could handle her.

Every meeting she'd attended had proven to be contentious. This one would most likely follow that pattern.

"All right. I'll try to start again."

Millie glared pointedly at Betsy before continuing.

"You all might have noticed Frannie is not here. Yesterday afternoon, she fell and broke her wrist.

"Oh no, that's awful." A few members chimed in together.

"Yes, it is. And awful timing for all of us," Millie said. "As you can imagine, this will make it impossible for her to do her job. She's asked her daughters who both live out of town for their help, and I was hoping she'd make it to this meeting to let me know if they're coming. She's probably resting." Millie looked around the table. "We might need volunteers. Would anyone here be able to help?"

Betsy smacked her hands on the table, and her diamond tennis bracelet flew off her wrist. She grabbed it back, muttering under her breath, "Figures he bought a cheap one," before responding to Millie. "Oh, that's just super. We've already paid Frannie, and now you're asking us to do our own flowers. That's ridiculous!"

"Stop complaining, Betsy," Grace said. "Let's try to work this out."

Betsy scowled. "What if her kids don't come? I've been generous with donations to support your event. I even bought tickets for my sister and friends, and now it could turn out to be a dud."

"Stop whining," Bridget muttered before adding, "What friends?"

Millie clenched her teeth. This was going from bad to worse. She tried diplomacy. "Samantha and I will be helping. Betsy, if you're so worried you could volunteer too."

"No way," Betsy continued to protest. "I've donated enough money to help you." Millie noted the humongous sapphire on Betsy's hand. Her donation was quite large and presumably a drop in the bucket for her.

"I'm not helping either," Annabel said, shaking her head. "Millie, you can solve this problem by yourself."

"I hate to say this, but you two are awful," Julie fumed. "This is for a great cause, and we need to work together."

Millie and Samantha exchanged a glance. In the past, Annabel hadn't had anyone who agreed with her on the committee. Now she had Betsy as a coconspirator.

Fortunately the other committee members agreed with Samantha and Millie and helped to rein in the troublemakers.

Millie shook her head. She wished she'd never allowed Betsy on the committee. Her constant complaints were wearing them out.

As for Annabel, in the beginning Millie had felt obligated to put her on the committee. Annabel's Coffee and Tea Emporium was a fixture in Houndsville, and they had needed all the shopkeepers to pitch in for the first Gala. The problem was Annabel despised Millie for outsmarting her and getting Christopher's farmhouse for her bakery when Annabel had wanted it for herself. Now she made it her mission to cause trouble for Millie.

"Okay everyone, enough," Millie said loudly.

"We'll wait to see if Frannie's kids come. I should know later today. In the meantime, this is our last meeting before the gala. We need to finalize everything else."

She paused briefly to sip her coffee and review her notes.

"As you know, this year we've added a silent auction. Our shopkeepers and even our local veterinarian have contributed items. Some of them are spectacular."

Millie read off her list.

"Thanks go to Harper McNeely, who has agreed to do a commissioned dog portrait."

"Wow! That's really special," Bridget said as everyone else nodded.

"Julie designed a lovely pendant."

This got the group talking among themselves. Julie's designs were very popular.

Millie went on to explain. "Julie's pendant is an eighteen-karat gold two-inch heart-shaped medallion with a large diamond-encrusted paw print in the center. And to help raise more money, since there is only one of those, Julie has designed a smaller one-inch heart-shaped medallion to be sold at her store. Those she is selling for three hundred and fifty dollars. And for each one sold, she will be donating fifty dollars."

The group nodded appreciatively at Julie.

"To continue, Bridget has gotten on board too. Her item is a group of dog books by various authors. Among the offerings she's donating from her personal collection several books by Albert Payson Terhune, author of *Lad A Dog*. Lastly she has the author of *Mollie's Tail*, a book about a rescued sheltie, coming to do a book signing a week from Sunday. A portion of her sales will be donated to our foundation."

"Oh, come on Millie, you're wasting time. We all need to get to our shops," Annabel huffed.

Millie ignored that comment. "Now to some smaller items. I have donated a five-hundred-dollar gift certificate worth a years' supply of dog treats at my very own Best Doggone Bakery. Colin, Stella, and Grace also donated large gift certificates."

Before Millie could say anything more, Annabel shouted nastily, "Figures, you're promoting your bakery."

"Annabel, I don't have the patience for whatever drama you're trying to stir up this morning."

Everyone looked uncomfortable even though they were used to Millie and Annabel's constant bickering.

Millie, for her part, sipped her coffee and carried on as if nothing out of the ordinary had occurred. Truth was, her stomach was in knots. Annabel managed to get under her skin every time she opened her mouth. Hopefully she hadn't forgotten anyone's donation in the process.

She took a deep breath and persevered. "Also, as we've done for past galas, many of our local shopkeepers will be donating a percentage of their sales for the week prior to the gala. This year all those who participate will be recognized in *The Houndsville Times* paper, and I will personally thank them at the gala when I give my yearly speech."

Millie sat up straighter and moved on to the next item on her agenda. "This next idea was Colin's—and a fun one, I might add," she said, smiling at him. "He's found someone with horse drawn carriages and is willing to take people on a lovely ride around Houndsville for fifty dollars. The entire fee will be donated to our foundation."

"Wow! I'd like to do that. Great suggestion, Colin," Julie said.

Millie put down her notes. "I'm done, but please make sure you tell all your friends to buy tickets to the gala and to support the local businesses who have so kindly helped us."

Millie nodded at Samantha. "Your turn."

Samantha leaned forward.

"I have one issue to cover. Several months ago, *Leisurely Living Magazine* did a spread on small towns in the USA. Houndsville was one of them, and according to their editor the article was well received. As a follow-up, they are sending back their top photographer, Vince Cordoza, who will be here this weekend to do a story on the Fur-Baby Gala, our foundation, and the good work we've accomplished for our community. Prior to the gala, they'll be taking photos and talking to people about places of interest."

Annabel slammed her hand on the table, imitating Betsy. "This is a small town. People won't like having their pictures taken."

"Annabel, you can't know that, and stop imitating Betsy," Millie snapped. "I thought I was clear before. I'll try again. Keep quiet if you have nothing positive to say."

"Annabel has a point." Betsy scowled. "I got to know that photographer the last time he was here. He's sleazy. He gets in people's faces. No one will want their picture taken by him."

"You say you got to know him? And what does that mean, exactly?" Samantha scoffed.

"None of your business," Betsy replied, her eyes boring into Samantha's.

Samantha's tone was withering. "Well, then thank goodness this is not your decision to make. Having *Leisurely Living Magazine* do a spread on Houndsville was great publicity for our town, and maybe other towns will be inspired by our idea for the Fur-Baby Gala."

"You mean publicity for your inn," Betsy mumbled under her breath.

"I heard that." Samantha's eyes narrowed to slits. "If you have a problem with their photographer, stay away from him. Am I clear?"

Betsy crossed her arms and glared at Samantha. "I gave you a huge donation. You should treat me better."

"You know what? I'm tired of hearing about your huge donation. Millie and I thought you were trying to make up for your past indiscretions. Now we know better."

Betsy turned her attention to Millie, glaring at her.

"You're the one who's going to be sorry. I'll not only stop my donations, I'll tell everyone in this stupid town of yours that I'm convinced you're funneling money meant for the foundation to your own failing bakery. See where that gets you."

Everyone gasped. Millie jumped to her feet. "How dare you! You know none of that's true."

"Do I? Anything is possible, and I'm sure I will find some believers."

Millie balled her hands into fists. "Is that a threat, Betsy?" Millie gritted her teeth and ground out, "You'd better make sure of your facts before you spread a wild rumor like that. It could land you in big trouble."

Samantha clapped her hands. "Betsy, enough with your threats." She glanced around the table. "Does anyone have anything to add before we adjourn?"

Millie plopped back down in her chair. "I do."

She fumed. Betsy had totally sidetracked her with her threats. Now she had something to say, and she grappled with the right words to express herself.

Everyone but Annabel and Betsy looked directly at her and nodded encouragingly.

She folded her hands in front of her. "It's been wonderful working together again to bring about our third annual Fur-Baby Gala. Most of you have stood steadfastly by me in this endeavor that is so dear to my heart. I owe you a debt of gratitude."

She breathed in deeply. She knew she should have left off the "most" in her comment, but she couldn't help herself. She hated Betsy and the way she used her money to manipulate people into doing her bidding. And she hated Annabel for being a constant thorn in her side.

She glanced around at everyone. "Together, we have changed many dogs' lives forever. It's something I'm very proud of, and I'm looking forward to continuing this tradition and to raising a lot of money Saturday night."

She smiled broadly. "But above all, we've worked hard to make this event successful, so let's have fun."

Millie surveyed her committee as just about everyone clapped resoundingly before standing up to leave. She refused to allow the two who didn't totally support her to bring her down and wondered once again why they were even here.

"Hey Samantha, can we talk?" Millie asked once everyone else had left the room.

"Sure. Let me grab a cup of coffee, and we can sit in my office."

"Sounds good," Millie said as she refilled her mug. They walked back into Samantha's office, and before they even sat down Millie blurted out, "How long do you think Betsy has been planning to drop that bombshell about me? If she carries out her threat, it could dissuade people from making donations at the gala."

Samantha shook her head. "I agree it's really bad that she's threatened you and the foundation."

Millie plopped down in one of the chairs by the window. "I'll have to figure out what I can do about it. I can't allow her to go around saying things like that. It'll ruin all my efforts to raise money."

Samantha ran her fingers around the rim of her coffee cup. "I know you'll figure it out. By the way, did you hear her muttering when her bracelet fell off? I wonder who gave it to her? Do you think it could have been Vince? She implied something had gone on with him."

Millie paused. "Maybe, but I could swear I've seen her wear it before. Doesn't matter anyway. She's a horrible human being, and I wish we'd never seen the likes of her."

Samantha tapped her fingers on her coffee mug. "Agreed. We knew she was despicable when she wanted to put those precious puppies to sleep. It was her big donation that blinded us, and we fell into her trap. Now she has us exactly where she wants us."

Millie frowned. "I'm afraid you're right."

Three

"Take a deep breath," Daisy mumbled as she walked purposely to her dad's office. It was still early. She should be able to catch him.

His assistant wasn't at her desk, and his inner office door was open. Her dad stood with his back to her, facing his bank of windows. He had his phone up to his ear.

"Dad," she said softly as she rapped on the door frame.

He turned around and glared at her while waving his hands as if to shoo her out. Obviously he didn't intend to talk to her.

Bummed out, she left.

She'd made an effort to be at the office early to find out how he felt about her going to Houndsville. Now she had no idea. And she had nothing to tell her mom, who was waiting for her call.

She wasn't sure when she would get another chance to talk to him. She knew he had back-to-back meetings lined up for the next several days.

Now he'd probably be annoyed with her for barging into his inner sanctum. She'd had no choice. Her mom was waiting to hear from her. She'd have to try again late in the afternoon when he usually returned to the office.

She headed toward her office, feeling stressed. The morning was not going as planned. She'd shortened Max's walk to get to the office early to talk to her dad. And now she had nothing to tell her mom. Only one thing would make her feel better. Chocolate.

Her chocolate buds were somewhere in her top desk drawer. She rummaged around until she found the super-sized bag she kept for emergencies. Peeling the silver foil was a bother, but once she popped a few in her mouth, she felt better.

Taking a few minutes before she started working, she swiveled her chair around to gaze out her small office window to the courtyard below.

Mostly what she saw were small bushes. She had a view of one maple tree, which she watched change with the seasons. Today some of its red leaves swirled around and drifted to the ground. Fall had her vote for favorite season, although winter, if it snowed, played a close second.

Startled by a knock on her door, she flipped her chair around as Edward strolled into her office for his daily morning chitchat and tossed *The Wall Street Journal* onto her messy desk. She smiled, happy to see him.

Today he was wearing slate gray trousers, a tattersall shirt with the sleeves rolled up, and a royal blue tie. His dark shaggy hair, always messy like it had never been professionally cut, and his blue eyes, set off by incredibly long lashes never failed to make her heart beat just a tad faster.

"Good morning, sunshine." His eyes focused on her. "How do you manage to look so ravishing this early?"

"Don't even bother to lie," she murmured. She never looked good first thing in the morning, and especially not today. She hadn't taken time to control her wayward blonde curls, and in her rush to speak to her dad, she'd forgotten to put on eyeliner and lipstick. But he was a drop-dead gorgeous ten even on his worst day.

While he walked over and looked out her window, she attempted to sweep her pile of chocolate buds under a file and wondered why his intimate teasing always managed to unsettle her.

The day they'd met, she'd found him irresistible and pretty much made a fool of herself. Nowadays, they talked every day, bantering back and forth, but she was still waiting for him to make a move to become romantically linked with her.

"Hey," Edward, said tapping her arm. "Earth to Daisy?"

"I'm here. Just thinking. I have a few things to tell you," she fibbed. She'd never admit to Edward her daydreaming was often about him.

"Unless it's urgent it will have to wait. Come on. The staff meeting starts at nine." Edward held up his left hand and pointed to his watch.

"Well, it is kind of important. Sit. We have almost half an hour. I need to talk to you."

She took a deep breath. She was pretty sure she knew what his reaction would be after she told him she wanted to go to Houndsville.

"O…kay. This sounds serious." He dropped down into the black leather armchair and slid his hand across her desk. Then with a grand flourish, he uncovered her messy stash of silver foil and peeled a chocolate bud before popping it into his mouth.

"Seriously, you didn't think I saw this? Chocolate so early in the morning? Daisy, what's up? Is it the upcoming trial? Are you worried about Corinne trying to upstage you?" He shook his head. "She considers herself exceptional, but she isn't nearly as good a lawyer as you are. We did that mock witness interview, and you were fantastic."

Hmmm. She'd always wondered if Edward might be attracted to Corinne, with her model-thin body, slicked-back blonde hair, and inscrutable brown eyes. Compared to Daisy's wayward curly blonde hair, turned up nose, blue-gray eyes, and a body that was in her mind too boyish—no boobs and no curves—Corrine's attractiveness was undeniable.

But it didn't appear Edward thought much of Corinne. That was great news. If someone was going to catch Edward, it had better be her. Besides, personally she despised Corinne. She treated everyone with disdain and seemed to believe she could manipulate anyone around her. She was one of the major reasons for Daisy's unhappiness at the firm.

She tilted her head and raised an eyebrow. "Wow. You're being particularly complimentary today."

He shrugged. "You seem uncharacteristically gloomy. I needed to see your usual sunny smile."

She gave him a fake toothy grin and chuckled as he nabbed a few more chocolate buds for himself.

Her dad was not one for compliments, and knowing Edward thought highly of her work was wonderful, but she needed to get back to the matter at hand. She swallowed past the lump in her throat, speaking quickly.

"My mom called. She broke her wrist. Problem is, she's in charge of the flowers and decor for the Fur-Baby Gala this weekend in Houndsville."

"Stop right now," Edward said, holding up his hand. "I know where you're going with this. My answer is unequivocally no. You cannot leave here to go help her."

She popped another bud in her mouth, allowing it to melt in her mouth before responding. "What if I drove there late on Friday and came back early Sunday morning?"

Edward shook his head. "I'm sorry. I still say no. You know your dad will want to work all weekend to make sure the team is ready for trial. Good luck with telling him you won't be here."

Daisy rolled her eyes. "I know. I got here extra early and tried to catch him before he got busy. No luck. He waved me out of his office before I could open my mouth. My plan is to try again later."

"Why can't your sister help?" he asked, staring at her.

"Umm…she's not really the creative type."

"And you are?" He snorted. "I can hardly imagine you arranging flowers."

Daisy narrowed her eyes at Edward. "Hold up. You think you know everything about me."

"Yup," he answered smugly. "Don't I?"

She shrugged. "Maybe not," she said, opening her desk drawer and fumbling around. "Aha!" she said, holding up a pair of scissors. "Hand over the flower arrangement on the credenza behind you."

"Whatever for?" Edward asked as he stood, grabbed the arrangement, and placed it on her desk.

Daisy moved the arrangement closer and unceremoniously dumped all the flowers and greenery out of the crystal bowl.

"What are you doing and what's that thingy for?" Edward asked, pointing to the round green sphere with metal pins in the bottom of the bowl."

"It's a pin frog. It anchors the flowers in place. Give me thirty seconds," she said as she threw some of the faded hyacinths in her trash, stuck the remaining ones into the pin frog, cut the stems of the silk roses, and lastly added the fernlike greenery.

She sat back and grinned broadly. "Looking better, right?"

Edward folded his arms across his chest. "All right, you wowed me."

"I did, didn't I?" She chuckled.

He had no idea she had any talents besides being a lawyer. After all, that was all she ever did nowadays. No time for anything else if you were on the partner track.

"My mom does own a flower shop. But for your information, before the divorce and before she ever had her shop and we lived in D.C. she used to teach flower arranging to the members of a local garden club. Sometimes Hyacinth and I joined the class."

She fiddled with one of the ferns, tilting it to the left. "I learned a lot. Hyacinth? Not so much. She can't arrange flowers worth a darn. That would be why my mom reached out to me for help rather than my sister."

"So you can arrange flowers. That's helpful to your mom, but it doesn't change my mind. You still need to stay here." He shook his head. "Besides, I'm not the important one. Your dad is likely to be furious at your request and…"

His cell pinged, interrupting them. He removed his phone from his pants pocket, peered at the screen, and glanced up at Daisy, "Sorry, I have to take this call."

He held the phone to his ear. "Hello, Ben. Give me a minute. I'm just leaving an associate's office." He stood and began walking toward the door but quickly turned around and walked back to her desk, scrambling around until he found her pen and a blank Post-it Note. He scribbled, *We can talk after the staff meeting.*

Daisy gave him a thumbs up as he left her office. No surprise—she was correct about his reaction to her going to Houndsville. She still hoped against logic her dad might tell her to go help her mom.

Belatedly she realized she hadn't told Edward about Max. He'd be happy since he knew how much she wanted a dog.

Daisy sighed. She had a few minutes before she had to get to the staff meeting. She opened her computer and attempted to concentrate on a real estate matter she'd been working on for Allan Gold, her dad's close friend and a client of the firm.

Her lawyerly mind found the work interesting, but her thoughts kept wandering back to her conversation with Edward. She flirted with him almost daily, but were her actions getting her anywhere? They met often for drinks at a local bar on Friday nights, but nothing more than that. He played it close to the chest. He enjoyed hanging around with her, of that she was sure, but what about more?

Her cell pinged with an incoming text.

Flowers, where are you? It's after nine.

Oh, no, I'm late. Those darn blue eyes of his. She grabbed a legal pad and ran out the door.

At four p.m., Daisy popped back into her dad's office. He was seated at his desk and not on his phone.

"Dad, it's me. I'm back. Can we talk now?"

He nodded. No pleasantries. His piercing dark eyes bore into hers, shaking her composure and tying her stomach in knots.

She wanted to turn around and run for the exit.

You can do this.

It was time to confront him head on. She took a deep breath and proceeded to his desk.

He didn't ask her to sit.

That suited her. She stood, grasping the top of the chair facing his desk to keep her hands still. Fiddling would alert him to her nervousness, and so would talking too fast.

"Mom fell. She broke her wrist."

She tried to slow down her breathing while she waited for his response.

"I'm assuming you're telling me this for a reason?"

Figured he would put her on the defensive. "Yes, Mom's biggest event of the year, the Fur-Baby Gala, is Saturday. She's asking me to come help her."

That was better.

"Again, you are telling me this why? You must have told her that's impossible right before trial starts on Monday."

Keep your eyes on him. Do not waffle.

Speaking forcefully, she said, "No Dad, I didn't. It's over the weekend. I really want to help her out."

"You'd better think twice. Not a good career move. Let your sister help. You need to be here."

She clenched her hands on the back of the chair.

"Dad, you know Hyacinth is all thumbs. She may be a math whiz, but flower arranging is not her thing."

Silence reigned as her dad picked up his favorite Montblanc fountain pen and scribbled doodles on a manila folder.

It seemed like time was suspended indefinitely. She observed him while waiting him out. Her dad was a handsome man with short gray hair, an aquiline nose, and a small mouth. Dark bushy eyebrows framed dark brown eyes, which to her were anything but warm.

He finally looked up at her. "Daisy, obviously the final decision is yours. If you decide to go, I won't think much of your commitment to the firm or to me. If that is your choice, I'm going to give someone else your witness for the trial."

"But Dad!"

"No buts, Daisy. It's my decision."

She gritted her teeth. "You really have put me in a no-win situation. Give me an hour or so to reach Mom and talk to her. I'll text you later to let you know my plans."

She trudged back to her office, wondering if there was something different she could have said, but from her dad's point of view, he was doing what he thought would be best for his firm and his client. Fair enough. Unfortunately he thought he knew what was best for her too.

Too bad he wouldn't even attempt to come up with a solution that could work for both of them.

Daisy dreaded calling her mom. It didn't seem fair to be unable to help her, but her dad had pretty much made that impossible. She sat at her desk, chomping on chocolate buds, pondering how to tell her mom she couldn't come. She might as well get it over with. After she popped one last bud into her mouth, she called her. Her mom answered on the first ring. She had probably been waiting for her call.

Daisy cringed.

"Bad news, Mom. I'm sorry. I can't come help you. Dad insists I stay to prep for our trial."

"Why? Even if you just come on Saturday, it would be helpful, and you could drive home early Sunday."

"Ultimately it's his call. The Parsons Pharmaceutical trial starts Monday. There's a dinner meeting on Thursday night. Friday we'll be prepping all day, and there's a good chance we'll be working through the weekend."

Daisy could have told her mom the truth—that her dad had given her an ultimatum. But there was nothing to gain by telling her mom. It wouldn't change the outcome, and it would only serve to make her mom think worse of her dad—if that were possible.

She was tired of all their fighting and wished they could be civil to each other.

"So your dad gets his way as always." Daisy could hear the exasperation in her mom's voice, and it made her flinch. "I'm really sorry you can't come. I could have used your help."

"I know, Mom." She clenched her cell tighter. She felt horrible. "I'm sorry too. I hope it all works out okay. Is Hyacinth coming to help you?"

"Yes, she's coming later today. I'll have to figure out a way for her to be helpful."

A laugh bubbled up from Daisy's chest when she thought of Hyacinth arranging flowers. She held back. It wasn't funny. "I'll call you next week."

"Bye, Daisy. We'll miss you."

Daisy ended the call. Now she'd have to tell Meghan. Rather than sending a text, she picked up her cell and called.

"Flowers. So when are you coming?"

"I'm not. My dad nixed it. For him, it's always been work before family. Ultimately that's why my parents divorced. I shouldn't be surprised."

"Sorry."

Daisy groaned. "I've always wanted to follow in his footsteps. Guess that means I need to think more like him."

Her stomach twisted into knots. She was fortunate to have a position in her dad's prestigious firm. It was exactly what she'd always wanted. Lately she wasn't sure that was still true.

"It seems he made this situation a choice between your mom and him," Meghan said.

"Yup." Daisy sighed. "And he won. I texted him to tell him I'm staying."

Meghan spoke softly. "Flowers, don't get mad at me, but he might have a point."

"I guess," Daisy admitted grudgingly, "but I still don't like it."

Four

Max stuck his nose in her face and whined.

She didn't respond.

Unfortunately he was undeterred. His rumblings increased in frequency and volume.

If only she could stay in bed and forget today was Thursday. She tried. It didn't work. Max was telling her he wanted a walk.

"All right, Max. I'm getting up."

She heaved herself out of her toasty warm bed and rummaged through her pile of dirty clothes until she found sweatpants and a sweatshirt that suited her mood—black. He mood only got worse when she walked into her kitchen and realized she was out of coffee.

It wasn't Max's fault. She had to be upbeat for him. "Okay Max, time for a walk. Let's go."

And actually walking Max was the highlight of her day. They walked briskly for fifteen minutes before she turned back toward her apartment to feed him and to change into work clothes. Again, she chose all black to suit her somber mood.

An hour later she slipped into her office unobserved. Just what she wanted. Normally she would have grabbed a cup of coffee in the break room or hung out with Edward in his office for an early morning chat. This morning she wasn't interested in conversing with anyone.

She flipped on her small desk lamp, signed in on her computer, and started to do some prep work for the dinner meeting tonight when an email from her dad popped up on the corner of her computer screen. She read it.

I'll need you to do additional prep work for tonight's meeting. See list below.

She took a deep breath and let it out slowly, trying to keep calm and not allow herself to feel sick and stressed out. She refused to believe her dad had done this as payback for wanting to go to Houndsville. Maybe he had done it to keep her busy, to keep her focused on the upcoming trial. It didn't matter. She would get the work done and do an exemplary job, like always. Just let her dad try and complain.

By the end of the morning, her vision started blurring from reading too many legal files. She needed a break and searched her desk for her stash of chocolate buds, only to find a few stray ones.

She needed real food. What to get was the problem—everything seemed to upset her stomach recently. Two weeks ago, trying to find some answers, she had seen a gastroenterolist, who'd explained her problem was stress related. When he'd found out she was a trial lawyer, he had bluntly told her she might need a new job, that her body might never adjust to the stress of her chosen career.

That was a daunting thought.

She called in an order to the nearby sandwich shop for a turkey sandwich, no lettuce, no tomato, and no mayonnaise, following the doctor's orders to stick to basics. She passed on ordering her usual double espresso and instead asked for a bottle of water.

Grabbing her handbag and her jacket, she headed out to pick up her food. If she walked briskly, she'd be there in less than ten minutes. Of course that depended on how long she window shopped, especially at her favorite shoe store. Today she forced herself to walk on the opposite side of the street, the only possible way not to be tempted.

Her order was brown bagged and waiting for her on the counter.

She grabbed it and headed back. The wind had picked up, and a light rain began to fall. She had to admit the weather suited her mood—dismal.

Back in her office, she scarfed down her sandwich while looking out her rain-streaked window. The rain had started in earnest, and the normal crowds of people on the street had disappeared. It was obvious winter was fast approaching, and more deep red leaves lay at the base of the maple tree.

A deep voice rang out. "Hello, Ms. Flowers"

She swiveled her chair back around. Allan Gold stood in her doorway.

"Hello, Mr. Gold. It's nice to see you. Come on in."

Allan Gold, who didn't fit her image of a billionaire hotelier and developer, was her favorite client. He wasn't at all snobby, but rather he was like a big teddy bear, warm and huggable with adorable dimples. She was sure he liked her too. He treated her as a beloved daughter.

He sat across from her, leaned forward, and looked directly at her.

She swallowed hard. Was something wrong?

"I can see you're wondering why I'm here. I'll get right to the point, if you have time."

She really didn't. She had to finish up the work her dad had given her for tonight's meeting. She folded her hands on her desk. "Please. I'm listening."

"Our last few phone calls have been unsatisfactory. You seem distracted. I get the feeling something's wrong."

The words rolled off her tongue before she thought about it. "I'm not sure I fit in here. The hours are ridiculous, I truly hate the daily backstabbing and the competitive culture, and I have no life outside of work." She didn't mention the dustup with her dad. Her feelings about that were too raw. All done, she looked down and studied her clenched hands. She took a deep breath. "I'm sorry. That was unprofessional of me."

"Maybe, but let's talk about this."

She wanted to hear what he had to say. He disarmed her with his gentle fatherly approach, so unlike her dad's. It made her want to open up to him.

"Look, I've been around long enough to know when something is not working, and as someone who has hired and fired people for decades, I hate to say this, but I don't think you're a good fit here either."

She squeezed her hands so hard her knuckles turned white. She was no longer sure she wanted to hear his opinion.

He frowned. "I want you to know that I see you working tirelessly and doing great work without the support from your dad you need." He paused. "I like your dad, he's a good man, just a lousy husband, and as a father and boss, tough as nails. It's obvious that deep down, you want to please him, but you do have choices about your career."

Allan continued. "Having said all of this, I have one strong suggestion. Stick it out for another year or two. See if the situation improves. If not, you'll have a great resume you can use to find a better fit. And keep in mind, if your goal is to make partner here, it's still attainable."

She had listened intently, but now she bristled and fought back. "Look, I've tried really hard to please my dad. Growing up, I spent countless hours on the weekends here with him. I always wanted to be just like him, but if you really think he is too demanding, why should I stay, especially if he's not helping me to get better? Why not leave now and find something more suited to me?"

Allan shook his head. Standing up abruptly, he walked over to her door to leave but not before he remarked, "Daisy, don't do anything rash. You might regret it later."

He left. She sat, feeling not only defeated, but sad.

That had ended horribly. Allan had only wanted to help, and she'd behaved immaturely. She'd have to call and apologize. The disagreement with her dad about helping her mom was at the root of her current discontent. She wished she could go home and bury her head in Max's fur. Somehow, being with him made her feel better.

Glancing at her watch, she saw she was running out of time to get her work done and still have time to run home and tend to Max before tonight's meeting.

Five-thirty and time to head back to the office. She'd fed Max and walked him longer than usual since she didn't know when she'd be back home. He padded behind her as she picked up her handbag and headed to the door.

Maybe she imagined it, but he looked sad as she kissed his snoozer and drew the door closed. She hated leaving him alone for the evening, especially after she'd been gone most of the day.

Four days with him and already she was in love with this big furry and funny dog. She sighed, wishing she'd given him an extra hug. She'd just have to make it up to him when she got home.

She drove back to work and found her office door partially open, a bag of chocolate buds on her desk with a note: "You're the best! Don't let anyone intimidate you. We'll talk later. Edward."

She smiled and aimlessly opened the bag, popping a bud in her mouth and allowing her mind to wander to the morning she'd met him. It had been her first day at the firm, and even now she could feel her face heat up. It wasn't her best performance. It was probably the most important day of her life. Her lifelong dream of working with her dad had finally come true. It started out fine. She remembered standing at the entrance to the building and running her fingers along the cool edges of the brass plaque of the William Flowers Law Firm.

That day she envisioned another name—Flowers and Flowers Law Firm, or even The Father and Daughter Team of Flowers and Flowers. She remembered smiling. She liked the second choice. It certainly was original.

Anyway, after stalling for a minute she walked, legs quivering, into the conference room. Her heart hammered in her chest as she wondered if her go-to little black dress had been the right choice and if she'd fit in with the other new hires.

Her first impression of the women in the room—never proven incorrect—was that they weren't her type with their sophisticated hairstyles, chunky jewelry, and designer handbags on the table in front of them.

Among the several men, one immediately caught her eye. Head down, he appeared engrossed in the book in his hands. She loved to read. Maybe he'd be friendly.

She moved toward the empty seat next to him and sat. He was reading one of her favorite authors, whose main character was a smartass lawyer. She was intrigued. She tapped his arm to ask, "First year associate?"

He gazed back dismissively, but he answered after a brief pause with one word. "Nope."

That was rude.

Didn't matter. She couldn't stop staring at him. He had long wispy straight hair almost totally covering the bluest of eyes she'd ever seen. Dark blue, like storm clouds.

Not willing to give up, she stuck out her hand "I'm Daisy. And you are?"

He sighed, turned his book over on the table, and with a raised eyebrow said, "I'm the firm's investigator."

Okay, so he wanted to give her a hard time. It was like throwing a red flag in her face. Now she'd never quit. "So Mr. Firm's Investigator, what's your name?"

He rolled his eyes and replied succinctly, "Edward Plant."

And here's where she should have taped her mouth permanently shut.

But no. Out popped, "That means we *have* to get married. Then I'll be Daisy Plant!"

He glanced back at her, his eyes boring into hers. "I don't know about you being Mrs. Plant. I hate daisies."

She flinched. Shocked.

He picked up his book and continued reading.

Daisy sighed.

Even after all this time, the memory still had her slinking down in her seat until she happened to glance at her watch. If only she'd whispered that morning. She'd never learned to speak softly. Better yet, she should have kept her mouth shut.

It was a quarter to seven. Almost time for the meeting. She grabbed the completed papers and her handbag, closed her office door, and walked down the hallway to the conference room.

Standing in the doorway, she observed each person on the team. First on the left was Tom. He was smart, funny, and the first chair on this case. She liked him. Next to him was Preston, entitled trust fund baby and a jerk, and then there was Susan, who drove her crazy with her indecisiveness. On the other side of the curved oval table sat Trevor, pretty boy but clueless, then Corinne, the epic troublemaker. Daisy hated that woman. Undoubtedly the feeling was mutual. Not a surprise since Corinne bristled when her dad gave Daisy the prime witness to prepare, a coveted position.

She walked over to the last empty seat and took it. Her dad nodded. No welcoming smile.

"All right, everyone." Her dad's booming voice put her on edge as he pointed to the console table along the far wall. "Help yourself to some dinner, and we'll get started."

The small group crowded around the table where there were burgers, fries, and Caesar salads sent in from a local steakhouse. It was one of her dad's favorite eateries. Hers too, to be honest.

She watched everyone pile food on their plates while she took a burger, no fries, and no salad. Being around her dad tied her stomach in knots. Food had no appeal.

"Okay everyone, eat up while I explain our strategy for the trial."

He droned on for the next thirty minutes, and when the pretrial business was completed, her dad asked if anyone had any questions or concerns. No one responded.

He cleared his throat.

"I have an important announcement." He looked directly at her. Her stomach twisted into knots. She had a bad feeling about what was going to be said.

"As of tonight, Corinne will be replacing Daisy."

No way. She couldn't have heard correctly. But then when everyone's eyes focused on her, she knew what he'd said was true.

Why had her dad done this after she'd agreed to stay?

She met everyone's eyes and tried to keep a smile on her face as if it didn't bother her. Hopefully they couldn't see how devastated she felt. With his one move, her dad had most likely destroyed her hopes of surviving in his firm. Above all, she couldn't let Corinne's positively gloating smile bother her. She gripped her hands together to keep them from shaking and made herself recall the words Allan Gold had said about not doing something she'd regret.

She sat up straight, and even though her stomach was rolling, she tried to remain stoically in her seat as her dad carried on with what seemed like an endless pep talk about the trial before calling an end to the meeting when she could finally escape the room.

After taking a deep breath and letting it out slowly, she pushed her chair backward, gathered up the work papers her dad had requested, and walked over to Corinne, who was busy accepting congratulations from her coworkers.

She swallowed hard but managed a forced smile. "Here are some documents you'll need for the trial." She couldn't help but add a little jab. "I'm sure you'll do an adequate job."

Corinne merely stifled a yawn with her hand and muttered softly behind it, "For sure better than you." Then she turned her back on Daisy.

Daisy shook her head. Did her dad know how much Corinne was disliked? Hopefully he'd find out, although Corinne was a master when it came to hoodwinking her dad. Playing office politics suited her deviousness.

Unobtrusively Daisy went back to her seat, swept up her belongings, and left the conference room. She needed to be alone. She flew down the hallway to her office, shut the door behind her, and leaned against it, trying to quell her upset stomach. Thank goodness she'd left most of her burger untouched.

Her vision to see The William Flowers Law Firm change its name to Flowers and Flowers was fading fast, leaving her feeling totally adrift. She shook her head, wondering for the millionth time why her dad treated her so badly. She shrugged. She might as well head home. Max was waiting for her. She grabbed her handbag, flipped off the lights, and hurried down the hallway to the elevator and the parking garage where her SUV was parked.

A minute later she slid onto her car seat and sat for a minute, drumming her fingers on the steering wheel. What would she do now? She reviewed the facts as she saw them.

Her dad didn't need her.

The fact that her mom did made her decision easy.

She was going to Houndsville.

Allan's words came to mind. He had warned her not to do anything rash. She sighed. Ultimately her decision to go to Houndsville could jeopardize the career she worked so hard for, but it felt like the right choice regardless.

She'd have to deal with the consequences later.

She revved up the engine and headed home.

For the first time in days, she felt relieved. Going to Houndsville was always the right thing for her. Her mom would be comforted to know help was on the way. She used her Bluetooth to call her.

"Daisy, are you sure?"

"Yes, Mom. It turns out I don't need to stick around."

"Okay. I won't ask why your dad changed his mind. That's wonderful. Having you around will be so helpful. Hyacinth is staying with me. Do you want to stay with me too?"

She stalled. She loved her mom and her sister, but she wanted privacy. "I'll stay at the Inn. Your place is really small. Okay if I meet you at the Inn tomorrow?"

She ended the call and then went on to type a text to her dad. No, he hadn't changed his mind, but she had.

I'm leaving tomorrow for Houndsville. Mom needs me, and you're all set with my replacement.

Right before she pressed send, Allan Gold's words to think twice before doing anything drastic reverberated again. She stalled for a minute, and even though right now she was too hurt and angry to take his words to heart, she pushed herself to add two last sentences.

I'll have my computer with me if you need anything. And in any case, I'll see you bright and early Monday morning.

Five

Daisy's cell pinged. Crap! The sun wasn't even up yet.

Once she'd gotten home last night, she'd indulged herself with a crying jag and tried to think about what she could have done differently, and she hadn't remembered to turn off her ringer.

She struggled to lift her head and squinted to read the display. Her eyes felt gritty and swollen.

She eked out, "Lisa, it's only seven-fifteen."

"I'm sorry." Lisa'a voice sounded strained, not her usual upbeat tone. "I have a problem."

Daisy waited to hear what she had to say. This didn't bode well.

Lisa continued. "My mom is not doing well. I'm not even sure when I'll get back home."

Daisy glanced at Max. Her stomach did a nose dive. Right now she was so glad he was not a human because this discussion was not one she would want him to hear.

She sat up. She was alert and totally awake now. "So what does that mean for Max?"

Silence met her. "Lisa? Are you there? What about your dog?" Daisy caressed Max, his body keeping her warm in her chilly room.

"Do you think you could keep him a little longer?" Lisa said. "If not, I guess I'll have to find someplace for him to go until I can get him."

Daisy sat, stunned, and then she reacted.

"Since you won't be here, *who* do you expect to dump Max in some place you know nothing about? Me?" she added through clenched teeth. Her hands were shaking. She had just unloaded on Lisa, but she was really upset.

Again silence, then a whispered response. "I have no choice, Daisy. I can't leave my mom."

Daisy let out a long, deep breath. At this moment, she tried to feel bad for Lisa, but for Max's sake, she was angry. To place him somewhere strange was just so unfair. And for how long?

She hadn't taken her eyes off of Max. No way could she desert him. Even that momentary thought had her feeling sick. Only one other option.

"Look Lisa, I have a problem here too. My mom needs my help in Houndsville over the weekend." She took a deep breath. "The only solution I can think of is to take him with me."

Her statement was met with an audible sigh. "Oh Daisy, that's perfect. I'm sure Max will like that better than any alternative."

Daisy pushed herself into a sitting position and leaned back against her headboard. "Okay, then this is the scoop. Max and I will leave here soon, and I expect to be back early Sunday," she said. "Keep in touch. I hope your mom gets better soon."

Daisy knew she was being short, but she couldn't wait to get off the phone. Now that she was taking Max, she had additional items to load into her SUV, and she'd already decided last night to leave on the early side. She was available, and she was sure her mom could use her help before the gala tomorrow.

"Well Max, looks like you're stuck with me a while longer." Daisy buried her head in his fur and whispered in his ear, "Truthfully, I didn't want to give you back anyhow.

"Max, we'll walk soon," she promised as she dragged herself into her bathroom and glanced in the mirror. Her hair was stuck in clumps, and black mascara stripes ran down her face, the result of last night's crying jag.

A hot shower and a quick blow dry did wonders to make her feel better, but it still took a ton of concealer around her eyes before she actually looked decent.

Thank goodness that last night, even in her muddled state, she had remembered to call the Inn and reserve a suite. She was all set, though she figured she'd better call back and tell them she was bringing Max. She knew the Inn was dog-friendly, but maybe they'd need to know. She rung them on her cell. Whoever answered the phone told her they would add Max as a guest to her reservation. That made her chuckle, a nice feeling after all the angst of last night.

Max seemed fine, so she decided to pack before walking him.

She reached into her small closet for her carryall. What should she pack? She wouldn't need a lot. Two sweaters, one navy cashmere, one dark green, and a pair of black leggings and of course underwear. She added a pair of sneakers. If it rained or if she did a lot of walking, they'd come in handy. She added gloves and a pompom hat for when she would walk Max at night. It might be cold.

Last thing she'd need was something dressy for the gala. She could wear the new dress she'd bought recently, and it was already in a garment bag, so all she had to do was stuff a pair of dressy shoes and a small evening clutch into her carryall.

She also packed her computer in a backpack. If a question came up about the case or some other work concern, she'd have everything she needed with her.

For traveling, she slipped on her jeans, a sweatshirt, and her favorite brown suede boots. Sometimes wearing a favorite clothing item made her feel good, but not so much today. Although she looked forward to helping her mom and was glad she'd get to keep Max a bit longer, she still hated what had transpired to make it possible.

All ready, she grabbed Max's leash and walked outside. A slight breeze blew her hair into her eyes. Good. She wouldn't be too warm in her clothes. She always preferred the cooler days of fall to the summer heat anyway.

After a shortened dog walk, Daisy loaded her suitcase, her backpack, and Max's tote bag in the cargo area, harnessed Max into a seat, and slid behind the wheel of her SUV.

She turned to glance at Max. "Okay big boy, our adventure starts now."

She turned on her favorite country music station and started driving. This trip could be just what she needed. After six months of nonstop work, she couldn't wait be with her mom and her best friend.

Oops! She'd totally forgotten about calling Meghan to tell her there had been a change in plans.

"Call Meghan's cell," she instructed Siri.

Meghan answered, and Daisy shouted, "Surprise! I'm on my way to Houndsville."

"What do you mean? Did your dad change his mind?"

"Not exactly. I'll fill you in when I get there. I'm already on the road."

"Oh, this is fantastic. I can't wait to see you, and Grace will love seeing her auntie Daisy. Plus, you'll get to meet Buddy and Bear. Call as soon as you get here."

Daisy couldn't wait to see Grace, Meghan's adorable eight-year-old daughter, and her special needs dog, Buddy, who was a blind and deaf double merle.

Better yet would be spending time with Meghan in person. Seeing her on the phone was fine. A hug or two from her friend was ten times better.

Daisy ended the call and realized she'd forgotten to mention she had Max with her. Oh well, her showing up with a dog would certainly shock everyone.

Next up, she called her mom to tell her she'd be arriving sooner than expected. No answer. She left a message with her estimated time of arrival.

It would take approximately forty minutes to reach the Bay Bridge, and after that she had another thirty minutes before she reached the edge of Houndsville on the Eastern Shore of Maryland. The last leg to the Inn would take an additional fifteen minutes.

She left D.C. with mixed emotions. She'd miss the final preparations for the trial, but she felt confident she had made the correct decision to help her mom. Besides, she'd be back before the trial started.

Along the way she tried to distract herself by singing along with some of her old favorites on Apple Play. It was too bad her dad's actions invaded her thoughts. Hopefully Meghan could help her make sense of it all.

Daisy and Meghan had met when the tennis coach asked Daisy to substitute for Millie in a doubles tournament. Daisy had hesitated, thinking she'd never be good enough to replace Millie, but Meghan had assured her she'd be fine.

Meghan and Daisy had destroyed the competition, won the tournament, and ended up best friends. That had happened Daisy's senior year, her first year in Houndsville.

She hadn't expected to make such good friends so quickly, but Meghan had welcomed Daisy into her small group of close friends, which included Millie, Carolyn, and Todd. Her first year in Houndsville had been wonderful, thanks to all of them.

In August when Meghan and Daisy both left for college, they'd sworn to remain friends forever.

Her cell rang, interrupting her musings. Looking at the display she saw it was Edward.

"I heard what happened last night. Are you okay? And where are you?" His rapidly fired questions told her he was worried about her. It had been a mistake not to call him.

"I'm sorry. I'm all right. I made a last-minute decision to go to Houndsville."

Daisy tapped her fingers on the steering wheel, waiting to hear Edward's response.

"I'm sorry I wasn't there to console you after what went down. Just my opinion, but you shouldn't have left. You should be here showing everyone you were okay with Corinne taking over for you."

She took a deep breath. "Look, I hung around after my dad did his best to throw me under the bus, but right now I believe I'm doing the right thing. Remember, I have two parents and one obviously needs me, the other one not so much." She tapped her fingers on the steering wheel. "Besides, everyone is well aware Corinne and I pretty much despise each other. No one who knows me would think I was okay with my dad's decision."

"Daisy, you might be surprised to learn that no one on the team approves of what your dad did. Include me in that too. They all dislike Corinne and are bemoaning the fact they have to listen to her boasting. They do think your dad's motive is to try and make you tougher. Everyone sees you as the nice one around here."

"That's really good to hear." She smiled for the first time in hours, mulling something over. "I have an idea. Let the team jointly tell Corinne they're really proud of her. That she's doing a good deed by taking over for me so I'm able to help my mom."

Edward snickered. "That's brilliant. Done. And I'll make sure to report back to you about her reaction. I wonder if she'll be able to keep a straight face?"

"More likely the person with enough nerve to confront her will be shut down with a nasty comment or two."

"Back to reality. Daisy, you still need to get back here—and soon. Don't blow this golden opportunity to work here. Not many people get to do that. Show your dad he made a mistake."

"Opinion noted. But this weekend, besides helping my mom, I'll get to spend time with Meghan, who I've told you had some issues with her own dad. I'm hoping for some life-changing advice."

She paused for a minute to gather her thoughts. "You have to know I don't feel good about what happened last night. And maybe I should have stayed and let this play out. I could have tried to show my dad I could work with Corinne, and I probably would have if my mom didn't need me."

"Sunshine, go help your mom. I'm sorry I wasn't around last night to give you a much-needed hug."

Although she almost drove off the road, she managed to respond. "I wish I had been there to receive it."

She adored Edward. It was just at times he struck her as somewhat like her dad. Work came first. Would he change if they became romantically involved?

She drove on and kept thinking about her conversation with Edward. Would it help if she called her dad? See if he needed anything from her? She shook her head. If he wouldn't talk to her, she'd feel even worse.

Not long after she hung up, she turned onto the winding driveway to the Inn.

If she had more time she would have driven down to the inlet. It wasn't very far, and it was the site of Allan Gold's development with a hotel complex and storefronts. It would have been nice to see how it was coming along.

As she drove up to the Inn, she noted new boxwoods and oak trees lining the driveway, evidence of new landscaping and renovation, which she had heard about from Meghan and her mom.

Small world. It was Allan Gold's daughter, Samantha, who had purchased it several years earlier. Her mom raved that it had been restored to its former glory.

Daisy really wanted to meet her.

A little farther off to the right, a new large wood sign attached to two posts indicated the turnoff to take to the Buckshead Spa where Meghan worked. Once the old carriage house, Samantha had turned it into a world-class spa. She slowed down to a crawl to get a quick view.

What a huge change. The once old and dilapidated building looked brand new. The gleaming white building had new windows installed with black trim framed by window boxes filled with mums. The old barn door had been removed and replaced with a shiny new black double entrance door with fixed glass panels on either side. Samantha had also added a small decorative pool with a fountain in the center. Two wrought iron benches flanked by two large planters with mums surrounded the pool to the right of the entrance.

It looked so enticing. She wished she had time for a treatment, but she knew that was impossible. She had to get back to D.C. No wonder Meghan was ecstatic to be managing it for Samantha.

She picked up her speed and drove farther up the lane. While she'd expected the Inn to look refurbished, the changes were dramatic.

New black shutters gleamed on the window frames and the small front porch had been extended around the entire front of the Inn. Black wrought iron tables and chairs were set up, and surprisingly several couples were sitting there. Daisy shivered. It seemed a bit cold for that, although she was sure Max would enjoy sitting there.

Neatly trimmed boxwoods replaced old scraggly bushes while a bright red front door and humongous bronze planters filled with yellow mums on either side of the main door spruced up the entrance.

As she drove around the circular driveway, a car pulled out leaving an available space behind a Range Rover parked near the front walkway. Perfect for now. She exited her SUV, grabbed her handbag, and unhooked Max, and together they headed up the steps. Later she'd return for her suitcase, backpack, and his tote bag.

The large red door opened into a small vestibule where a gorgeous arrangement of white lilies, her mom's signature blooms, sat on a round mahogany table. Its sweet fragrance wafted in the air.

A few steps farther, and she stopped to gaze around. Wow!

The mid-sized room and what she considered the hub of the Inn had been transformed. Loveseats and barrel chairs upholstered in mint and forest green stripe made for a comfortable yet elegant seating area, along with a gorgeous dark wood cocktail table covered with knickknacks and books. Add in the fabulous contemporary artwork on the walls, and the space was both unique and welcoming.

"Come on, Max. Let's get checked in." She wondered where check-in might be until she spied someone with curly red hair seated behind a free-standing escritoire topped with a computer. The woman waved them over.

"Hello handsome. Want a treat?" the redhead asked as she walked around the desk to pet Max and pointed to a beautiful beige ceramic jar with a large bone on top used as a handle.

"I'm sure he'd love one," Daisy said, lifting off the top and taking out something that looked like an Oreo cookie.

"These are for dogs?"

"Yes, courtesy of our local dog treat bakery."

"Oh, you must mean Millie's place. I'm looking forward to seeing it."

"Oh, you know about that?"

"Well, sort of. I used to live here, but back then it was where we went to get ice cream. I'm Daisy Flowers. And this is Max," she said, giving him the treat. "I'm here to check in."

"Hi, I'm Sandi. We've been expecting you. Your mom called earlier and said if you had time to stop by her shop. She'll be there all afternoon."

"Thank you." Daisy watched Sandi's fingers fly over the keyboard. She looked to be in her early thirties, but her bouncy curls and bright red lipstick made her look even younger.

"Ms. Flowers," Sandi said, looking up from her computer, "we've put you in the Blue Suite. It's ready for you if you'd like to go there now. May I ask if you have any luggage?"

"Yes, a carryall, a backpack, and a tote in my SUV. It's parked right out front."

"If you want, you can leave it there. We'll make sure it gets to your suite."

"Thank you." Daisy dug around in her purse. "Here's my key fob." She handed it to Sandi. "I want to get to my mom's. I'll check out our suite later."

"Of course," Sandi said, tapping away at the computer. "Before you leave, could you please swipe your credit card?"

"Sure. By the way, does the bar still offer takeout?" Daisy asked as she swiped her credit card.

"Yes. Today's special is a shrimp salad sandwich and fries. It's delicious, but if you don't want that, the burgers are good too."

"Do you think I could get the shrimp salad quickly? It sounds perfect."

"Absolutely. I'll ring the bar and get them to pack up a lunch for you. When it's ready, they'll let me know, and I can bring it to you. We'll charge it to your room."

"Thanks. I'll go wait over there." Daisy pointed to a small seating area in a nook by the window.

"Come on, Max."

The small chintz-upholstered loveseat looked inviting. She sat there while Max settled on her toes. She bent down to pet him.

"Okay. You sit and be comfy while I look over some work files."

She opened her computer and looked at a file on the upcoming trial. Even though she wasn't in D.C., she should still be prepared if her dad wanted her opinion on anything.

She had reviewed a few pages when she glanced up and saw Grant Stamford walking in, holding a squirmy puppy in his arms. Her heart skipped a beat. He was still hot, just like he had been in high school when she'd had a serious crush on him. She thought about calling out to him, but he seemed to be on a mission as he stalked over to the reception desk. She heard from snippets of his conversation with Sandi that the puppy in his arms had been wandering around outside.

"Any idea who she belongs to?" He held up the dog so Sandi could see its face.

"Nope," Sandi answered. "But it looks like a purebred collie. I can't imagine anyone letting it run loose."

That confirmed what Daisy thought. The puppy was a tiny Max.

Grant frowned. "Luckily she's friendly and was happy to be picked up before something awful happened."

Daisy watched Grant gently tickle the puppy's tummy. This was a guy who really loved dogs.

"If you have no idea who she belongs to, I can bring her to the clinic to scan for a microchip."

He shook his head. "I doubt she has one. She's pretty young, but I'll check anyway."

Daisy's attention was abruptly drawn to a well-dressed woman stalking across the lobby and heading straight toward Grant. She tapped his shoulder forcefully.

He turned toward her, and immediately his expression changed to one of pure disdain. Daisy stared, wide-eyed. He really didn't like this person.

The woman wasn't deterred. She crossed her arms and shrieked, "Grant Stamford, what are you doing with Peanut?"

"Ms. Clarkson, what can I do for you?" he asked calmly, although Daisy could see his stance become stiff.

"Why are you holding Peanut?" she asked rudely.

"I found her in the parking lot. I wasn't about to leave her there where she could get hurt."

Daisy knew that name. She cringed. This person must be the infamous Betsy Clarkson. Daisy had never met her, but she knew a lot about her. More than she wanted to know.

Watching this was uncomfortable. She looked around. One man reading a newspaper looked up, and another couple seemingly waiting to talk to Sandi moved farther off to the side.

Watching Grant, he looked and sounded like a man trying to keep his anger in check. He was probably thinking about Betsy's past behavior. The story Meghan had told her about Betsy and her dog, Cleo's, puppies was absolutely horrendous. She shook her head.

It wasn't difficult to understand why Grant had a problem with Betsy.

"Well, hand her over now," Betsy demanded.

"Not until you tell me why she's running loose and not wearing a collar. She's a puppy. She could easily have been killed." He stood his ground and glared at her. "Some people shouldn't be allowed to have a dog."

Yikes! Grant, as a veterinarian, should be less judgmental, certainly in public. She guessed he just couldn't stand Betsy and wasn't thinking clearly. This situation must have aroused his natural instinct as a vet to protect Peanut.

"Well, then lucky for her. She's not mine. She's my sister's."

Grant still hadn't handed over Peanut. "And where is this sister of yours? Did you make her up?"

Betsy stomped her foot and turned around. "Stephanie, where are you? If it weren't for you, I wouldn't have to deal with this asshole. Come show him that Peanut does have a collar."

Betsy waved her index finger at a petite woman obscured by a six-foot ornamental tree. "Oh, come on over already. He won't bite. It's me he hates."

Stephanie flinched as if someone had hit her. She walked over hesitantly. She appeared to be clenching a dog collar and a leash in her right hand.

"Hello," she said haltingly. "I'm Stephanie. I'm sorry for any confusion I caused. Peanut is just learning to walk on a leash." She held up the pink leash and matching collar. "My sister and I were on our way to the spa when a loud noise spooked Peanut. She slipped right out of her collar." Stephanie swiped her fingers around her eyes. "We've been trying to find her. I was scared I'd never see her again."

Betsy scowled at her sister. "Stephanie, stop being so melodramatic. Peanut's fine. Take her, and let's get out of here."

"She's safe now," Grant assured her. "I'll hold her while you put her collar back on. Let's make sure it's tight enough."

Stephanie smiled weakly at Grant before hooking the collar around Peanut's neck. "It's fine now," Grant said, checking it. "You should know lots of dogs can slip their collars, especially when they're frightened."

Betsy rolled her eyes at Stephanie. "I've had enough of this. I'm leaving to go to the spa. Do what you want."

Grant totally ignored Betsy and spoke to Stephanie as if she were a child. It did seem like she was shy and socially awkward. "Go buy Peanut a harness. Some dogs can still slip a harness if it's not on properly, so you might consider getting a second leash and attach one to the collar and one to the harness. That way, if one fails, you have a backup."

"I'll do that." Stephanie managed a shaky smile.

Grant put Peanut down on the floor. "Be careful with her, and remember to go get her a harness." He watched Stephanie walk with Peanut until they were out the door.

He turned back to Sandi and gripped the desk with his hands. "Sorry about the commotion. That woman brings out the worst in me." He took a breath. "Anyway, I almost forgot what I came here for, and now I'm out of time." He took an envelope out of his jacket pocket and handed it to her. "Could you please give this to Samantha? It's the gift certificate Harry was supposed to give her for the silent auction. Tell her I'll see her tomorrow at the gala."

He started to walk away but turned back to Sandi and muttered, "We'd all be better off if she left town. She's a menace."

"Yes, she is difficult, to say the least," Sandi murmured.

Daisy assumed it must be difficult to be a vet and have people around like Betsy who were careless and irresponsible. Maybe she could get him to focus on something else. Before she could think too hard, she waved and called out, "Grant. Over here."

He looked straight at her. She gulped. Would he recognize her? She caught a fleeting glimpse of confusion before he smiled.

"Daisy Flowers." He ambled over. "My brother mentioned you might be coming to help out your mom. It's nice to see you." His hazel eyes sparkled just like she remembered.

He plopped down on the loveseat beside her. He was so close. She tried not to fidget.

"If you've been sitting here, I guess you heard that entire exchange. That woman never fails to irritate me—and worse. I can't forget what she planned for Cleo's pups."

"Meghan told me all about that. It looks like her sister has her own problems with her. Makes a person wonder why they were together."

She stole a glance at him, examining him more closely. How was it possible there was another gorgeous guy out there with the exact same smile and hazel eyes who was engaged to her best friend, Meghan? Nicholas and Grant were identical twins, and only a few people could even tell them apart. She imagined it would be fun for two best friends to be married to twins.

He seemed to relax, noticing Max. "I would have expected Nicholas to tell me you had a collie, especially since he and Meghan have two now. This one here is quite the looker," Grant said, running his hand along Max's back. The dog put his paw on Grant's knee.

"He wants you to pet his paw. I know it's weird, but he loves it."

"Okay, big boy."

She watched him using his large hands to caress Max's paw and wondered how it would feel to have him run his hands over her body instead?

Her heart skipped a beat. Where had that errant thought come from? She eked out, "Yes. He's great."

"Did you see the puppy I found?" Grant said. "That was a collie too. Lots of collie folks in this town."

She caught herself second-guessing her opinion of Grant. Although she'd had this crush on him, he had been known to play pranks that were sometimes hurtful. Maybe she needed to give him a break. Those had been tough years for him and his family after his parents were killed in a car accident.

Today she saw a man who loved dogs and had infinite patience with Stephanie. Even considering how obnoxious Betsy behaved, and if you discounted his numerous scowls, he'd handled the situation well.

"So, Daisy, you want to join me for a quick cup of coffee?"

She was caught off-guard. "I thought I heard you say you were out of time."

"Yup, I was in a rush until I saw you." He winked.

Her heart skipped a beat or two. He always had been a smartass.

She paused. "I can't. I'm supposed to be helping my mom get everything ready for the gala."

"Too bad. We could have caught up on old times."

It was probably a good thing she'd turned him down. The good old days. Did she want to be reminded of them? She'd think about that later. "I'm not sure that would be a good thing. You weren't always nice to me or my friends in high school."

She cringed. *Did I just say that?*

She shook her head. She was mad at herself. Whenever she felt trapped or flustered, bad stuff popped out of her mouth. She stole a glance at Grant, and for a fleeting second, he looked dejected. She even saw the telltale twitch in his right eye. She'd never noticed it back in their school days, but Meghan had told her that was the only way she could tell the brothers apart. And to this day, Meghan had sworn her to secrecy about that little detail.

Crap. She frowned. She'd ruined everything. She was about to apologize when his eyes twinkled and he grinned. "I know I was pretty bad back then. But now I'll just have to make sure to change your mind." He leaned toward her and grasped her hand in his. "You'll be at the gala?"

"That's the plan." She avoided looking at him, feeling her face getting warm.

"Then I'll see you there." He stood, smiled down at her, and strolled off.

She'd never even gotten around to telling him Max wasn't her dog.

Six

Five minutes later, after Sandi brought her takeout, Daisy paused outside the Inn's front door. It had turned out to be one of those late fall days that are especially enjoyable. A slight breeze and a warm sun.

"Come on, Max. We need to get moving."

She sure was glad she had on comfortable boots. It was a steep walk from the Inn, which was off the main thoroughfare, to her mom's shop on the Commons, as it was called by the locals.

Her mom's shop, Frannie's Flowers, was on the same street as Bridget's Bookstop, Julie's Jewels, and Stella's Shoes, a few of her favorite haunts. It was a shame she was in a hurry and didn't have time to shop.

She glanced across the street to the Houndsville Park where one dog was catching a frisbee and another was chasing a kite a little girl was flying. Houndsville was definitely a dog-friendly town and had surely played a part in Millie's success with her Best Doggone Bakery. She couldn't see it now, but she remembered that in the center of the park was a monument with a commemorative bronze plaque. It honored Robert Brooke, who brought his hounds to the Eastern Shore of Maryland for hunting the foxes that threatened the crops and livestock, naming the town Houndsville in their honor.

She walked along, savoring the fact that here she was in Houndsville with a dog she totally enjoyed. So different from where she'd been just yesterday.

She viewed her mom's shop up ahead. She loved that her door was spectacularly different from all the others on the street. It was a high-gloss hot pink painted with pastel roses and vines, the perfect entrance into a cornucopia of flowers.

She flung the door open, only to come to a full stop. "Sorry, Max," she mumbled as she almost tripped over his paws. She saw her sister sitting on a high-top stool with a small sheltie on the floor next to her.

"Hyacinth! It's so good to see you." She stepped forward, dropping Max's leash to fling her arms around her sister.

."Hi to you too," Hyacinth said. "But hey, wait a minute. Who is this?" She pointed at Max.

"This is Max. Isn't he gorgeous? He's my neighbor's dog,"

"I'm confused. If he's your neighbor's dog, what's he doing here with you?"

"Lisa, my neighbor, had an emergency out of town. She couldn't find a dog sitter and asked if I could help her out. So here we are."

She watched as Max checked out the tiny sheltie. "And I suppose that's Mom's foster Max is sniffing?"

Hyacinth's eyes opened wide. "You know about Sidney?"

"Meghan told me," Daisy murmured.

"That's good. Mom was afraid you'd freak out."

Daisy ignored her sister's comment. No point in bringing up the dog issue. She turned and placed her handbag and her bagged lunch on the front counter and bent down to pet Sidney. "He certainly is tiny compared to Max."

"Yes. I think Mom said he weighs around eighteen pounds."

"Hey, where is Mom?" Daisy asked.

"On the phone," Hyacinth said, pointing to a spot behind a flimsy beige curtain. "She left one of the refrigerator doors ajar, and she had to trash some of the flowers. She's freaking out because Samantha was specific in wanting all white flowers, and it seems the distributor wasn't sure he could get her any replacements by tomorrow."

"You're right. I am a mess," Frannie said, shaking her head as she drew back the curtain. "It's been a terrible week. My assistant quit, I broke my wrist, and then last night, I left the refrigerator door open."

She walked up to her front counter. "One good thing. The distributor has agreed to deliver the flowers we need. It's worth it even if I have to pay him a small fortune. She looked over toward the door. "Whose dog is that?" she asked, pointing to Max.

Daisy patted Max. "I just explained to Hyacinth that he belongs to my neighbor. She had an out-of-town emergency, and he's with me until she comes back."

Her mom looked at her. "I'm happy for you. I know you've always wanted a dog."

Daisy didn't want to have this discussion. She pointed to her mom's right wrist and laughed. "A hot pink cast. Figures."

"You know pink is my favorite color." Frannie grinned.

"Yes, I sure do. I'm surprised this whole shop isn't pink. So Mom, now that I'm here, what needs doing?" she asked.

"A lot, since I'm pretty much unable to do anything, but we should start getting everything ready to take to the Inn. I made a list of what I'll need. It'll take a while to find everything. My back room is not exactly well organized. Once you find all the items, if you could pack them up and load the truck, that would be great.

Then tomorrow, once the distributor arrives, we'll transfer the flowers from his truck to mine and head to the Inn."

"That doesn't sound too bad," Hyacinth said.

"Well, if you finish all that and we still have time, I could use help with some other orders."

"Mom, don't worry. We'll get everything done," Daisy said, patting her mom on her forearm. "By the way, you asked about Max, but how is it you didn't tell me about getting a dog yourself?"

Her mom sighed. "I wasn't sure how to tell you. And let's just say I was conned by a pro." She smiled tentatively. "At least it's working out nicely."

"You mean Millie?" Daisy said.

"Yup. She stopped by here, supposedly, to get some flowers for her home. She hardly ever does that. I should have known she had an ulterior motive when I saw her walking a dog other than Luke or Annie."

"So how did she persuade you?"

"It was more like coerced," Frannie said. "She told me she was hoping to find a temporary home for him until the rescue group found him a permanent one. It's like being a foster parent."

"Mom, you do know she's probably hoping you'll be a 'foster' failure."

"'Foster' failure? What's that?"

"A foster parent cares for the dog until the rescue finds it a permanent home. If you end up keeping it and becoming its owner, technically you 'failed' as a foster. I guess it happens so often someone gave it a name."

"Well, I guess that could happen. I'm really enjoying his company."

Daisy shook her head. So many times she'd tried to tell her parents that dogs made wonderful companions. It made her sad they'd never listened. She didn't want to dwell on the past anymore. It was over.

"Mom, before we start, I'm going to sit down for a minute and eat the sandwich I brought with me. I also want to call Meghan and tell her I've arrived."

"That's fine." Her mom walked over and hugged her. "I'm just relieved you're here. When Cynthia quit so suddenly, I was already in trouble, but after I broke my wrist, I panicked. I knew I'd never be able to get the Inn ready for the gala by myself."

"Mom, no worries. Hyacinth and I are here. We'll get it done."

Daisy sat at the front counter, opened her lunch bag, and pulled her cell out of her purse. As she started munching on a few fries, she called Meghan.

"Hi, I'm at my mom's. You—"

"Flowers, I'm so sorry to cut you off. Can you fill me in later. Betsy's here. She's so demanding. I can't possibly talk."

"What! You mean she has an appointment with you?" Daisy asked incredulously. "You, of all people, can't stand her."

"She spends a fortune here, and although Samantha despises her, she won't turn away her business. Besides, if we didn't give her an appointment, she'd lie and tell the whole town the spa is no good. True or not, it could hurt."

"But why you? Surely Betsy knows how you feel about her."

"Oh, that's easy. Betsy insists on having me attend to her. It makes her feel superior. Plus, she'd love to entice me to do something inappropriate so she could get me fired. Little does she know that is never going to happen."

"What a loathsome person."

"You have no idea. Oh no, here she comes. Gotta go."

Drat. Daisy really wanted to tell Meghan about Grant's dustup with Betsy and that she'd talked to him afterward.

"Well, she certainly was in a rush," her mom commented as Daisy put her cell back in her purse.

"Yes. She's got Betsy Carlson to deal with. Fortunately Meghan is used to dealing with difficult people." She handed a fry to Max and one to Sidney. "Remember me telling you that when she lived in California she worked as a make-up artist for the starlet Gwendolyn McMasters? Meghan describes her as a prima donna. If Meghan could handle her, she'll never allow Betsy to get to her."

Daisy finished off most of her sandwich and shared more of her fries with Max and Sidney "Okay Mom, put me to work."

Frannie picked up several notebook-sized pieces of paper clipped together and handed them to Daisy. There were scribbles all over the papers. It was hardly legible. *Uh-oh.* This was going to take a lot longer than Daisy had anticipated. She'd hoped to get back to the Inn on the early side so she would have time to review some of the legal work she was working on for Allan.

"We're on it." The sisters headed to the back room.

Daisy placed her arm around Hyacinth's shoulder. "Be honest. Why are you really here? You hate arranging flowers."

"That's true, but Mom was desperate. She didn't think you were coming. I was her last resort." She shrugged. "My help was better than none, if only slightly."

Daisy grinned. "Are you sure that cute detective didn't have something to do with you coming here?"

Hyacinth's face turned an interesting shade of red. "Okay. I'll admit he's been bugging me to come back."

Daisy grinned. "So Mom's broken wrist came in handy. Good. I haven't met him, but if you like him, that's good enough for me."

"Okay, so I've been honest with you. Now it's your turn." Hyacinth put her hand gently on Daisy's arm. "Tell me why you seem so uncharacteristically uptight lately when we talk. Did Mom's wrist come at a good time for you too?"

"Shh, you're right of course, but Mom doesn't suspect anything. And anyway, how'd you know?"

"Educated guess. Dad would never give you time off to help Mom. Plus, knowing Dad, I figured sooner or later things might blow up."

"Well, you're right, but let's talk about that later. We need to get to work, and this list of Mom's is impossible to decipher."

They started hunting down the things on the list. "I had no idea Mom was so disorganized. I hope we don't end up forgetting something and have to run back here tomorrow," Hyacinth said.

"Agreed." Daisy wiped her brow.

Two-and-a-half hours later, they studied the pile of cartons packed with the tablecloths, the tools they'd need to arrange the flowers, and the vases for the flowers. "I never thought it would take this long. I should take Max outside, and I'd love some water or something to drink."

They walked back up front where their mother was struggling to arrange some greenery in a vase.

"Mom, leave it. We've got to take the dogs out, but I'll help you with that when we come back inside," Daisy said.

By the time all the orders were finished and ready for pick-up, and there were many, it was almost five.

"Mom, I'm going to head back to the Inn. I need to unpack, and it's time to feed Max. After that, I'll eat an early dinner and try to get some sleep."

She didn't mention that she'd hardly slept last night. She didn't want to answer any questions. "I'll need to be up early to walk and feed Max so I can be at your shop first thing."

"That sounds good. And thank you again for coming to bail me out. See you tomorrow."

Hyacinth put her hand on Daisy's forearm. "Sis, thank goodness you're here. We all know the flower arrangements would have been a disaster if I were the only one helping Mom. I would have ruined her good name."

Daisy smiled. "Thanks, sis. For a change it feels good to be needed."

Twenty minutes later, Daisy unlocked the door to her suite, hoping she would like it as much as she liked what Samantha had done in the lobby.

The staff had turned on the lights in the small foyer, creating a warm welcome for her and Max. She took a few steps into the living area. Yup, this certainly was the blue suite. Everything, top to bottom, was a lovely shade of blue, from the sky blue walls to the blue carpet and two upholstered sofas done in a blue and white silk stripe. Even the lampshades were a blue floral print.

"Oh, look, Max. They left something for you."

A small blue and white striped box was sitting on the foyer table with an attached note that read, "For the fur-baby in your life."

Daisy laid down her handbag and opened the box. Ahh, there were three cookies like the ones from Millie's bakery.

"Here, Max." She gave him one, which he gobbled up in one bite. "Come on, let's go exploring."

Same as the rest of the suite, it was all blue. The bed had a floral blue print spread that was swallowed up with sumptuous blue pillows.

And on the night stand was another box and a bottle of champagne with another note: "Happy to have you staying with us. Enjoy!"

"Oh look, I get a treat too," she told Max.

With everything being blue, she wondered about the bathroom. She peeked inside and laughed out loud. From the fluffy towels down to the toilet paper, tissue, and soap, everything was blue.

Who even made colored tissues or toilet paper anymore? Obviously Samantha had found it somewhere. All in all, Samantha hadn't missed a single detail. It was awesome. Lucky for Daisy, blue was her favorite color.

Seven

Saturday morning, the day of the gala, Hyacinth and Daisy met up at their mom's shop and loaded the flowers from the distributor into her truck. Hyacinth stuck out her hand for the keys. "All right, Mom, the truck's all loaded. I'll drive. Daisy, you drive Mom's car, and I'll meet you at the Inn. That way, Max can go with you."

Frannie frowned. "Hyacinth, have you ever driven a box truck?"

"No, but how hard can it be? It's only a few miles. I'm going to grab my handbag from the shop. I'll meet you at the Inn."

Frannie shook her head. "You should let me drive."

"Mom, I'm driving. You're the one with the broken wrist."

Her mom reluctantly handed the truck keys to Hyacinth. "Please be careful."

"Mom, she'll be fine." Daisy loaded Max in the back seat of her mom's car while her mom climbed in the passenger seat.

It took only a few minutes to get to the Inn. Daisy pulled into a space near the front door. She allowed Max to jump out of the back seat while holding on to his leash. She looked around.

Millie and another woman were stringing white and yellow twinkle lights on the bushes at the front of the Inn.

Daisy pointed. "Mom, there's Millie. I want to go say hello." Daisy waved and ran over with Max.

Millie dropped the lights she was holding to run and hug Daisy. "I am so glad to see you. You're a lifesaver. But hey, I didn't know you have a dog."

"Nice." Daisy grinned. "You haven't seen me in ages, and all you care about is Max?"

"Well, it is a big surprise, but of course I want to hear what's going on with you."

The other woman stringing the lights walked over. "Hi, I'm Samantha. She held out her hand to shake Daisy's. "It's nice to finally meet you. My dad talks about you a lot. He's always telling me what a great lawyer you are."

"Thanks. That's really nice to hear. And Millie, this is not my dog. This is Max. Long story, but he belongs to my neighbor. She's out of town, and since I was coming here, he had to come with me."

Daisy's cell pinged. "I'm so sorry. I'd better see if that's work calling." She dug into her handbag to find her cell. Could Edward be calling again?

She peered at the screen. Hyacinth's name appeared.

She frowned. Why would she be calling?

She answered. "What's up?"

"Seems as though I can't drive a box truck after all. I hit a curb. The tire's flat."

Daisy walked off a ways and whispered, "You have got to be kidding."

"Nope. You'd better ask mom to get help."

Frannie walked over to her. "What's wrong, Daisy? Who's on the phone? You look upset."

That was an understatement. There was no way to be tactful. "Umm," she stammered, "Hyacinth hit a curb. She says one of the truck's tires is flat."

Frannie gasped. "I knew it. It's my fault. I should have insisted I drive. It's not that easy to drive a box truck." She ran her fingers through her hair. "This is awful! How will we get everything to the Inn?"

"Mom, now is not the time to panic. We'll figure it out."

Daisy pulled her cell from her handbag. "Let's find a tow truck to come and fix the tire."

Frannie shook her head. "All right, I'll call, but what if they can't get her soon enough?"

"I have another idea. Hyacinth is stuck only a few minutes away. I'll drive over to where she's stuck and fit as much as I can in the back of my SUV. If the tow truck can't get there soon, I'll make as many trips as I need to, and eventually, we'll get everything here."

"You think you can make that work?" her mom asked, wringing her hands.

Daisy gave her mom a quick hug. "Yes, I do. And I'm going right now. We have no time to spare. You keep Max with you."

Daisy glanced at her watch. It was after eleven. They really were running out of time. She dug through her handbag, found her key fob, and pressed the button to locate where the valet had parked her SUV.

In minutes, she was on her way and driving like a bandit fleeing a robbery. She spotted Hyacinth leaning against the side of the truck, tears streaming down her face. With no time to waste, she checked both sides of the road, did an illegal U-turn, and parked her SUV behind the truck.

Hyacinth ran over. "Daisy, why are you here? Shouldn't you have stayed to help Mom?"

"Think about it. Everything Mom needs is in the truck. We need to fit what we can in my SUV."

"Oh, this is awful. I've ruined everything."

"Not if we hurry. Come on, let's move. You open the back of the truck. I'll pull down my seats. We can do this."

Hyacinth wiped her eyes with the back of her hand and sprinted to the truck. Daisy pulled down her back seats to allow more room for the cartons and went to help Hyacinth.

"Is Mom totally freaked out?" Hyacinth asked as they grabbed a few boxes and carried them over to the SUV. Together, they pushed the boxes tight up against the front seats and filled the space almost up to the roof. Daisy was glad it was only a short trip to the Inn. She would have a hard time seeing while she drove.

"Mom's handling it okay, and she'll be better once we've delivered the stuff to her. Come on, we're filled up."

Daisy didn't see any reason to upset Hyacinth more by telling her their mom was definitely freaking out.

They drove to the Inn. Daisy waved to Millie and Samantha, who were on the ground laying out iridescent paw prints on a red carpet runner. Millie stood up and hightailed over to them. "Thank goodness you're here. You weren't gone but a minute, and your mom started pacing back and forth. We tried to keep her busy sticking on these paw prints, but that didn't help. Finally I told her to take Max to Samantha's office. Her dogs, Bailey and Berry are there. I figured the three dogs would keep her busy until you got back."

"Well, it would have been better if everything fit in one trip, but it didn't. Can you help us unload so we can head back for another round? We have to make at least one more trip," Hyacinth said, wringing her hands.

Millie looked at them. "Sure. Let's get the SUV unloaded. After that, leave it to me. I'll get the stuff to your mom. Rob can help."

They worked together, the SUV was unloaded in no time, and Daisy and Hyacinth headed back to get another load.

They worked in tandem to pack in more cartons until they had them all loaded. All that was left were the buckets of flowers. They had to be loaded carefully. Damaged flowers would definitely add to her mom's problems.

"There are two buckets left. Can you possibly fit one in between your feet and one on your lap?" Daisy asked.

"You bet I can, if it means we'll get everything in."

Three minutes later, they were done.

"We're ready to go." Daisy got behind the wheel. "Hey, where are the truck keys?"

"Crap! Right here." Hyacinth pulled them from her jacket pocket and held them up.

Daisy put out her hand. "Well, give them to me. I'll leave them under the front mat for the tow truck driver."

"Good idea. By the way, I know you fibbed earlier," Hyacinth said, climbing into the front seat. "If I were Mom, I'd be furious with me. I should never have insisted I drive."

Daisy patted her sister's hand. "Let's just go."

Daisy drove extra slowly so none of the buckets would spill or tip over. By the time they got to the Inn, Daisy felt like a sweaty mess.

Hyacinth groaned. "Daisy, I'm afraid to see Mom."

"Forget that. She'll be so relieved to see us she won't yell at you. Besides, you know Mom blames herself for not insisting she drive the truck."

Millie and Samantha and Rob were waiting. It didn't take long until they had everything in the Crystal Room.

They found their mother trying to unpack one of the cartons.

"Mom, I'm so sorry," Hyacinth said apologetically.

"Come here, you two." Frannie pulled both kids in for a tight hug. "Let's kick ass and get this room looking gorgeous."

Daisy winked at Hyacinth. Their mom would be fine.

For the next few hours, they worked tirelessly to lay out the tablecloths, arrange the flowers, and hang twinkle lights.

"Hooray, we're all done, and with time to spare." Frannie swiped her one good hand across her sweaty forehead.

Daisy took a moment to relish it all. Twelve tables. Each one covered with a floor length black cloth, topped off with a gold glittery square and surrounded by ten gold lacquered chairs. The all-white flower arrangements with the photos of someone's rescue dog prominently displayed in the center of the flowers were sure to catch attention.

Frannie turned to her two daughters. "I'm going to flip on all the lights to see the full effect."

She did. The trio gave each other an exuberant high five. The Crystal Room sparkled. The magnificent crystal chandelier in the center of the room shimmered with prisms of light playing off it and spread its glow to all the tables. The numerous palm and ficus trees loaded with hundreds of gold twinkle lights blinked on and off around the perimeter of the room. Even from where they stood the patio bushes covered in hundreds of twinkly lights could be seen through the huge French doors.

Hyacinth waved her hands around the room. "Mom. This room is ready for a party."

"It does look spectacular." Daisy blew her hair off her damp forehead. "And now that we're done, I'm going to get Max and head to the bar for a glass of wine. Do you and Hyacinth want to join me?"

"Thanks, but I'm whipped, and my wrist hurts," Frannie said. "I'm going to head home."

"I'll come with you," Hyacinth said.

"What time do you plan to come back?" Daisy asked.

"I'm not sure. Probably around seven." Hyacinth glanced at her mom. "Is that good for you?"

"Sure. That's fine," Frannie said.

"Then I'll see you two later." Daisy walked off to get Max from Samantha's office and head to the bar.

The Oak Room had always been her favorite spot in the Inn. Today she stopped to admire the highly polished mahogany bar along one wall with a mirror behind it and two shelves filled with bottles of liquor glistening in the recessed lighting in the bulkhead. On the opposite wall, a fireplace burned, making the space cozy and intimate.

She lingered with Max in the doorway, trying to see where to sit. Two women were seated at one of several booths against the far wall, an older couple were sitting at a freestanding table in the center of the room, and a handful of men and women were seated at the bar. *Hmmm*, the two leather wingback chairs by the old fieldstone fireplace were empty. *Perfect.* Meandering over to one, she sat facing the fire, enjoying the warmth from the flames.

Max found his own favorite personal space and sat with his head on her toes. Within seconds, he was asleep.

She'd enjoyed working with her mom and Hyacinth. Doing something creative had been a relief from her usual work. Sadly she wasn't looking forward to returning to D.C.

She leaned back and closed her eyes until someone tapped her shoulder. "Want company?" Samantha held up two glasses of wine.

"Sure, I'd love that, and thanks for the drink." Daisy smiled and grasped the wine glass.

This was nice. She'd like to get to know Samantha better.

"I have to tell you the Inn looks amazing, and my suite, well, that's something else. Love the blue toilet paper."

Samantha laughed. "Thanks. It's been rewarding to fix it up and see people's reactions." She sat forward. "So, you like working with my dad?"

"I do, very much. He's been like a mentor to me."

Daisy sipped her wine. Could she ask Samantha a personal question? She seemed friendly enough, so she jumped right in. "I'm curious, and I hope you don't mind me asking, but why didn't you want to work for him? Seems like that would be a no-brainer."

Samantha's green eyes shined as she discussed her dad. "He's wonderful, but I wanted to try to build something of my own.

Besides, he gets lots of media attention. I hated that as a child—and still do."

"Was it difficult to make the decision to break out on your own?" Daisy asked.

"Yes, of course. I love my dad. He wanted me to work with him, and nothing would have been easier." She ran her fingers along the edge of her wine glass. "But branching out on my own was my dream. He gave me the support I needed to do that."

Daisy debated whether to say anything. She opened up a little. "Unlike you, I always thought I'd work with my dad. Even as a kid, I wanted to follow in his footsteps, and I think he expected that too. I haven't been working for him long, but nothing is as I thought it would be. Now I'm not even sure working for him is right for me."

Samantha leaned toward Daisy and put her wine glass down. "Look, it was a gamble. I wasn't sure I would succeed on my own. I can hardly believe how it turned out so perfectly."

Samantha glanced at her watch. "Darn. I have to go. I need to finish setting up the silent auction and check to make sure the caterer has everything he needs."

She took one last sip of wine and put her empty glass on the table. "Daisy, it's scary to make a big career move, but if working for your dad isn't working, you owe it to yourself to do something about it. Look, I hardly know you, but you seem sad. I never thought I'd be happy in a small town, but I've made lifelong friends here, and I met Harry, the best husband ever. I couldn't be happier. You could do the same for yourself."

Samantha left, and Daisy softly caressed Max. She wished they could have talked some more. She really liked that Samantha had chosen to come talk to her. The Inn felt like the exact opposite of the atmosphere at the firm where everyone was competitive with each other and had no interest in making friends. Gosh, the only friend she really had at work was Edward. She felt more at home here in just the past day than she had in D.C. and her dad's firm in the last six months.

She drank the last of her wine. "Come on, Max. I'm sure you'd like to walk."

They left the bar and headed outside to the small, enclosed dog park.

Her cell rang as she headed up to her suite. She pulled her phone from her jacket pocket and answered.

"Mom, what's up?"

"I know you'll be disappointed, but I'm not coming back tonight."

"Oh, no! Why?"

"Even with all your help, I must have used my wrist too much. It hurts. Hyacinth is still coming. She said to meet her in the lobby at seven-thirty."

"Okay, I understand, but why is Hyacinth coming so late? The gala starts at seven."

"She insists she's here to visit with me. She said she'll have more than enough time at the gala if she meets you at seven-thirty."

"All right. So if you're not coming tonight, how about we meet for an early breakfast?"

"Sure. We could go to Millie's bakery and get coffee there if you want. That way, I could bring Sidney along."

"Perfect. I'll call you in the morning. And tell Hyacinth I'll be waiting for her at the front door. Tell her to be prompt."

"Will do, and have fun at the gala. You'll have to tell me what people say about the flowers."

"Mom, they'll love them." Daisy ended the call and headed up the steps to her suite.

"Come on, Max. I need to feed you."

She walked into the small galley kitchen and grabbed the tote with all his food. She filled his bowl and put it on the floor for him. While he ate, she called Edward. There was no answer but a text message popped up from Meghan. *Can't wait to see you!*

She replied, *Same for me!* followed with three heart emojis.

Glancing at her watch, she saw she still had time to relax before she showered.

She walked into the bedroom and plopped down on the sumptuous bed, fluffed up the pillows, and invited Max to join her before she turned on the TV.

Eight

Ping, ping, ping.

Daisy struggled awake and reached over a sleeping Max to answer her cell.

She peered at the screen and slid the arrow over to accept the call. "Hi, Meghan," she mumbled, rubbing her eyes.

"Daisy, are you sleeping? Do you have any idea what time it is?"

Daisy checked the time on the nearby alarm clock. Six forty-five. Oops! She'd fallen asleep. She'd lain down on the bed and turned on an episode of *The Big Bang Theory*, a show she loved to watch. Only she'd missed it all.

"Oh, no! I'm supposed to meet Hyacinth in forty-five minutes."

"Well, you'd better hurry up."

She glanced at Max. He had his head propped up on the pillow next to hers, and his eyes were closed.

Her original plan had been to take a long, hot relaxing shower after she walked and fed Max. At least he'd been fed. She didn't have much time. She tickled Max awake. "Come on, buddy. I'd better walk you. I'm going to be gone for a while tonight."

With no time to waste, she nudged him off the bed and snapped on his leash. She practically ran out of her suite, then outside to allow Max time to walk around the doggie park before she headed back to her suite.

Fifteen minutes later she was shampooed and showered.

Unfortunately she didn't have enough time to blow out her unruly blonde curls. Her natural look would have to do. Fortunately she had a sparkly pair of imitation diamond barrettes in her makeup case. They would work. She pinned her hair back from her face and moved on to makeup. Smoky eye shadow and mascara, blush and lipstick. Meghan, the world's best make-up artist, might notice she hadn't used both thickening and lengthening mascaras. Meghan insisted you needed both for optimum results. No time for both now.

In the closet hung her little black dress. She allowed herself a fleeting moment to ogle it.

Not long ago, she and Edward had been on a much-needed caffeine run to the nearby Starbucks when she'd spotted it in a window of one of the fancy dress shops. He'd insisted they had time, and she should go try it on.

Its pencil-thin straps and rhinestone-studded bodice accentuated her small waist, and the silky layers all the way down the dress enhanced the scant curves of her boyish frame. Edward hadn't needed to tell her to buy it—his expression had been all she'd needed to see. Shame he wouldn't see her wearing it tonight. It might have enticed him to kiss her. She indulged for a moment and wondered how that might have felt.

She stood on tiptoes and stretched her arms to remove the dress from the hanger. It got stuck, and when she pulled on it, she heard a rip. *Oh, no.*

She scrunched her eyes shut, not wanting to see what had happened. One of the thin straps was hanging by a thread.

She burst into tears.

The only other clothes she had were casual jeans, leggings, and sweaters.

It was only a dress, and she was overreacting, but it felt like a metaphor for her life. Nothing seemed to be going the way she wanted or expected.

She gritted her teeth. She could sit here and mope and feel sorry for herself or she could pull herself together and do something. If she was going to go to the gala, the dress had to be repaired.

Maybe Sandi or someone at the reception desk could help her. She picked up the house phone to call but then remembered having seen a sign posted earlier informing guests the desk would be closed from four to eleven.

What were her options?

Some inns or hotels had those little fix-it sewing kits, not that she'd ever used one. Samantha had thought of everything else, why not a sewing kit?

First place to check would be the bathroom. She flew in there and started pulling open all the vanity drawers. Nothing in the first three. She slowly opened the last one, praying she'd find something, and there it was, a little gold mesh bag in the back of the drawer.

She held her breath and unzipped it. She pulled out a sample-sized body cream, a shower cap, and then she hit the jackpot—a tiny plastic sewing kit containing a needle and a few strands of different colored thread.

I can do this. After all she was a trained lawyer. She could certainly sew a strap back on a dress. How hard could it be?

She walked back into the bedroom, sat on the bed, threaded the needle, and without much of a plan started sticking it into the fabric and attempted to reattach the strap to the dress.

She had no idea what she was doing, which was obvious every time she pricked one of her fingers.

Five minutes later, the strap was reattached. It looked a little askew, but it would have to do. She was running out of time.

She slipped on the dress and checked herself out in the mirror.

Oh no! It was twisted and off center.

Her mother had tried many times to teach her to sew. Why hadn't she paid attention? Actually it was so bad, people might think it was a new fashion statement. She had no choice but to go with it.

With no time to spare, she slipped her feet into her four-inch black satin sandals and glanced down at her feet. Her shoes were spectacular, and they boosted her five-foot-three stature into the not-short range.

All set, she kissed Max on his snoozer, placed his green plush toad under his paw, and slipped her lipstick into her small evening purse.

Unbelievably she was right on time.

A large banner hanging from Sandi's desk read, "Welcome to the third annual Fur-Baby Gala," and wherever she glanced, she saw clusters of white and gold candles, giving the lobby a warm and elegant glow.

By the front door stood the pièce de résistance. An enormous portrait of two shelties sitting on a cream colored brocaded sofa was displayed on an easel. She recognized Luke, and the other sheltie must be Annie. It was signed by Harper McNeely. A small handwritten sign was attached to the top of the easel.

"Tonight at our silent auction, bid on your own commissioned painting by Houndsville's esteemed local artist, Harper McNeely."

She could imagine Max having his portrait done and how much she would treasure it. If only he were hers. She shook off that thought and walked out the front door to watch for her sister.

A long line of cars awaited valets. People walking into the Inn smiled and pointed to the iridescent paw prints on the red carpet.

Bushes and trees glimmered with twinkle lights in the moonless night sky, giving the whole place a fairy tale glow. Maybe it was the reminder of stringing Christmas tree lights when she was a child, but somehow twinkle lights always made her feel good.

She shivered and ran her hands up and down her arms, her little black dress doing nothing to keep her warm. Just as she turned to go back inside, she recognized her mom's car turning into the circular drive and coming to a stop. The valet ran over to open the door. Hyacinth gingerly climbed out of the car. Daisy put her hand over her mouth.

She could hardly believe she was looking at her big sister. Most days, Hyacinth wore business attire, her long dark hair pulled back into a simple ponytail.

Not tonight. Her long hair curled around her face, framing her pretty blue eyes, and she looked stunning in a soft lemon colored dress that hugged her rail-thin body. Of course Daisy's eyes landed on her shoes. Her tiny ankles were encased in navy suede sandals that made Daisy's eyes pop. Who had highjacked her sister and turned her into a girly girl?

Hyacinth strolled up the steps and gently kissed Daisy on her cheek.

"Sis, you look amazing." Daisy grabbed Hyacinth's hand and pulled her up the steps to walk inside.

"And I love your dress," Hyacinth said. "It suits you, but I hate to tell you your strap is crooked."

Daisy moved back quickly. "I know. Don't touch. I ripped it and did a quickie repair."

Hyacinth burst out laughing. "No wonder it's crooked. You actually sewed something."

"I had no choice. Hopefully no one else notices. Come on. Let's party."

Hyacinth shook her head. "Okay, but for the record I'm impressed you sewed." Still holding hands, they zigzagged through several groups of people toward the Crystal Room.

A crowd had gathered around a huge screen suspended from the ceiling.

"Wait," Daisy said. "Let's see what this is all about."

It quickly became apparent this was a video of a rescue operation. It depicted dogs cowering in filthy conditions with rescue workers carrying them to a waiting van. Daisy gripped her sister's hand tighter.

The final scene, a year after the operation, showed Millie with rescue workers and some of the rescued dogs looking happy and healthy.

While the people standing around clapped, one strident voice remarked, "They're obviously showing us this so we'll donate more money."

Daisy thought she recognized that loud voice. Sure enough, when she peered through the throng of people she spotted Betsy

Carlson, and standing beside her, looking totally out of place and embarrassed, was her sister in a lacy pale yellow blouse and a long navy skirt.

"That loud voice is Betsy Carlson's," Daisy said. "Let's get away from here."

"Who?"

"A major problem. I'll tell you all about her later. The music sounds great. Let's see what's going on."

A crowd of guests stood in the doorway. They had to maneuver past them to get into the room.

"Wow!" Daisy mouthed to her sister. "The room looks even better at night."

They weren't the only ones who thought the room looked amazing. Daisy heard another person standing near her comment, "Ooh, look how pretty."

Hyacinth tapped her to look at another couple who stood open-mouthed. The husband said, "I've never seen this old room look so good."

"I knew it," Hyacinth said. "The guests love the way the room looks. I can't wait to tell Mom."

Daisy glanced around. Women with glittery dresses and fabulous hair styles stood talking to men looking suave in dark suits. Tuxedoed waiters passed hors d'oeuvre trays and soft jazz filled the air. The twinkle lights and the crystal chandelier beamed down on everyone, creating a magical scene.

She craned her neck. "I wish I could find Meghan. I thought I'd see her right away. Oh, wait, I do see Allan Gold."

"You know him? The billionaire?" Hyacinth asked, surprised.

"Yes, he's a client." She looped her arm through Hyacinth's. "Come with me. I want to say hello."

Daisy hadn't known he would be here, but it wasn't totally surprising. He always talked about his daughter and her accomplishments. It made sense he would be here to support her.

She waved as she dragged Hyacinth over to greet him. His arm was wrapped around Julie Jewels, the owner of the jewelry shop next to her mom's store.

He smiled as she approached. "This is delightful," he said boisterously. "I know your mom lives here, but I didn't expect to see you. Don't you have a big trial coming up?"

Daisy winced and avoided answering his question. "Allan, meet my sister, Hyacinth. Our mom is the florist in charge of the flowers and decor for tonight. Unfortunately she broke her wrist earlier this week. We came to help her."

Allan shook hands with Hyacinth. "I hope your mom is okay. She's not here with you?"

"No," Daisy said, shaking her head. "She said her wrist hurt after setting up today. She wanted to stay home tonight."

"It's a shame she's not here. Everyone is remarking about how extraordinary the Inn looks. I hope she feels better soon." Allan put his arm around Julie's waist. "Have you met Julie?"

"Yes, I have. Her store is right next to my mom's. It's impossible not to stop and gawk at window displays. Her jewelry is quite special." Daisy smiled at Julie. "It's nice to see you again."

"You also," Julie replied.

Julie was wearing an emerald green dress with a plunging neckline and an eye-catching pendant around her neck.

"Your necklace is amazing. I assume you designed it," Daisy said, staring at a round medallion with a paw-print encrusted in diamonds.

Julie smiled. "Yes, I made an identical one for the silent auction."

In Daisy's mind, Julie and Allan looked like a power couple who fit together perfectly.

"So let's go see what else is being auctioned," Daisy suggested.

Hyacinth tapped Daisy on her arm. "Hey Daisy, I see a friend who I want to talk to. I'll catch up with you in a few minutes."

Suddenly a flash popped in Allan's face. "Who the hell was that?" Allan shook his fist at the photographer. "I'm going to complain to Samantha. I don't want a photographer following me around here."

"Calm down," Julie said, putting her hand on his arm. "That was Vince Cordoza. He works for *Leisurely Living* magazine. After they did an article on smalltown living, Samantha worked hard to persuade them to come back to do a spread on the gala. The press coverage will be wonderful for the Inn and Millie's foundation. Don't mess with him."

Allan shook his head. "Sorry. I got caught off guard. I'm not used to being photographed in Houndsville. Come on you two, I need a drink. Let's go to the bar."

"Good idea," Julie said. "Maybe we can catch a waiter and see what nibbles are being passed around. Millie told me the food would be divine, and I'm hungry."

Suddenly Daisy realized she hadn't eaten anything, and she was starving. She hoped Julie was right and the food would be good.

The threesome had only taken few steps when a well-dressed elderly couple stopped Julie. He couldn't wait to tell Julie he had bid on her pendant for his wife.

Julie thanked him profusely.

"What an adorable couple. He looks besotted with her," Daisy whispered to Julie as the husband grabbed his wife's hand and walked off with her. "Someday I hope I find someone who loves me that much."

Julie looked at her and smiled. "Hang around Millie long enough, and she'll have you matched up and married in no time flat."

"I've been told to watch out for her meddling, that she's dauntless," Daisy said.

"Let's go, you two. You're dawdling." Allan grabbed Julie's hand and steered her toward the bar. A large crowd was gathered in the area. Allan signaled to one of the bartenders. He came right over. "What can I get you to drink?"

Allan ordered a Johnny Walker Black for himself. Julie and Daisy each requested a glass of white wine.

With drinks in hand, they moved away from the bar and were approached by a waiter who had tiny crab cakes on his tray.

"Those were delicious," Daisy said after finishing hers. "I didn't realize how hungry I was."

"I agree," Allan said and placed his hand on Julie's arm. "Would you mind terribly if I had a word with Daisy alone? Could you find someone to hang out with for a few minutes?"

Daisy froze, barely holding on to her glass. What was this about? Was something wrong? Her stomach clenched up.

"Sure," Julie said. "I'll go check out the silent auction."

Allan looked at Daisy. "Stop staring at the floor. Nothing is wrong. Funny, you do the same thing in your office. You avoid eye contact when you're nervous and don't have an answer for a legal issue."

Daisy lifted her eyes and looked at him. He was right. If only she could relax. It was just too difficult not knowing what he wanted to talk to her about.

"I told you nothing's wrong. Just bring your drink and follow me. We'll go to Samantha's office."

Allan zigzagged through the crowd with Daisy behind him, dragging her feet.

When they got to Samantha's office, he held the door open for her. The office was small, and since she'd never been there before, she stood waiting for him to tell her where to go.

"Let's go sit over there." He pointed to two upholstered chairs with a small table between them by the window.

She picked one and sat primly with her hands wrapped tightly around her wine glass.

"Take it easy. Drink your wine." He sat in the other chair, put his glass down on the table, and leaned back.

"I know you're wondering what's up. I'll get right to the point. I find myself in an unusual position. Your dad is my friend, and he might find issue with what I'm about to do, but I'm going to do it anyway."

He paused. "I won't beat around the bush. I want you to come work for me."

Daisy's heart skipped a beat. She was tongue-tied. This was a major compliment, and she should say something.

Allan chuckled. "It's not often I render an attorney speechless. I know this is a shock. Don't say anything yet. Let me talk."

He crossed one leg over the other and took a sip of his drink, looking totally at ease. Did he hope that would lead her to do the same? If only she could. Her heart was beating a mile a minute. She could hardly relax.

"I know you talked with Samantha today. It was her idea for me to offer you a job. She cornered me when I got to the Inn tonight. She's never done that before, but she said she spoke with you earlier and felt an immediate connection to you."

Daisy smiled. "That's so nice. I felt the same about her."

"Well," Allan added, "she already knew I thought highly of you, and she got the sense you're unhappy working for your dad. She suggested I help you and offer you a position. She says I'll be lucky if you accept."

He smiled before adding, "I agree wholeheartedly with her."

Daisy frowned. "But you—"

"I know what you're going to say. I told you to stick it out with your dad. Samantha disagrees. I've decided to listen to her. I'm offering you a position as director of development. For now, you'll be based in Houndsville. You'll be working on my new project on the inlet."

Daisy gripped the glass in her hands and took a deep breath. No doubt this was a major opportunity for her.

A million thoughts zinged through her brain all at once and collided at one conclusion. "It's wonderful to have someone believe in me and my capabilities. If only my dad did too, I'd be much happier."

Her whole body started to tremble. Could she give up her life-long dream of working with her dad? Would he even care if she left?

She wanted very much to lean over and hug Allan, but thinking that was unprofessional, she tried to put her hug into words.

"Allan, from the moment I met you I liked and admired you. You've listened to me…really listened, and I'm not sure how to thank you properly for giving me this opportunity."

"Does that mean you're accepting my offer?"

She thought about it for a minute. "This is a huge decision. I'd like to think it over for a bit. Get used to the idea."

He smiled graciously. "That's appropriate. If you want, we can talk tomorrow in more depth about the details of the offer." He tapped his fingers on his glass. "Regrettably I need a response from you rather soon. I originally had someone else in mind for this job, but I can wait on your answer for a few days. I have some international interests, which means I'll be traveling extensively, and I need someone looking out for me on site as soon as possible."

"All right," Daisy said, swallowing past the lump in her throat. "And thank you again. When I get a chance, I'll thank Samantha too."

He nodded and stood up. "Julie will be looking for me. Let's go. You should go find your sister and share the news."

"No, that's okay. I need some time to process this. I'm going to sit here for a few minutes." She smiled tremulously. "I'll meet you back there soon."

"All right," he said, turning to leave. "Remember, I'll need an answer, let's give it until next Monday."

He left her there.

Various scenarios ran through her brain. None seemed fool-proof. For instance, if she left the law firm, would her dad ever talk to her again? She wasn't sure she could handle that. And what if she accepted Allan's job offer and ended up not liking it? What then?

I'm terrified that whatever I do, I'll make a mistake.

Nine

The crowd had grown larger as she wandered back into the Crystal Room. All around her people had drinks in their hands and were chatting and laughing.

They appeared trouble free. She wished she felt like them.

She heard someone calling out her name and turned around to see Grant waving as he headed in her direction.

She smiled, and her heart skipped a beat. His navy blue suit showed off his broad shoulders and fit him like a glove. A scarlet tie was knotted perfectly under a white spread collar.

What was it about spread collars that made a guy look sexy? With a bright glint in his playful hazel eyes, he had her complete attention. He was exactly the distraction she needed.

"So you like the way I look?" he murmured, softly teasing her.

Guess her wide open mouth had given her away. "Mmmm. I guess so." She tried to avert her eyes from him, to downplay her reaction. She certainly found this new Grant intriguing.

Seeming to sense her unease at his poking fun at her, he pleaded, "Join me for a drink?"

She'd left her glass in Samantha's office. Another glass of wine might help her to loosen up. "Yes, definitely, but wait a sec." She held up her hand and pointed to the right. "I finally see Meghan and your brother. Give me one minute." She raced to her best friend, nearly tripping in her spiky heels, and threw her arms around her. When she let go, she stood back to check out Meghan and her fiancé, Nicholas. Grant's identical twin.

Meghan's hair was in a ponytail wrapped with a gold cuff. Her luminous violet eyes were enhanced with lots of navy shadow and mascara. Her curvy frame was ensconced in a shimmery navy dress, and she'd completed the look with an amazing pair of silver-heeled navy stilettos. Of course Daisy adored the shoes.

"Good you called earlier," Daisy said.

"Yeah, Flowers, next time set an alarm," Meghan said before leaning forward and whispering in her ear, "You and Grant?" Her mouth puckered, and her eyebrows scrunched together over her nose.

Daisy bit her lip to keep from laughing. Meghan would laugh too if she could see her own expression. She'd practiced for years and still couldn't get the one raised eyebrow correct.

"Shh," Daisy mumbled. "He asked me to get a drink with him. Not to go to bed with him."

"Is that why your face is turning red?" Meghan teased as she watched Grant walking over to join them.

"Hello, Meghan, Nick," Grant said, first hugging Meghan and then wrapping his arm around his brother. "Come on. I promised Daisy a drink."

"Good idea," Meghan responded, pointing to the bar. "Looks like Millie and her crew are there. We can party together."

Meandering around the guests, Nicholas and Meghan led the way, stopping several times to say hello to other couples. Daisy saw her sister and waved her over.

"Hey sis, having fun?" Daisy asked.

"Yes, but I wish Tucker was here. He's fun, and I would love for you to meet him."

"Well, he's not, so you can join us. You remember Grant?"

"Yes, I do. Hi, Grant."

Together they joined Millie, Carl, Samantha, and Harry.

"Now that we're all together, let's get drinks." Grant placed his arm around Daisy's shoulder.

She melted into him, her body tingling.

To even peek at Hyacinth or Meghan could prove disastrous. Undoubtedly Meghan would make silly kissy faces, and Hyacinth would do something just as bad.

"The bar's crowded, so why don't you guys order drinks? We'll wait here," Samantha suggested.

"Good idea, Sam," Harry said to his wife. "I know what you want. Everyone else, give us your orders, and we'll get the drinks."

After the count was taken, the guys all strolled off to snag a bartender.

"Hey, everyone," Millie said. "Take a peek to your left. Something weird is going on. I have no idea why Christopher is here, but he's having a cozy conversation with Betsy. Don't look now, but he has his hand on her arm. It looks like they're more than friends."

"Oh my goodness, I remember him," Daisy mumbled to Millie. "He was the kid at the ice cream store. He looks almost exactly the same. Only difference is he's not as chunky as he used to be. Probably doesn't eat as much ice cream now that he sold you the farmhouse."

Millie chuckled. "Yes. That's him. I thought he couldn't wait to leave Houndsville behind and start somewhere new."

"So what's he doing here?" Daisy asked.

"Give Millie time and she'll get the scoop." Meghan chuckled and so did Daisy.

"Oh, now I get it. Ice cream scoop," Samantha said, laughing too.

"Shh, let's listen," Millie said, putting her fingers up to her lips. Their whole group, including people standing nearby, could hear them clearly as they were quite loud.

Christopher scowled. "You had me buy those expensive tickets for a cruise. Now you say you're not going."

Betsy took a sip from her glass, looking totally disinterested. "I'm tired of all your whining. I can't stand the thought of spending ten days listening to you complain."

"That's rich after you had me buy you that diamond tennis bracelet and the expensive designer clothes you said you needed for the cruise."

Millie whispered, "Yikes, he's trying to grab the bracelet off her wrist."

Betsy pulled away from him. "You're a petty little man. You made me think you were rich and could afford to take care of me. Now all you do is complain about spending money you don't seem to have."

He got in her face and spat out, "You disgust me. I wish I'd never met you."

"So leave me alone." With that, she ripped the bracelet off her wrist and threw it at his head. She sneered when he ducked and stalked off to the bar where she flagged down one of the bartenders.

"Yikes, that was ugly," Millie said. "And did you see Vince standing off to the side? I believe he got a photo of Betsy throwing the bracelet at Christopher. That could certainly make a juicy bit of gossip, depending on what he plans to do with it."

"What are you women whispering about?" Harry asked Millie as he and the other guys handed out the glasses of wine to the women.

"Apparently Christopher and Betsy know each other quite well," Millie answered.

"Shh, she's heading our way," Meghan murmured.

Betsy's eyes seemed to focus on Daisy, and she pointed at her. "I remember seeing you yesterday ogling Grant Stamford. Were you jealous that he was with me and not you?" She ran her fingers down her body and cackled. "He only likes tall voluptuous women like me. He wouldn't be caught dead with someone like you."

Daisy stood wide-eyed and horrified. How embarrassing. It was made worse by the throng of guests standing nearby who seemed caught up in Betsy's continuing tirade. "You thought you saw me leave the Inn, but I came back inside and watched you cozying up with Grant after he was done with me. Good luck with that."

Betsy must have hit a nerve. Grant's face lost all its color. She couldn't believe how well Betsy lied and commanded an audience. Grant clearly hated her, and she obviously got pleasure embarrassing both of them.

Daisy could feel her face heating up. "Are you sure I can't strangle her?" Daisy half-kidded, although there were gasps from the crowd, and they moved away, possibly fearing a fight might break out.

"No, you can't," Grant said, grabbing her hand. "Ignore her. She's a horrible human being. Come on, we'll all go see what's happening with the silent auction."

"Great idea," Meghan, Millie, Samantha, and Hyacinth chimed in together, forming a circle around her. Daisy glanced around at all of them. Having Betsy humiliate her had been awful, but having her friends, Grant, and her sister rally to her side felt amazing. A warmth spread throughout her body. Right here, right now, she felt protected and loved.

As a group, they maneuvered around the people to get to the back of the room to where the auction items were displayed on a large table. The guys hung back as the women walked over to survey the items and the bids.

The first item they looked at was a large wicker basket filled with books from Bridget's Bookstop. The books were mostly dog-themed titles, a few old Nancy Drews, and several Hardy Boys. There were about ten bids.

"Hey sis, look at this." Hyacinth pulled Daisy over to look at another item. On display was a sample flower arrangement by their mom, but the actual bid was for an arrangement made to the winner's specifications.

Daisy touched one of the flowers. "It's not real. What a great idea for Mom to do a custom arrangement out of silk flowers. That way people can pick their favorite flowers and colors, and it'll last a long time."

The next item was a box of sample cookies from The Best Doggone Bakery, but the actual bid was for six months of free dog treats.

"Meghan, you'd better bid on this. It's perfect for you," Millie said.

Meghan looked at the bidding sheet and grabbed the nearby pen. "Done. I hope I win."

"Come on. There's more to see," Samantha said.

The women circled around the table to what appeared to be the two hot items of the night, if the number of people hanging around was any indication. One was the Harper McNeely commissioned painting, the other Julie's pendant.

"Hey, you guys," Millie said. "It's almost time for me to make my speech. I'm going to the ladies' room to freshen up. Anyone want to join me? You can come back here and see the other items later."

Everyone nodded.

"I'll go tell the guys to find tables near the lectern," Samantha offered. "Wait here."

The women waited for Samantha to return, and then the group of them weaved their way to the ladies' lounge. Samantha opened the door, and like ducks in a row, they filed inside.

Millie, being first in, stopped in her tracks. "Uh-oh." She turned to her friends. "Trouble ahead."

At first Daisy couldn't see who was seated in the small anteroom, but she did recognize the woman's shoes. She'd seen those same shoes earlier, on Betsy's feet. Embellished cobalt satin Manolo Blahnik pumps, the most coveted shoes of the season, and they cost a small fortune. Eleven hundred bucks.

Now she knew why Millie had said trouble ahead. Betsy was seated in front of the large rectangular mirror fluffing her short dark hair. Her sister, Stephanie, stood next to her. The silence in the room was palpable. Daisy cringed. She thought about turning around and leaving. This could be an unmitigated disaster. And no one could get to the mirror or even the toilets without dealing with Betsy.

"Well, well, if it isn't Betsy Clarkson," Millie announced loudly. Daisy took that as a warning and banded together with her friends.

Betsy shifted her body to face Millie directly. "Oh, how perfect! Millie Whitfield and all her cohorts in one place. How lucky could I be?"

She smiled nastily. "Wouldn't you know I have some news that you're going to want to hear? It's just too bad your hotshot veterinarian brother can't be here to listen too."

Meghan put her hands on her hips. "If you had something important to tell Millie, why didn't you tell her earlier when you were so busy harassing our friend."

Betsy shrugged. "I forgot. I promise you'll want to hear it though."

"If you have something to tell me, you'd better hurry. I'm supposed to be making my speech soon," Millie retorted.

"Oh, dear," Betsy said with a disdainful flip of her hair. "Maybe I ought to wait until later. I wouldn't want to put you off your game and have you ruin your minute of glory."

"Betsy, spit it out," Millie said, clenching her hands into fists. Daisy seriously wondered if Millie was going to take a swing at Betsy.

"Okay, you asked for it. I know where there's a puppy mill. And the dogs don't look so good."

Stephanie seemed about to say something. Betsy quelled that temptation with a glare.

"You're bluffing. How would you know that? It doesn't make sense."

"Why not? I've been thinking about breeding Cleo again and was checking around to locate a dog to mate her with."

"If there is someone running a puppy mill nearby, I can't believe I haven't heard about it. But even if that's true, why tell me? Why not call a rescue group or animal control?"

Betsy sneered. "You think I care if someone wants to run a puppy mill? No sweat off my back. Besides, then I'd miss riling you up. It's fun to see the emotions flitting across your face. I know you're already thinking about those poor dogs and how you can help them. But I'm just not quite ready to reveal my information. I expect you to grovel for it."

"Betsy, please tell me," Millie said softly. "How could you want something bad to happen to any dogs?"

Daisy was surprised to hear Millie ask Betsy nicely, but then she realized Millie knew exactly what she was doing.

Betsy had told Millie to grovel, and if that was the only way Millie could get the information she needed to rescue these poor unfortunate dogs, Millie would do it. Smart woman. Yelling and screaming would get her nowhere.

Betsy cackled. "Oh, I like this new Millie. Show up at my house tomorrow morning at nine. If you're nice, I'll tell you then."

Millie gritted her teeth. "After my speech would be better." She was barely holding her temper in check.

Betsy snickered. "Do you want the scoop or not? Stephanie and I are leaving. I'm not interested in hearing your speech. If you want the information, be at my house nine sharp. And don't be late. I'm not going to wait around for you."

"Fine. I'll be there, and now if you don't mind, I need to refresh my lipstick."

"You'll need more than lipstick to make your face look good." Betsy smirked as she grabbed her purse and strolled out the door, her heels clicking on the wood floor. Stephanie glanced at everyone, seeming to still want to say something, but she scurried after her sister.

"That was awful," Hyacinth said as everyone circled around Millie.

"Do you believe her?" Meghan asked. "She's such a witch, and we know she lies."

Millie looked at her friends. "Why would she make this up?"

They all glanced at each other and shrugged. "That's obvious. To get to you," said Hyacinth.

"The only way to find out is to go to her house." Millie sighed.

"Do you want me to go with you?" Samantha asked.

"I could come along too. Might be good to have a lawyer present," Daisy added.

"Let me think about it," Millie said as she applied her lipstick.

"Oh no, Samantha, I hear the band playing the song you told me would be my ten minute signal until my speech." She stuck her lipstick back in her purse. "Someone take my handbag. We'll have to figure this out later."

Ten

As her friends headed to their tables to meet the guys, Millie walked to the microphone. She took a deep breath and exhaled.

Samantha had made sure to place the microphone and lectern strategically where everyone could see and hear her. She palmed her sweaty hands on the side of her dress and grabbed onto the small lectern to steady her nerves before looking out into the crowd. It seemed like this year the group was larger than ever. They grew silent as she began to speak.

"Good evening, ladies and gentlemen, and welcome to the third annual Fur-Baby Gala. We're thrilled you're here to celebrate with us after another successful year for our charitable foundation."

She took a steadying breath. "For those of you who aren't familiar with our foundation's goals, I'll give a quick overview."

She took a deep breath, memories filling her head. "Everything started three years ago when our local sheltie rescue group extricated eighty-seven dogs from a dire situation. Short on funds to get them the proper vet care, I came up with a plan to raise the needed money. With help from our local shopkeepers, a leading businessman who made a huge donation, and proceeds from the first Fur-Baby Gala, we succeeded beyond our imagination. As a result we formed a charitable foundation to help other dogs."

Many of the guests clapped, allowing Millie time to gather her thoughts and gaze around the room. She must be doing okay. They were paying attention.

She continued. "I can proudly report our foundation has helped shelters and rescue groups outside of Houndsville and contributed money where it was needed for lifesaving operations. And this year we've added a silent auction to raise more money. We hope you'll take a look at the fantastic items and bid if you are able. The auction will be open for another two hours. Winners will be notified tomorrow."

She relaxed when her eyes settled on Carl, and he nodded slightly at her.

"One last thing. Tonight, also a new first, we hired horse drawn carriages to take you on a leisurely trip around downtown Houndsville. The cost is fifty dollars, and all proceeds will go to support our foundation. We have two carriages, and they are out front and ready to roll."

Almost done, she relaxed.

"Remember as you leave to collect your Fur-Baby Gala baseball cap as our thanks for attending tonight's festivities. You'll find them in baskets by the front door."

Millie turned to leave the microphone but stepped back to add, "Don't forget to hug your fur-babies today and every day."

She looked out at the tables as the small audience erupted in applause, and to her surprise, she caught sight of her three brothers and Carl standing together with all her friends, whistling and clapping for her. She smiled, left the lectern, and circled around the tables, shaking hands and receiving congratulations from many of the guests before reaching Carl, who stood with open arms. She welcomed his hug and allowed herself a moment to take a deep breath.

"Great job," he said. "You should do this more often. You really kept everyone's attention."

Millie sighed. "I'm just relieved I did okay. Right before the speech, a bunch of us ran into Betsy in the ladies' room. She was in rare form. She insisted she knows about a puppy mill around here."

"What? How would she know about that?" Carl frowned. "Besides, we all know she lies."

"Listen to Carl," Samantha said.

Meghan nodded. "I agree."

"All right, so could we please get me a glass of wine and a slider or two?"

"Sure," Carl answered. "Come on. Anyone who wants food, follow us."

Carl put his arm around Millie and steered her as they threaded their way through a throng of guests. Daisy and Grant joined them. The others stayed behind.

Even before they reached the bar, they were stopped by her bakery partners and more friends.

"Good job, Millie," Julie said while Allan slipped his hand into his pocket and pulled out a check he handed to her. Millie thanked him profusely. He was always extremely generous. It was his one-hundred-thousand-dollar donation at the very first Fur-Baby Gala that had allowed the foundation to thrive so quickly.

And as they left that group, several more couples crowded around to congratulate her for being a great public speaker.

"Hooray! We finally made it," Millie said, leaning against the bar and slipping off her shoes to give her feet a rest.

Carl laughed. "I know you hate that you're short and would love to be taller, but your feet don't seem to agree."

"Same for me." Daisy chuckled.

Millie sighed. "Yes, wearing these stilettos is a bummer."

"Can I get you something to drink?" a bartender smiled and asked.

Carl pointed to one of the wine bottles. "Yes, please. Two sauvignon blancs."

Grant nodded. "Two for us also."

Carl tapped Millie's arm. "Stay here. Talk to Daisy and Grant. Rest your feet. I see a tray of sliders at the end of the bar. I'll grab some for all of us."

Sitting next to the sliders were plates and napkins. Millie watched as Carl piled some sliders on a plate, picked up some napkins, and walked back. "Food for the best speaker of the evening and for friends who agree."

With a chuckle, Millie picked up a slider. "That's because I was the only speaker."

Carl chomped one and Grant followed suit while Millie recounted her heated conversation with Betsy in the ladies' room.

"Millie, stay away from her," Grant said. "You already know she's trouble."

"Yes, I do, but I have to find out if what she said was true. There may be dogs that need rescuing. It will just be a quick visit to her house."

"Mil, I'm counting on you to be careful." Carl put his hand on her arm.

"Always," she replied.

"Yeah, sis, listen to—" Grant's cell pinged, diverting everyone's attention. He reached into his pants pocket, pulled it out, and looked at the screen. "It might be an emergency. I have to take this."

Millie knew there was a problem when Grant said he'd meet the person at the clinic in less than fifteen minutes.

"Who was that?" Millie asked.

"A new client who is panicked about their puppy. I don't want them to worry. I told them I'd meet them at the clinic."

"You mean you have to leave?" Millie said, frowning.

"It doesn't sound serious. I should be back soon." He walked over to Daisy and spoke to her for a minute before the two of them walked off.

Millie slipped her shoes back on and tapped Carl's arm. "Come on. Let's mingle. I should try to drum up more donations."

A half-hour later, Millie stopped Carl and leaned on his shoulder. "My feet are killing me. Please find us a table where we can sit down."

"You sure? I don't want you to moan later that you should have tried to get more money for the dogs."

"Of course you're right, but I think I've done my best."

Carl led her over to the table where Nicholas and Harry sat. She half-heartedly listened to them telling jokes while she mulled over a plan she'd been formulating in her head.

It didn't take long, and once she had it all figured out, she wanted to implement it right away. All she needed was Carl's, Grant's, and Daisy's unknowing cooperation. She glanced at her watch. Grant had been gone for a while. She suspected he might already be back.

She tapped Carl on his shoulder. "The party's winding down. Do you think it would be okay if we disappeared for a bit and went on the carriage ride? It should be fun."

Carl arched an eyebrow. "Millie, you have that devious look in your eyes. Are you plotting something?"

"Uh-oh. There's talk Grant is your next victim," Harry commented. "Should I forewarn him?"

"Oh, come on. I'm harmless," Millie retorted.

Harry laughed. "Tell that to Samantha. Anyway, I refuse to be a party to whatever you have planned. Time for me to find my wife." He sauntered off.

Nicholas nodded to Carl. "She's your problem. I'm off to find Meghan." He walked off in a hurry and didn't look back.

Carl narrowed his eyes on Millie. "Leave Grant alone. Stop intruding."

"Who, me?" Millie murmured, looking downward.

Carl placed his hand on her arm and peered into her eyes. "Hmmm, as always, I'm sure I know exactly what is going on in that head of yours."

Millie didn't respond.

"Come on, Millie. You don't even know if Daisy already has a relationship with someone back in D.C."

"You're right, she might have someone in D.C., but what if Grant would be better for her?"

She placed her hand on Carl's arm. "It's just a carriage ride. I'm going to find Daisy. Meet me at the front door in ten minutes."

She winked and walked off.

The crowds had thinned out as she headed toward the lobby, thinking that was where she might find Daisy. Instead she spotted

Annabel poking her finger in Christopher's chest, her face contorted angrily while Christopher stood with his hands on his hips.

This could be interesting. She figured she had a minute to eavesdrop.

She hid behind a nearby ficus tree where she could hear them easily.

Annabel hissed." You gave me your word you'd get Betsy to help me with my renovation. Now that the money is due, she's not coughing up one penny."

Christopher groaned. "That's because she found out your shop is in trouble. She told me she didn't plan to lose money on a failing proposition. Betsy would never do anything that didn't benefit her."

"Oh, that's rich. I introduce you to Betsy, you two hook up, you're happy, and I'm screwed. I should have known better than to trust her."

"Yeah, you should have. FYI, I'm done with her too."

Millie shook her head, shocked. Here she'd thought Betsy and Annabel were friends. Seemed like they were using each other for their own purposes. She'd heard enough. They deserved each other.

A group of partygoers headed her way. She snuck out from behind the tree and blended in with them to keep Annabel or Christopher from seeing her as she resumed her mission to find Daisy. She was running out of time when she finally glimpsed Daisy and Meghan chatting.

She walked up to them.

"Hey, anyone want to go on the carriage ride with Carl and me?" Millie held her breath, waiting for a response. She counted on the fact Meghan would have to get home to Grace.

"I don't think so," Meghan said. "We should be leaving soon. My parents are babysitting, and by now, they've probably had enough."

Millie smiled inwardly. *So far so good.*

"You should just go with Carl," Daisy said. "Have a romantic carriage ride."

"Oh, I think it'd be more fun with you and Grant."

Daisy raised an eyebrow and observed Millie. "But Grant left to go to the clinic."

Millie gazed back, trying her best to appear relaxed like she had nothing to hide.

"He said he wouldn't be long. Maybe he's already back."

There was the distinct possibility Daisy had figured out what Millie was up to, but a carriage ride would be perfect for her to get to know Grant better.

"If he's back and wants to go, I guess that will be okay," Daisy agreed amicably.

Millie shrugged. Did Daisy suspect her of playing match-maker? No matter. So far her plan seemed to be falling into place.

She swallowed the "hooray" that bubbled up from her chest. "All right. Give me a minute to find Grant, and I'll meet you near the front door."

As she walked off, trying not to look too excited, she muttered, "He'd better be back." She had no time to look for him. She pulled her cell out of her purse and called him.

He answered. "Why are you calling me? I'm back. Well, actually I'm walking in the door now."

"I couldn't find you," she blurted out. "I want you to go on a carriage ride with Carl and me."

"Why me?" he asked. "Your voice sounds funny. Are you plotting something?"

"All right. I already asked Daisy, and she said yes. She even knows I planned to ask you."

"Mil, you're meddling." He paused. "I'll play along but only because this is your special night."

"Ha ha. You're not fooling me. You like Daisy. That's why you've agreed."

Millie shrugged. Who cared about his reason? She'd gotten what she'd wanted.

"Okay, come on then. Meet us at the front door."

Good. Her plan was a go. Grant was playing along like a good little brother should.

Eleven

Millie let out a huge sigh of relief when she saw Carl standing at the front door. She hadn't been sure until that moment he'd go along with her plan. She walked up to him. "Grant's coming, and so is Daisy."

Sure enough, Daisy walked up first and then Grant arrived. He grabbed Daisy's hand and smiled at her.

"Good," Carl said. "I made sure one of the carriages is available. The driver is waiting for us." Carl held open the door. One by one, they walked down the steps to the waiting carriage.

Millie halted suddenly and tapped her fingers on her forehead.

"Oh no! I totally forgot I told old Mr. Swanson I'd find him before he left. He said he wanted to make a large donation." She elbowed Carl in his side, hoping to convey he should play along. "Come on, we need to find him."

She glanced at Grant. "You and Daisy will have to go without us."

And before anyone could say anything, she grabbed Carl's hand, turned away, and practically dragged him up the steps and back inside.

Carl put his hand on her arm to stop her.

"That was classic, Millie." He raised an eyebrow. "I know Mr. Swanson already gave you his donation earlier."

"So what? It's much better for Grant and Daisy to be alone."

"Millie, I was actually looking forward to the carriage ride."

Millie peered at Carl and burst out laughing. "Now who's fooling who? You couldn't care less. You just want to make me feel guilty. It's not going to work. Daisy is perfect for Grant."

Millie smiled at him and murmured, "She loves dogs and she's best friends with Meghan. Two best friends married to twin brothers. What could be better?"

Game on. So far so good!

Grant looked at Daisy, and they both burst out laughing. "Boy, that was so obvious, though I have to admit I never expected her to bail on us," Grant said, taking her hand. "Come on. We should still go. We'll have fun."

"I'm not sure I know what to say." Daisy shook her head. "But I agree, it should be fun."

The carriage reminded Daisy of the ones she'd ridden around in Central Park with her parents and Hyacinth when they were very young children. It was shiny white inside and out with gold trim. The reddish brown horse had a purple plume in its mane.

The driver, an older man, greeted them jovially. "Hi there, I'm Benny." He looked them over from head to toe. "And by the looks of it, you're lovers out for a moonlit ride."

Daisy's face heated up. Grant gave her hand a gentle squeeze.

"Hey mate, don't tease her. I'm just getting to know her. You don't want to ruin it for me." He winked.

Grant held on to the side of the carriage and climbed in then held out his hand to help Daisy onto the white leather seat. She gulped. The small seat meant they'd be butted up against each other.

Benny handed them a warm plaid throw. Grant placed it over their knees, and she pulled it up higher to keep her warm.

The horse started off at a slow walk, breaking into a trot as they moved along.

Daisy was acutely aware of Grant's body pressed up against hers, and with the carriage bumping along, it unsettled her. Was Grant feeling it too? She tried to start a conversation.

"Nice job on your sister's part. Do you think this was what she had in mind the whole time?"

Grant gave her his lopsided smile that made her stomach flip-flop. "Does it matter?"

"No, I guess not. You seem to be okay company for now."

"Geez, a compliment? I'll take it." He chuckled and placed his arm around her shoulders. It felt comfortably cozy, and she nestled in close to him, a warm feeling settling in her belly.

The clip-clop of the horse's hooves lulled her into closing her eyes.

I want Grant to like me.

She opened her eyes and bolted upright, grazing Grant's chin. Where had that thought come from?

"What's wrong?" Grant looked at her, concerned.

She stalled. She held up her hands and blew on them. "Oh, that last bump jolted me. Didn't you feel it?"

Grant stole a glance at her sideways, and she was caught off guard when his eyes met hers and then settled on her lips. Her heart hammered in her chest. It appeared he wanted to kiss her, but what did she want? She didn't have time to think about it. He leaned toward her, and his lips lightly touched hers. Her whole body tingled, and she started to kiss him back when Benny asked," Do you folks live around here?"

She froze and raised her head just as Benny turned around.

"Oops!" He turned his head back around. Too late. The moment had passed. She sighed.

Grant shook his head. "I do. Daisy is a visitor. Do you think you could give her the tour we paid for?"

He sounded annoyed, but Daisy quickly realized he just was disappointed when he took her hand in his and murmured, "Later?"

She could have replied, but she didn't. She wasn't sure what to say.

Benny, for his part, did. "My pleasure."

And for the next fifteen minutes, Benny prattled on about the stores, the park, and lastly the new development down at the inlet, which he thought was great because there would be boat docks.

"You like boating?" Daisy asked, making idle conversation to cover her awkwardness with Grant.

"Sure. What's not to like? Take out the boat, spend a few hours on the water with a shitload of beer and a fishing rod."

As Benny reversed his direction and headed back toward the Inn, Grant questioned her about Max. "You mentioned earlier that Max was not your dog. So what is he doing here with you?"

"My neighbor across the hall had an emergency out of town and asked me to dog sit. I said yes, having no idea I'd end up here helping my mom. Once I decided to come, I had to bring Max with me."

"Why don't you have your own dog? You seem very fond of Max."

"My job," Daisy said. "I'm hardly ever home. And yes, Max is great."

"Maybe you need a different job," he joked.

"That is a possibility," she murmured.

He raised an eyebrow. "Sounds like you're not fond of your job. What do you do, by the way?"

"I'm a lawyer. I work at my dad's law firm in D.C."

"Isn't that a cushy job?" he asked, rubbing his chin.

"Could be, I guess." She shrugged.

"You sound sad."

Daisy answered as she saw it. "I'm not sure working at his firm is right for me.

"Sorry." He glanced at her. "That has to be difficult. Time for a change?"

She took a deep breath and let it out slowly. "Maybe."

She wasn't about to say any more. She'd probably said too much already, although she would have loved to share Allan's job offer with him. She had an innate feeling he'd understand her dilemma.

She sat quietly watching the scenery as Benny continued to guide his horse back to the Inn. Daisy sighed as they passed by the spa.

"I wish I had time to go get a facial or a massage, but I have to leave tomorrow morning to get back to work."

A minute later, Benny pulled up near the front door.

Grant gently removed the blanket, leaving it on the floor, and stood up. He stepped down onto the pavement and held out his hand for Daisy. "Let me help you."

"I'm fine. She stood up to step onto the ground. The heel of her shoe snagged on the blanket and she started to fall. "Oops"

Her arms flailed, and she stumbled. Grant caught her in his open arms.

"So you didn't need my help?" He chuckled as he wrapped his arms around her, embracing her.

"Nope." She shook her head, trying to get a handle on the butterflies in her stomach. She didn't want to move, not ever.

Held in his arms, she felt safe and treasured.

Where was all this coming from? They hardly knew each other.

She gazed into his eyes. "Thanks for the ride."

She knew she should say more, but she needed to get away, and fast. Her attraction to him was growing by the minute, and she was at a loss as to what to do about it. She guessed she could have made a joke and implied Millie might have made another match, but it was way too soon.

Instead she added, "I'm going to head up to my room and get Max. I need to take him outside."

"Want me to join you?" he asked casually while folding up the blanket and putting it back in the carriage.

She paused for a moment. She wanted him to kiss her again, to continue the connection she thought they'd had going on between them, but she was conflicted.

She placed her hand on his arm. "Why don't I just meet you when I come back from the walk? I won't be long."

She needed a few minutes of time alone with her thoughts. For the past six months, she'd pictured herself in a romantic relationship with Edward. Now her feelings for Grant had muddied her thoughts tremendously.

"I'll hang around. We can have a drink then," Grant answered.

Twelve

Daisy unlocked the door to her suite, put her handbag down on the table in the foyer, and reached down to slide off her shoes.

She tiptoed into the bedroom.

Max looked so comfy with his snoozer on her pillow.

He lifted his head and raised his right paw. She chuckled. "All right. One paw rub coming up."

She rubbed his paw for a minute. "Come on. Time to go outside."

She changed into jeans and sneakers and threw on her cashmere sweater and wished she'd packed her leather jacket.

She leashed Max, and they headed back downstairs and out the door.

Daisy shivered. It felt colder than during the carriage ride, but then she'd had Grant's warm body cozied up next to her to keep her warm. She kind of wished she hadn't turned down his offer to come with her.

Too late now. She headed around the right side of the Inn. She had already decided not to go to the doggie park but rather to walk along the well-lit flagstone pathway that crossed the circular blacktop driveway toward the spa. She had to leave in the morning, and she really wanted to peek inside the spa before she left.

She was surprised to see no one else walking around. It felt a little creepy. Maybe she should have gone to the doggie park after all. She shook off that feeling. There was lots of light with the full moon shining down through the clear sky.

Up ahead in front of the entrance to the spa, she spotted a fountain backlit with colored lights. Several benches surrounded the fountain. She moved forward with Max to go sit on one of them. She stopped. Someone with their back to her was sitting on one.

Max whined and pulled her toward the bench. She wasn't eager to talk to anyone, but Max always expected everyone would want to pet him. She figured the person would hear Max and turn around to wave or shout out a greeting, but they didn't.

This was starting to feel weird in a bad way. She contemplated heading back to the Inn, but what if they were drunk and had wandered out here and fallen asleep? She should wake them, right?

She wasn't really given a choice. Max pulled her along, and she chuckled nervously when she was close enough to recognize the person's shoes. Manolo Blahnik embellished cobalt satin pumps. Only one person had been wearing those shoes tonight.

"Betsy," she called out.

No answer.

Prickles ran along her spine. Something didn't seem right. She swallowed hard. Betsy hadn't moved.

She moved closer, one step at a time. Max sniffed Betsy's hand and then seemed to be sniffing her chest.

"Wake up, Betsy." Daisy reached out and tapped her shoulder.

She didn't react. She didn't even twitch.

She reached out to shake Betsy. Her hand brushed against something cold and hard and sticky on Betsy's jacket. What could it be? She looked down, a dark red stain fanned out in a circle on her chest. Was that a bloody knife she saw?

Her hand shook. Was that sticky stuff blood? She couldn't look. A sick feeling rose in her stomach. Her knees wobbled. She stumbled over to grab the edge of the nearby empty bench to sit so she could find her cell. She had to call 911.

Blood always made her woozy and light-headed.

She pried open her eyes. The moon and the stars shone above. She tried to grab on to where she might be. It was all so hazy. Someone held her tight, their arm around her shoulders. She gazed sideways and saw Grant.

She felt chilled. She scrunched closer, unsure of her surroundings. She slurred. "Where are we?" She knew before he could answer. She bolted upright, knocking into his chin.

"Oh, no! Betsy! Max?" She trembled from head to toe.

Grant hugged her tight against his body. "Daisy, it's okay. Max is fine." He pointed to the ground in front of her. "My foot is on his leash."

She desperately needed to pet him, to reassure herself, to feel his soft fur. She bent forward. Everything spun. She leaned back against the bench to overcome the dizziness.

"Uh-oh! I think I might throw up."

"Take it easy. I'm pretty sure you fainted." Grant held her tight.

She stammered. "Betsy?"

"I called 911."

She squeezed Grant's forearm tight. "She's dead, isn't she?"

"I believe so." Grant nodded as sirens blared.

"I found her. It was awful." She sobbed against his chest.

"Shh, take deep breaths." His hand squeezed her arm while he whispered over and over. "I'm not leaving. I'll take care of you and Max."

Her heart rate slowed, his words comforting her as she tried to focus on feeling safe instead of the fact that Betsy lay motionless on the nearby bench. She bent forward again, and this time Max nuzzled her hand. "Max, thank goodness you're okay."

Seconds later, an ambulance, red and blue lights flashing, tires screeching, halted nearby on the driveway. She shivered.

"The police are here now. They'll take charge."

She scrunched up against Grant, and he held her tighter. She buried her head in his shoulder, cowering. She dreaded the inevitable questions she knew would be coming at her.

Two EMTs jumped out of the ambulance. Grant pointed to the bench where Betsy lay inert.

Within seconds, they heard more sirens and more flashing lights. A police car zoomed to a stop, and a short, beefy officer climbed out of the cruiser. He trotted over to where the EMTs were working on Betsy. After a minute or two, the EMTs moved away from her body. The police officer had a brief conversation with them before walking over to Grant and Daisy.

"Excuse me. Was it one of you who called 911 and reported a possible death?"

"I did," Grant answered succinctly.

"And your name, sir?"

"Grant Stamford, and before you ask, the lady is Daisy Flowers. She's the one who found the…" He paused.

"Thank you. I'm officer Pincer, and I'll be securing the area. Detective Hartley has been alerted and will be here shortly. He'll need to ask you some questions."

Grant nodded. "That's fine, officer, but would it be okay if I take this woman and her dog back to the Inn? She says she's light-headed, and she's shivering."

The officer gave them a curt nod. "I'll have Detective Hartley find you there."

"Do you think you can stand up?" Grant slowly removed his arm from around her shoulders.

"I'm not sure. What about Max?" she whispered, afraid she might collapse in a heap on the ground. "I'll help you, and don't worry about Max. I've got him. Just lean on me." Grant gently grabbed her hand. With his other hand he held on to Max's leash.

"Brrr, your hand is ice cold. Here, put this on," he said, taking off his jacket. "The sleeves should be long enough to cover your hands."

At that moment, Daisy caught sight of Millie and Carl being held back by one of the officers. Millie appeared to be arguing with him.

Daisy's hand wavered as she pointed. "Grant, look, it's your sister and Carl. We had better get to them before Millie freaks out."

Millie started running toward them with Carl following behind, and when she got close, she threw her arms around Grant's neck, hugged him, then stepped backward and looked him up and down. "When I heard the sirens, I thought you might be hurt."

She grabbed Daisy's hand and stared at her. "Uh-oh, something's wrong. You're shaking."

Millie glanced at her brother. "Daisy's obviously not okay. What's going on?"

Grant shook his head before mumbling, "It's Betsy. She's dead."

"What?" Millie gasped and glanced at Carl. He put his arm around her. "She can't be dead. We just talked to her."

A flash popped. Daisy held her hands up to cover her face and murmured, "Please go away."

Millie shook her head. That's Vince, the LLM photographer. How did he get here so fast?"

"Sis, let's go." Grant grabbed Daisy's hand. "We can talk inside. I want to get Daisy away from here. She needs a quiet place and a warm drink."

Carl steered Millie back to the Inn. "People are starting to trickle outside to see what's going on, and we don't want to be questioned."

The foursome walked briskly and shortly made it back inside the front door. "Let's go sit over there." Carl pointed to the little nook off in the corner. "We can talk there."

They had just sat down in the small seating nook when Samantha ran up to them with Harry and Hyacinth trailing behind. "Hey, do you know what's going on outside?" Samantha frowned. "We heard sirens."

"We'll fill you in," Millie said. "You won't believe it. Betsy's—"

"What's happening?" Meghan interrupted, coming to a halt in front of Daisy. "You look awful." She didn't wait for an answer. She pulled Daisy toward her and hugged her.

"I thought you two had left already," Millie said.

Nicholas answered, "We had just gotten into the car when we saw all the police and ambulances heading to the spa. We came back to make sure everyone was okay. Will one of you please tell us what's going on?"

Daisy shuddered. "Betsy's dead. I found her." And with that said, she hid her face in Meghan's shoulder and sobbed.

"Oh, no!" Samantha waved her hands in the air. "Grant, you need to get Daisy out of here. She just had a major shock. Take her to the bar and get her something hot to drink." She peered around the lobby. "Let me check to see if the police or anyone needs me, then I'll try to meet you there."

Everyone exchanged glances, gathered around Daisy, and hastened down the short hallway to the bar.

Samantha was correct the bar was not busy. There was one rowdy group of young people gathered around the bar laughing boisterously. That was probably a good thing. They appeared totally unaware of anything going on around them.

Carl and Grant quickly rearranged a few tables to make one larger one where they could all sit together. Grant pulled out a chair for Daisy, making sure there was room for Max to sit by her feet. "I'll get you something to drink."

Hyacinth sat to the right of Daisy, leaving the chair on her left for Grant. She scooted her chair as close to Daisy as it would get and reached out for her hand.

Carl, Millie, Nicholas, and Meghan sat across from them.

Daisy felt numb. One loud-mouthed person at the bar invaded her haze while her group was eerily quiet. None of them would miss Betsy, but it was obvious they were all shocked by her sudden death.

Hyacinth broke the silence. "Sis, I can't imagine what you just went through. It had to be terrifying. Can you tell us what happened?"

Daisy took a deep breath. "All right. Here's a short version. I went on the carriage ride with Grant, and afterward I went to my suite to get Max. I needed to take him outside."

Carl laid his arm around Millie's shoulders while everyone else scrunched closer together and leaned across the table to better hear Daisy.

Meghan held up her hand. "Stop! I want to hear about Betsy, but I thought Millie and Carl went on the carriage ride too."

Millie looked off somewhere in the distance, not meeting anyone's eyes.

"No, it was just Grant and me." Daisy blushed.

Of course by now she knew Millie had set it up to happen that way, but Meghan would certainly approve. She'd love it if Daisy and Grant got together.

And while Daisy's thoughts were on all this, Grant returned carrying a mug and placed it in front of her. "Coffee. Try to drink some."

He pulled out the chair next to her, being careful not to jostle Max, and sat.

"Thank you." She wrapped her cold hands around the mug before taking a sip. "Ahh, that feels good."

She glanced at Grant. "I've been telling everyone what happened earlier. I'm at the part after the carriage ride when I went to my room and got Max to take him out. We walked toward the spa. I wanted to peek in the windows. I never made it that far."

Her voice quivered. "I found Betsy slumped on one of the benches near the front door. Thinking she might be drunk, I went to shake her. She didn't move, and I got something sticky on my hand."

She trembled. "The next part is a little hazy. I thought I saw blood on her chest."

Hyacinth grimaced. "Oh, no! Blood and Daisy are not a good mix."

"Yes, it seems that hasn't changed." Daisy shook her head. "I vaguely remember feeling dizzy and going to sit down to call 911. It's all a mystery after that until I woke up with Grant next to me. He's actually the one who called 911. A few minutes later, it was lights and sirens."

"So that's why we heard all the sirens," Meghan said.

A cell pinged. Everyone looked to see if it was theirs. Hyacinth swiped hers. "Hi. I was just getting ready to call you. We have a problem. Can I put you on speaker?" She mouthed to Daisy. "It's Tucker."

He paused. "I guess that's okay, but let me ask you. Did you say you were attending the gala tonight?"

"Yes."

"I just got a call. I'm heading there now. Seems there was a suspicious death outside the Inn."

"Yup, and my sister discovered the body."

"Your sister Daisy?"

"The only sister I have."

"Where are you? Are you still at the scene? And are you with her?"

"One question at a time, Tucker. No, I am not at the scene. It happened outside, and I'm inside. And yes, my sister is here with me now."

"Stay put. I'm on my way. I'll check in with the officers at the site. Afterward, I'll come find you."

Tucker disconnected before she had time to tell him they were in the bar. "So I know you all heard Tucker." She looked at Daisy and Grant. "I assume he'll want to ask you some questions."

Samantha walked in carrying a large tray with several carafes of coffee, mugs, cream, sugar, donuts, and treats for Max. "Here's something for all of you. You will probably be here awhile."

She placed the tray in the middle of the table.

Daisy reached out and took one of the cookies for Max. He was being such a trooper. She bent down, petted him, and gave the treat to him.

Samantha pulled up another chair and sat. "Phew. I just saw Vince, the photographer. He looked rattled. Thank goodness he didn't stop me to ask questions."

"The minute we left the crime scene he stuck a camera in our faces," Grant piped up.

Millie scowled. "He sure got to the murder scene fast. I'm surprised he hadn't already left. Most of the guests were gone."

Daisy wrung her hands. "Oh, no! That photo he took could turn up in the paper."

"What I don't understand is how it wasn't that long ago that we saw Betsy in the ladies' room," Meghan murmured.

"Tucker's going to the scene first," Hyacinth added. "Then he said he'd come find me. He'll figure it all out."

Millie grabbed Carl's hand. "I'm scared. The police could suspect me. The other day Betsy implied I stole funds from the foundation and funneled them to the bakery. And then I had that awful dispute with her before my speech."

Carl squeezed her hand. "You told me about the argument in the bathroom, but you never told me about her implying you were stealing from your own foundation. That's absurd. When did she do that?"

"At the last planning committee meeting. Everyone who was there heard her."

"So tell Tucker," he said.

"I will." Millie sighed. "I have what I consider an even bigger problem. How will I ever locate this puppy mill now that Betsy's dead?"

"Millie, not now. We can worry about that tomorrow."

Thirteen

Daisy watched the hands on the clock over the bar. It seemed like forever until Tucker arrived. Daisy recognized him from Hyacinth's description. Tucker Hartley's hair was light brown with some blond highlights, and he had brown eyes hidden behind glasses. He was taller than Hyacinth but built solidly. Dressed in khakis and a white button-down, he strode in confidently. He nodded at Hyacinth and walked up to her.

He leaned over and spoke softly to her. "I'm glad you're okay."

"I am, but take it easy on my sister." She then introduced him to everyone at the table.

He looked directly at Daisy. "I know this is not the best time, but I'll need to speak to you since you're the one who found the body"

Grant stood. "You might want to talk to me first. I'm not sure Daisy knows very much. She was passed out when I found her."

"All right," Tucker agreed. "How about I talk to both of you? Is there a room where we can talk privately?"

"You can use my office," Samantha said. "Here's the key." She took a key from her pocket and passed it to Grant.

Daisy stood up reluctantly and handed Max's leash to Meghan. "Watch over him?"

"Of course," Meghan answered.

Millie cleared her throat. "Wait a minute, Tucker. Before you go, I should tell you I had what could be considered a public fight with Betsy a few hours ago."

Tucker stopped and studied her. "A physical fight?"

"No, of course not." She shook her head. "We had a heated argument. She taunted me with something about a puppy mill. She knew it would rile me up right before my speech."

Carl placed his hand on Millie's arm. "Mil, that's enough. Leave Tucker alone for now."

"Mrs. Whitfield, I'll be in touch. You can tell me everything then."

Tucker turned to Grant. "Lead the way."

Grant put his arm around Daisy, and along with Tucker, they left the bar. The crowds were gone, probably frightened off by all the sirens. They passed only one couple on the way to Samantha's office.

Grant opened the door. "We can sit at the conference table."

He pointed to an archway leading to a small room mostly taken up with a large table.

"Daisy, sit here." He pulled back a side chair for her and then sat next to her. Tucker sat in the armchair at the head of the table.

"I'm really sorry to put you through what you saw again, but I have to ask you some questions. I'll try to make this quick."

She shuddered. "Of course. Fire away."

Grant put his hand on top of hers. She squeezed his hand back to let him know she was grateful for his gesture.

Tucker took out a small notebook and a pen and opened to a clean page. Reading upside down, she noted he had already labelled the page with "Betsy Clarkson murder investigation." She was surprised he hadn't asked to record their conversation.

"I'll try to keep this short tonight. I just need some basics for now."

His first question made her shudder. "You found the body?"

"Yes."

"Did you know the victim?"

"Not well," Daisy answered.

"Can you tell me what you were doing outside in the dark?"

"I hadn't taken Max out for a while, and he needed a walk."

"Max?"

"Yes, my friend's dog."

"Your friend's dog? What friend?"

"A friend from back home. I'm dog sitting him while she's away, and when I had to come here to help my mom, he had to come with me."

"Okay. Did you see anyone around the area before you found the body?"

"No. And if there was someone nearby, I imagine Max would have been whining."

"And why is that?"

Daisy smiled tremulously. "Oh, that's easy. Max loves people. Whenever he sees someone, he whines. He wants to go up to them, to be fussed over."

"Why didn't you walk in the doggie park? It's practically right outside the front door."

"I could have gone there. It was just that I haven't been to the Inn since before the renovation. I was curious to peek in the windows of the spa. My best friend works there, and I wanted to see what it looks like inside."

"In the dark? Why not wait until it was light outside and go visit your friend while she's working?"

She shrugged. "I need to leave early tomorrow to get back to D.C. for work. I won't have time in the morning. Tonight, I had time, and Max needed to walk." She ran her fingers through her hair. "It seemed like a good idea at the time."

Tucker raised an eyebrow, looking skeptical.

Too bad. So she had made a bad decision.

He continued. "Walk me through what happened as you were walking."

She concentrated, but she was too traumatized to remember much. "We walked across the driveway toward the spa. It looked pretty with the fountain lit up. I walked closer, and Max started whining. I didn't see anything at first, but then I saw a person slumped on a bench with their back to us. It seemed weird, but Max kept whining and pulling me along. I thought the person might be drunk and need help."

Daisy briefly closed her eyes. This was the awful part, and it all tumbled out.

"Betsy had a jacket or shawl over her shoulders, so when I went to shake her, I vaguely remember touching something that felt wet and sticky. I had no idea what it was. It was dark. It appeared there was a dark stain on her dress. After that I don't remember much until Grant started talking to me."

Tucker's eyes bored into hers. Was he trying to see if she was holding something back? Or was he waiting to see if she had anything else to add? She met his gaze with her own. She couldn't think of anything she'd forgotten.

"All right. I know from Hyacinth you don't live here. You'll need to stick around for a few days. I'm sure you understand that I'll need to question you again."

"Oh, no. I have to be back in D.C. I'm sure Hyacinth told you I'm a lawyer. Our firm has a big trial starting Monday. I have to be there."

"I can't allow you to leave. It doesn't matter that you're Hyacinth's sister. Imagine the news media reporting that the person who found the body is leaving town. And if someone gets wind I'm dating this person's sister, I'll be toast. Best thing for you now is to go get some rest."

Daisy swallowed past the huge lump in her throat. Now she'd have to call her dad. She dreaded that, especially when she remembered him telling her she was jeopardizing her career if she came here. Would he really consider firing his own daughter? She'd have to deal with that later. Right now, she listened to Tucker question Grant.

"I understand you found Daisy. Where?"

"She was slumped out cold on one of the benches around the fountain pool."

Tucker scrunched his forehead. "And what made you go looking for her?"

Grant squeezed her hand. "We had just been on a carriage ride together. When we got back, she said she was going up to her room to get her dog, Max, to take him for a walk. I asked if she wanted company, and she said she'd like to be alone."

Grant frowned. He looked unhappy at having to say that.

He added quickly. "She assured me she wouldn't be long. Since I wanted to see more of her, I told her I'd hang around until she came back."

Grant paused before continuing. "She left me to get Max, and I went to talk to my sister and her husband. Millie chastised me for not going with Daisy. She wouldn't listen to me when I tried to tell her Daisy wanted to be alone. She kept harping. She went so far as to tell me Daisy could fall and no one would know."

Grant paused to rake his fingers through his hair. "There's no point in arguing with Millie. If you had an older sister you'd understand. It's just easier to give in, so I agreed with her. I went to go look for Daisy."

Grant rambled on while Tucker took notes.

"You have to understand my sister is trying to get us together. This was her way of doing that. Although I hate to admit it, I'm glad I listened to her."

He took a deep breath. "When I got close to the spa, I saw two benches with a person slumped on each one, and when I spotted Max I knew Daisy was one of them. I ran over to her first. She was my main concern. It was scary until I realized she was breathing, so then I went to check out Betsy. I saw blood and called 911."

"So tell me, how did you know where to find Daisy?" Tucker asked.

"I didn't. First I looked outside in the area you called the dog park. She wasn't there. I started to get a little concerned, and then I remembered when we were on the carriage ride, she had talked about wanting to see the spa. I figured she might have taken Max in that direction."

Tucker scribbled more notes in his little black book.

"Thank you for your candor. That's all for now. If you think of anything else, call me."

"We will." Grant stood up and grabbed Daisy's hand. "Your hand is still like ice. Let's go back and get you some more coffee."

As soon as they left Samantha's office, he turned to her. "That was intense. I never imagined I'd be questioned about a murder. I could sure use a drink."

They walked back hand in hand.

Hyacinth ran up to them. "Did Tucker treat you two okay?"

"He was fine. I can see why you like him," Daisy answered, feeling exhausted and not wanting to talk about it. "I'm going to go sit and get some coffee."

Grant let go of her hand. "I'll join you after I get a drink."

"Oh, there's Tucker," Hyacinth said. "I can't wait to talk to him."

Daisy stalled. She tried to listen to their conversation. She caught snippets of it.

Hyacinth drilled him. *Good.* Better him than her.

"I can't deny that your sister is a suspect. She'll need to stay in Houndsville so I can question her further."

Her stomach flip-flopped. It was bad enough Tucker had just told her she had to stay in Houndsville, but now she might be a suspect too. *Great.* If that turned out to be true, she'd need a lawyer. She sighed. So much to process. She headed over to sit with Meghan check on Max—and to get a cup of coffee.

Meghan grabbed Daisy's hand. "Hey Flowers, do you want me to spend the night with you? It could be like old times. We could stay up all night watching reruns of some of our favorite shows."

Hearing her nickname and thinking about the events of the evening, both good and bad, her eyes started filling up with tears. She didn't want to cry in front of anyone.

"I'll be okay." She shakily poured herself a cup of coffee. "Max is great company. Besides, what about Grace and Nicholas?"

"While you were in with Tucker, I called my parents to tell them what was going on. They told us not to worry, that Grace and the dogs are wonderful and to do whatever we needed." She patted Nicholas's hand. "He'll miss me, but he'll be all right."

Daisy lied. "I'll be fine. I'm so tired, I'm sure I'll fall asleep instantly."

Grant came over, drink in hand. He smiled and placed his other hand on her shoulder. "I'm sorry. I have to head out. I have to be at the clinic early."

"That's fine. I'd really like to lie down. I'll walk out with you."

Daisy spoke softly, trying not to draw attention. She wanted to talk to Grant without interference, especially from his sister.

She whispered goodbye to Meghan, pushed back her chair, and walked out with Grant and Max.

They strolled a little ways down the hallway. She put her hand on his arm to stop him.

"What's up?" He peered into her eyes.

She stood stiffly, trying to ignore how flustered she felt. "I wanted to thank you for tonight. I couldn't have gotten through this ordeal without you. You surprised me, first on the carriage ride and especially afterward. You're a lot different than I remember from high school."

Quickly, before she had time to reconsider, she stood on tip-toes and hugged him. She let go.

He grinned. "Hey, maybe I'm not so bad after all?"

"That could be true." She smiled back at him and went to kiss him on his cheek, but he moved, and his mouth landed on her lips.

Her eyes flew open. She deepened the kiss until unfortunately she heard footfalls behind her and backed away. She touched the spot on her mouth where his lips had met hers.

He smiled, his hazel eyes sparkling.

"I'll call you."

She watched him walk away. Grant must have felt her eyes on him. He turned and waved before he disappeared out of sight.

Fourteen

Monday morning around six a.m., Millie slipped out of bed wanting to get an early start on her plans for the day.

She slipped her feet into her slippers and padded off to the kitchen to get some much needed caffeine. With her mug in hand, she sat at her kitchen table and gazed outside into the still dark skyline.

She thought back to Saturday night. It had ended tragically with Betsy's death. And then yesterday had been awful. It had passed in a blur of emails, texts, and phone calls in which she'd had to calm down donors and some of her foundations' board of directors while trying to avoid worrying about being a suspect in Betsy's murder. She never heard from Tucker.

The sun was just coming up when Carl joined her a little while later. He brewed himself a cup of coffee and came over to sit next to her.

"Rough night, huh?" He placed one of his hands on top of her smaller one.

"Yup. For the second night I couldn't stop thinking about Betsy's death and that sooner or later, Tucker's going to question me. I'll likely be one of his suspects."

She sighed. "At least the gala went off without a hitch. And with Frannie's broken wrist, that could have been a disaster."

She could feel tears forming in her eyes. She swallowed hard, trying to hold them back. "I'm worried sick about how Betsy's murder might affect our ability to raise money for all the dogs needing help. I was hoping this year to get more funds than ever so people who couldn't afford veterinary care could apply for a grant to help them out."

Carl raised an eyebrow. "Come on. Tucker will question you, but you're hardly a major suspect, and as to the foundation, are you sure you're not overreacting about what effect Betsy's accusations and murder will have on it?"

"Well, I might have agreed with you if I hadn't spent yesterday answering texts and emails and even a few phone calls from donors who claimed Betsy had accused me of stealing money from the foundation and threatened to expose me. Maybe the donors suspect me of killing her to shut her up."

She ran her fingers around the lip of her mug. "And get this. Two of the eight board members were worried about their own reputations. Instead of worrying about Betsy, even though she was an awful person, they're worried about themselves."

"Have faith. The police will find the murderer."

Millie tapped her mug. "Well, I hope you're right and that it doesn't take too long. Anyway, I asked the committee members to join me for breakfast this morning. I thought it would be good to talk about what's going on."

She frowned, thinking about what this would mean.

"I dread having to mention that some of the donors are threatening not to honor their pledges. They've worked so tirelessly to make every gala a success, to raise lots of money, and now to top it off, Tucker might want to question some of them as part of a murder investigation. They all attended the gala."

Carl sipped his coffee." True enough. How do you think Daisy is doing with all this?"

"I checked in with Meghan. She told me last night that between her, her mom, and Hyacinth, they were making sure Daisy was okay. Thank goodness Grant found her when he did."

"Not exactly what you planned, huh?"

Millie bit her lip. "No, but I have to believe it will work out okay."

She pushed back her chair and picked up her mug and his. "Refill?"

"Sure," Carl said.

"So how come you're up so early?" Millie stuck a pod into the machine to fill her cup.

Carl dragged his fingers through his already mussed hair. "Not to complain, but it's hard to sleep with your bedmate squirming around all night."

"Sorry." She put a second pod into the machine and waited for it to fill Carl's mug.

She brought both mugs back to the table and sat.

Carl sipped his." Mil, it's only natural that everyone will gossip about this until some other news hits the fan, but I don't believe this will ultimately reflect poorly on you or your foundation. Your work speaks for itself." He twirled his mug around in his hands. "You'll do so many good things this year that by the time next year's gala rolls around, all everyone will think about is what to wear. Don't get ahead of yourself. Everyone knows what the foundation means to you and will rally behind you."

She leaned toward him, kissing him. "What did I do to deserve you?"

He fully supported her even when she tested his patience. Lucky her.

She sighed. "Let's hope you're right."

"As to Betsy, no one will miss her," he mumbled.

"That's for sure. Earlier this week, Samantha and I tried to figure out how to get rid of her."

"Rid of her? Mil, be careful who you say that to. It sounds like you might mean permanently."

"Oops," she said. "I meant get her off the planning committee."

Millie shivered and wrapped her hands around her mug.

This talk made her nervous. Her friends and even her brother would be considered suspects.

Even after she was dead, Betsy was still a problem.

"Millie, another word of caution. Stay focused on the bakery. Even though you have three partners it's not fair to them for you to be off attempting to solve this murder while they're working. Let Tucker do his job. Don't try to play Nancy Drew."

"How did you know I was thinking about Nancy and her cohorts, Bess and George?"

"Aw, come on, Mil. Do I need to tell you that instead of drinking your coffee, you're running your fingers around and around the lip of your mug? That's a sure sign you're contemplating something you'd rather not tell me."

Millie put her hands in her lap. "You're right, of course. I'll let Tucker do his job." She took one last sip of coffee and went to put her mug in the sink. "I'm going to get dressed and go to the bakery. I'll be there for a bit before I head over to the Inn for our meeting."

Carl studied her face, and apparently satisfied, he took his mug and placed it in the sink too. "I need to get to work. We're pouring concrete today."

He came over and kissed her before he left with the parting words, "No funny business."

Millie stayed at the table, deep in thought. She hadn't exactly lied to Carl. She planned to give Tucker time to solve the murder, at least for now. Her first move would be to find out about the puppy mill. How to do that, she hadn't figured out yet.

Fifteen

Daisy rolled over and peered at the bedside clock.

She blinked. Seven forty-five.

It was Monday, and she really had to call her dad. She grabbed a few pillows, plumped them up against the headboard, and lay back while aimlessly tickling Max's tummy.

Her dad would be expecting her back in the office this morning. She just hadn't been able to face calling him yesterday. No telling how he'd react when she told him she had to stay in Houndsville and that she was a suspect in a murder.

Max whined softly. "Yes, it's late, and you want to walk. Just give me a few minutes."

Inevitably, at the thought of dealing with her dad, her stomach knotted up. She closed her eyes and tried to picture how this call might go. Probably not well, yet she couldn't put it off any longer. She grabbed her cell from the bedside table and tapped in his number.

"Hello, Daisy," he said succinctly

There went her short-lived hope he wouldn't answer and she'd be able to leave a voicemail.

"Hi, Dad. Can you talk?"

"Yes, I have time now." She paused, caught off-guard. Usually he'd tell her to call back later.

She hesitated, swallowing past the lump in her throat. The words tumbled out. "There was a murder at the Inn after the gala. I found the body."

"Yes, I am aware of the situation," he answered calmly.

"How?" was the only word that popped out. This might end up worse than she'd expected. Now her dad would be angry she hadn't called him earlier.

"Allan called yesterday. He said he saw you at the gala."

Now she felt bad. Her dad had heard about the murder already.

She ran her fingers through Max's fur. Her nerves ratcheted up tenfold. She rambled on. "Yes, I saw Allan there. His daughter owns the Inn where the gala was held." Another thought popped into her head, making her heart race. She hoped Allan had kept his offer to himself.

Her dad continued. "He told me it was quite a fiasco. His main reason for calling was to tell me you might need my help."

Images from Saturday night flashed through her head. She tried to dismiss them and concentrate on the call. Was her dad offering his help? Would he come to Houndsville? It was a daunting thought, and at the same time surprising, in a good way.

"Dad, I'm sorry. I'm a mess. I should have called you yesterday. I know you expected me back at work today. The lead detective already questioned me and informed me I have to stay to answer more questions."

"That's understandable. I'm glad you're safe."

She held back tears. *Wow!* Her dad had voiced an emotional response.

"Thanks, Dad. I'll keep you posted on what's going on. Oh, and I have my computer here so I can work if you need anything done." And then she couldn't help herself. She added, "Guess it was good Corinne replaced me."

"I'm debating whether to send Edward to help you. As the firm's investigator, maybe he can shed some light on other suspects."

"I'd like that. Thanks, Dad." He made no comments about the trial or Corinne. That was it. He ended the call.

She quickly threw on her jeans and the same sweater she'd now been wearing for days. After hooking Max's leash to his collar, she headed downstairs and out the front door to the doggie park.

Two black cocker spaniels with an elderly couple wandered over to check out Max, and then a small mutt with a very wiggly butt dragged his person over to meet all of them.

A woman walking a labradoodle rushed over. "Did you hear there was a murder here?"

Her question started a barrage of comments, and everyone had an opinion about the murder. Daisy cringed. Not wanting to participate in the conversation, she left the group and walked Max around the perimeter of the area.

A few minutes later, she waved goodbye. Back in her suite, she fed Max and brewed herself a cup of coffee.

Caffeine was the perfect remedy for lack of sleep.

"Okay, Max your bowl is empty. It's my turn to eat now. Let's head to the bar." She leashed him again and grasped her handbag. Outside her door was a newspaper lying on the carpet. Most likely it was the Houndsville Times. Did she want to read it?

She picked it up and with Max in tow headed downstairs to the Oak Room. Normally she would have sat at the bar on a stool, but that wasn't an option with Max. She sat at one of the small tables. He parked himself on her toes.

The waitress zipped over and zeroed in on Max.

"He looks like that Lassie dog that used to be on television."

Daisy smiled. "Yes. He's a rough collie. Just like Lassie."

"Well Max, I'll have to see what I can find for you," she said, handing Daisy a menu. "And can I get you something to drink while you're deciding what to order?"

"Yes, coffee please, and I don't need the menu." She handed it back to her. "I'd like scrambled eggs, two orders of bacon, and toast. Oh, and an extra plate for Max, please."

"Coming right up."

The waitress left, and Daisy hesitantly peeked at the newspaper. Right on the front page was a photo of the Inn and a headline that read "Mutts, Murder, and Mayhem at the Buckshead Inn."

She started to read the article. Oh no! It identified her as finding the body while she was walking her dog, Max. She sighed in relief that there wasn't a photo.

She had better call Hyacinth and see what was going on.

Hyacinth picked up on the first ring. "Hi, sis."

Before her sister uttered another word, she spat out, "Did you see the Houndsville Times?"

"No. What's wrong?"

"There's a photo of the Inn, and it mentions me as having found the body."

"Oh, no. Are you okay? I wanted to call earlier, but I was afraid you were still sleeping."

"Who gets to sleep late with a dog?" She stroked Max's back. "Anyway, they left a paper at my door. I'm downstairs getting breakfast and just started reading it while waiting for my food. Mom will freak when she sees this."

"She already has. She called me. She's on her way to find you. She's worried about you."

"Yup, you're right. She's walking into the bar with Sidney now. I'll catch up with you later." Daisy ended the call, placed her cell on the table, folded the paper, and stuffed it in her handbag.

Daisy waved.

Her mom, dragging Sidney behind, hurried over to her table.

Her mom eyed her. "Well, you look okay for someone who discovered a dead body."

Daisy blanched. "Shush, Mom. Not everyone sitting here needs to know that. And yes, I'm fine. Just tired. It was hard to sleep. Do you want something to eat?"

"No, I ate earlier, but I would like a cup of coffee." Her mom sat down, leaving room for Sidney, who scrambled to sit right next to Max. "Look at that. They like each other."

"And it seems you really like having him." Daisy was sure her mom would soon be joining the ranks of foster failures.

"So tell me what happened. How is it that you found Betsy?" her mom murmured. "Fill me in, and don't leave out a single detail."

Daisy gave her mom a quick synopsis. She was almost done when the waitress delivered her breakfast, along with a treat for Max.

"Could you also bring my mom a cup of coffee?"

Hoping her mom would stop with the questions if Daisy was eating, she picked up her fork and dug into the eggs. Max, whose head could reach the table, looked longingly at the bacon.

"Yes, Max. You and Sidney can have the bacon, and there's even a cookie for you to share."

After tearing the bacon into small pieces, she started to give each dog a piece when her mom caught her off guard by innocently asking, "Did you call your dad?"

"Yes, Mom. I did." She exhaled. "He already knew. Allan Gold got to him first."

Whatever her mom was about to say was interrupted by a cell-phone making a quacking noise.

Daisy watched her mom fish around in her handbag, wondering if she'd get to answer before whoever was calling gave up.

She finally retrieved it and answered. "Hi, Millie. I'm sitting in the Oak Room with Daisy. Can I call you back?"

Daisy couldn't make out Millie's response, but her mom told Millie she'd see her soon.

"Millie's invited everyone on the committee to eat breakfast together. She said for you to come with me."

"Why me?" Daisy asked.

Frannie shrugged. "I have no idea."

"Mom, will you call Hyacinth? Maybe she can meet us later. I'd like to see Millie's bakery, and she can come along."

"I need to go find some of my tools that are still here. I'll call her after that."

After her mom left with Sidney, Daisy picked up the newspaper and read the article about the murder. It ruined her appetite. She gave the rest of the toast to Max.

"Hi! I have something for you."

Samantha opened her tote bag and handed Millie a gavel and placed a sound block in front of her. "I know this is an informal breakfast meeting, but I thought you might like using this to get everyone's attention. It's certainly better than a spoon and a glass."

Millie laughed. "Thanks." She glanced around the table. Her whole committee, even Annabel, had shown up for their breakfast.

She tapped the gavel on the block. "May I have everyone's attention?"

Everyone nodded. She continued. "I thought it would be good to get together and chat in light of the fact that Betsy was murdered during the gala."

"You're probably the one who killed her," Annabel muttered loud enough for everyone at the table to hear.

"Annabel, stop. No one is in the mood for your accusations this morning." Julie rolled her eyes.

"Yes," Frannie piped up. "We're tired of your rants"

Bridget looked around the table. "Those of us sitting here know Betsy was a troublemaker and made enemies easily. Anyone could have murdered her."

"Could everyone please stop?" Samantha implored loudly. "Millie may have some more information for us by now."

"Sorry, I don't. People have been calling and texting, worried about the impact the murder might have on the foundation."

"Is it bad?" Colin asked.

"I'd say so." Millie frowned. "But right now we have a more pressing issue."

"What could be more urgent?" Stella asked.

Millie ran her fingers through her hair. "Saturday night before my speech, I had a run-in with Betsy. She insisted she knew about a puppy mill nearby and then refused to tell me where it was."

Bridget shrugged. "Why would she do that? Why not tell you right away?"

"Maybe she made it up. To get you riled up," Stella answered.

"Possibly." Millie sighed. "She certainly was capable of doing just that."

"Oh, no," Julie cried out. "She was killed before she could give you the information. Yikes, Millie, that means the owner of the puppy mill killed Betsy to keep her from telling you and getting their business shut down. You'd better tell the police."

"Let's not jump to conclusions. As Stella points out, she may have made the whole thing up. I need to get inside her house to see if she wrote down an address or a name."

Everyone gasped. "Millie, that could be dangerous," Colin said.

Millie shook her head. "I don't care. There could be dogs in danger. She chewed her lip. "Of course there's the possibility Betsy confided in someone else. Maybe a friend, if she had any, and I could get the information that way."

All at once, Millie's head—and everyone else's—turned to Annabel, who sat up straighter.

"Stop staring at me. I don't know anything."

Annabel squirmed around in her seat, making Millie wonder if she was being truthful. Millie raised one eyebrow higher than the other.

"All right," Annabel uttered reluctantly. "Betsy told me she knew something that would make Millie jump through hoops."

"She didn't tell you any more than that? Anything that might help us?" Samantha demanded.

"No. She was giddy about it though." Annabel refused to look at anyone. "But if none of us knows anything, why are we still sitting here? I don't know about the rest of you, but I need to get to my tea room."

"So leave. No one made you come here." Millie made a sweeping motion with her hands.

"Gladly," Annabel snarled.

Millie watched her scurry out before proceeding. "Gad, that woman drives me crazy. Anyway, just a bit of business. I need someone to confirm the silent auction winners and call them. I expected to do that yesterday, but I honestly forgot with everything that was going on."

Colin raised his hand. "I'll be happy to help."

"Thanks." Millie smiled at him.

"Last thing," Millie continued. "If you saw or know anything suspicious please contact the detective in charge, Tucker Hartley."

Bridget piped up. "I saw Betsy talking with that photographer, Vince. I remember telling my husband because I thought it was strange after she had called him a slimeball at our last meeting."

"And I heard she had an affair with Patrick Jetson," Stella added.

"Yikes, he's a jerk," Colin said. "He comes into the store sometimes. He's quite pretentious."

"Well, you should both call Tucker. That's it for now. We're adjourned."

Millie had formulated a plan and was anxious to leave when Daisy walked over to her. "Hey Millie, my mom and I were planning to walk to the bakery. Want to join us?"

Millie hesitated. "Not right now. I have to go somewhere."

Daisy frowned and narrowed her eyes. "That sounds mysterious. Uh-oh, you're planning to go to Betsy's house, aren't you?"

Millie didn't answer.

Daisy shook her head. "If you're doing that, I'm going with you, no buts. Mom, you take Max. I'll meet you back at Millie's bakery."

"Are you sure you're up for this?" Millie peered at Daisy. "We could get in trouble."

"I've already found a dead body. What more could happen?"

Sixteen

Ten minutes later, Millie drove slowly past Betsy's house, which was located on a cul-de-sac. "Well, there's no police presence that I can see, but we can sit here for a minute to make sure."

Daisy stopped chewing her fingernail just long enough to point to the vehicle in the driveway. "Whose truck is that?"

"Betsy's."

"So I assume you have a plan to get inside?" Daisy swallowed past the lump in her throat.

"Nope. We're just going to wing it."

Daisy rolled her eyes. "Are you serious? We drove here, and you have no plan?"

"I'm just messing with you. Meghan told me when they came to see the puppies every week Betsy told her to walk right in, that she never locked her door. I'm praying that's still the case."

"Yikes! So we're hoping that what Meghan told you ages ago is still true today."

"Yup. Although I did watch a YouTube video with instructions on how to open a door with a credit card. I have it on my phone."

Daisy groaned. "Oh, great. Now as a lawyer, I'm possibly going to watch you break into someone's home."

"That's about right."

Daisy opened Millie's car door. "Well, let's get this over with before I chicken out."

"Okay," Millie said. "I say we start around back. That way, if someone is watching the house, they're less likely to see us."

"Somehow I feel like you're Nancy Drew and I'm Bess. I hope we don't get in trouble like they often did."

Millie was reminded of her conversation with Carl when he'd told her not to go off playing Nancy Drew. She swiftly put that thought out of her head.

Millie led the way around the side of the house. She glanced behind her to make sure Daisy was following her and laughed nervously. "Hey, walk normally. You're all hunched over. You look guilty, like you're sneaking around."

"Great, now I'm getting lessons on how not to look like a burglar."

Millie kept walking until she found a patio door. She tried to open it.

"This one's locked, and my instructions won't work on this kind of door."

"Oh, this is just super. Now we need a certain kind of door?"

"Yeah, one with a knob."

"Let's just leave. This is getting worse and worse."

"No way. I bet the front door has a knob."

The front door did have a knob. Millie tried opening it. No luck—it was locked. She handed her phone to Daisy and took a credit card out of her pocket. "Watch the video and tell me what to do. And don't forget to try and cover me in case anyone is watching us."

"This is freakin' crazy. I don't know why I ever volunteered to do this." Daisy's voice quivered as she watched the video and relayed the instructions.

"Look, we did it!" Millie shoved open the door. "We're in."

"Oh, no." Daisy froze. "What if there's an alarm?"

"In that case, we run fast." Millie giggled nervously.

"Oh, great. That's your solution? Millie, you really didn't think this through at all."

"Look, what did you expect? I've never done this before, but so far no alarm is going off. Let's make this fast. Look around for a paper with an address or a breeder name that might lead us to a puppy mill. I'll check out the kitchen, you try the den."

They each headed in opposite directions. Daisy saw a desk and headed that way until she thought she heard a distant sound of a siren.

"Millie, run. There must be a silent alarm connected to a police station."

They bumped into each other in their panic to get out, but they made it into the car before the police showed up.

Daisy wiped her brow. "That was way too close. No more playing Nancy Drew for me. I'm done. Let's go."

"Don't tell anyone where we've been," Millie murmured as she opened the door to the bakery.

Daisy shook her head. "As if I would."

Before they took a few steps, Frannie came running up and whispered, "I've been a wreck waiting for you."

Before they could say anything, Carolyn came rushing up and threw her arms around Daisy.

"Oh, my goodness! Are you okay? Finding Betsy's body must have been so scary."

Daisy shivered. She really didn't want to talk about the murder, although it might be a distraction from her recent adventure with Millie.

"Yes, it was terrifying," she eked out as Todd and MaryEllen joined them.

"Hey, you two look like you've seen a ghost. What's going on?" Carolyn asked.

"We went to Betsy's house," Millie said blatantly. "I needed to see if I could find something about this supposed puppy mill."

Daisy shook her head. "You told me not to say anything."

"So, I can't keep a secret. It's okay. They won't tell anyone. Right?" Millie stared down her partners.

Carolyn screeched. "Millie, you're not thinking clearly. Do I need to tell you that on the off chance the person running this puppy mill was the person to murder Betsy, and he or she was worried there was something in the house, they could have gone there too? You could have endangered yourself and Daisy."

"Yeah, Mil," Todd added. "Not to be overdramatic, but think about Carl and the rest of us. If something happened to you, we'd be devastated. And what about Luke and Annie? Frankly I'm not sure Luke could survive that. I remember you telling us he was a rescue where one of his owners died in a car accident, and when you first rescued him he was so quiet and forlorn. Do you want that for him again?"

Millie hung her head. It was obvious she'd never do anything to hurt Luke, or for that matter, her family or her partners. She loved all of them dearly.

MaryEllen came up and put her arm around her. "Millie, a murderer is on the loose, and you need to leave this to Tucker."

"Okay, I get it."

"So, I might as well ask," Carolyn said. "Did you find anything in your attempt at breaking and entering?"

Millie shook her head. "We did not. Let's end this conversation. I was hoping to show Daisy around the bakery."

Daisy had been looking forward to seeing the place—it looked awesome—but hearing Millie's partners voice their concerns made her think she never should have allowed Millie to go to Betsy's in the first place. Now all she wanted was to leave.

"Where's Max?" she asked.

"He's hanging out with some of our regular patrons. Come on. I'll introduce you."

Millie dragged her over to a large group camped out on one of the sofas and surrounding chairs. She met MaryBeth and her Bichon, Matisse, and Susan with her two rescues, Piper and Jax.

"It's nice to meet all of you. I'd like to stay, but I need to get back to the Inn and see to my work correspondence."

She couldn't wait to get out of there. She sighed. She was just glad no one had gotten hurt on their adventure.

Seventeen

Her phone pinged. Daisy opened her eyes and peered at the clock and then at Max stretched out in what seemed to be his favorite spot with his snoozer on the extra pillow.

He lifted his head. "I know." She looked at him, petting his paw. "These early wake-up calls are getting to be annoying."

She picked up her cell and looked at the display. Houndsville Police Department.

She moaned. It was not even seven a.m. She slid the icon to the right and said, "Hello?"

"Ms. Flowers, it's Tucker. Sorry, I know it's early. We've established a timeline for the murder, and I'd like to talk to you. Let's say around ten."

"That's fine. I'll be here at the Inn. I'll tell Sandi at the front desk where you can find me."

"Thank you. I'll see you soon."

She laid her cell back on the night table and absently petted Max.

"Come on, big boy. Let's get up and go for an early walk."

There was no sense lying here worrying about Tucker's questions when she'd told him all she knew.

Thinking it might be cold outside, she layered the clothes she had with her. She grabbed her gloves and pompom hat—they'd come in handy—along with her cell.

Her plan was to stick to a walk along the perimeter of the Inn. She wasn't in the mood to go to the doggie park where she might have to pretend to be sociable if there were other people around.

They started out walking along the curving driveway.

A young couple, arm in arm, walked toward them from the opposite direction and stopped to pet Max. Then she passed by a group of three women, who simply waved.

They continued walking on the grassy edge until they got to the end of the road and had to turn around. Daisy started to cross over to the opposite side. There was a curve in the road, and suddenly a car seemed to come out of nowhere. The driver swerved to avoid them, but Daisy jerked Max's leash in an attempt to pull him backward toward the curb, and unfortunately she tripped and crashed into him.

He yelped, and when she looked down he was holding up his left paw.

"Oh, no! Max, I am so sorry." She knelt down to rub his leg and paw.

One of the three women had obviously seen what happened and hollered, "Are you okay? Do you need help?"

"We're fine," she shouted back. She didn't want to involve strangers when she felt stupid for not paying better attention. At least she knew who to call.

Shakily she pulled off her gloves, felt around in her pocket for her cell, and called Grant. She briefly explained what had happened.

"I can bring Max to see you, if you think I should."

"Daisy, he's probably fine. I doubt you did any harm to him. See how he does as you walk him back to the Inn." He paused. "I have a better idea. I'll come to you. I planned to leave soon anyway. I just have to wait for Harry to get here."

"Thanks. I appreciate it. I'll walk Max back, and we'll be waiting for you in the lobby." She ended the call and let out a relieved sigh. If he came soon, she'd still have time before Tucker arrived.

"Come on, Max, we'll go slow."

They ambled back toward the Inn with Max hobbling beside her. She felt terrible. It was totally her fault Max had gotten injured.

They didn't wait long before she spotted Grant walking into the Inn. He waved and raced over to her.

"That was quick," she said.

"Harry came in right after I talked to you. How's Max?" He sat next to her and bent down to pet him.

"He did walk back. I guess I overreacted. I'm sorry."

"It's okay. You've never had a dog before. Hey, Max. Let me have a look at you." He nudged him to stand up. Grant lifted Max's right leg and gently bent it back and forth. Max didn't flinch. He checked his left leg and then his paws. "He looks okay."

Daisy swiped her hand across her forehead. "Phew. That's a relief. I hated thinking I had hurt him."

She gently stroked his fur. "Is there something I should do for him?"

"Not really, unless he starts limping again. If he does, we can take an X-ray, but I don't believe that will be necessary. For now, let him take it easy."

"No problem."

She glanced at her watch. "Tucker called this morning. He's coming here to question me again."

Grant relaxed back against the sofa throw pillows. "I don't have to get right back to the clinic. We could sit in the bar and get something to eat. Then I can stay with you while you talk to Tucker."

"I'd really like that," Daisy said. "I can tell Sandi to send him to the bar when he gets here, but before we go there, I should probably take Max for a short walk. He never peed or pooped earlier."

Max started whining. Daisy shook her head and chuckled. "You'd think I'd know by now if he hears his name and the word 'walk' I'm done for. Now I have no choice but to take him outside."

"Well, this time you can have company." Grant smiled warmly at her.

"Sounds good to me." Daisy smiled back. She liked it a lot that Grant wanted to be with her.

They walked to the reception desk to give Sandi the heads up to send Tucker to the bar when he arrived and then headed out the front door.

Max bounded down the Inn steps, pulling Daisy behind him.

"Well, he seems totally recovered from his mishap." Grant looked at her. "I do think it might help if you taught him to walk better on a leash."

Daisy shrugged. "Of course you're right. It's just that I won't have him long enough. Let's go across the driveway to the doggie park."

Only two dogs, a Chihuahua and a black lab, were inside the fence, and both greeted Max with wagging tails. Their owners chatted with them, and then Daisy suggested they walk Max around the perimeter.

Grant stopped her after one lap. "Let's head back and get coffee before Tucker gets here."

As Grant closed the gate, her eyes were drawn to a black sports car pulling up in front of the Inn. Not many people drove a black Porsche. She watched to see who exited the car.

"Edward," Daisy hollered and waved before turning to Grant and saying, "I'll be right back."

She ran across the driveway with Max beside her. Having heard her, Edward stood next to his car and waited for her. She one arm-hugged him and pressed her cheek against his while Max whined to be petted.

"I can't believe you're here," she said, unwinding her arm and staring up into his eyes.

"Of course I'm here. You needed me, but who's your new friend?" He pointed to Max.

"I'll tell you about him later. How come you're here?"

"I thought your dad told you I was coming."

"Not exactly. He mentioned something about possibly sending you when I called yesterday to tell him about the murder."

"Well, here I am." He opened his front door and pulled out a bag of silver chocolate buds. "I thought you might need these."

"Wow! You brought me chocolate." Daisy eyed him up and down. Her heart raced when he looked at her with his dark blue eyes shadowed by long hair. He was so darn handsome.

"Your dad called me last night and told me to get here and help you. I packed up first thing this morning and got on the road."

So her dad was worried enough to send Edward.

"Well, thanks for delivering the buds, but it's even better to see you. And your timing is perfect. The lead detective will be here soon to grill me again."

She was so intent on talking to Edward, she barely noticed Grant strolling up to her and standing stiffly by her side. *Oops!* She had totally forgotten about him.

She stammered, "Edward, meet Grant Stamford."

Grant stuck out his hand to shake Edward's. Edward obliged and glanced from Grant to her.

Daisy babbled. "Grant's a vet. Max tripped earlier, and he came to check him out for me."

"I didn't know vets made house calls." Edward shrugged.

"Only for my favorite patients," Grant replied.

Daisy gulped and shifted from one foot to the other. Edward, a guy she liked immensely, stood with Grant, whom she had recently kissed and considered date-material.

She felt her face growing warm as the men checked each other out.

She wondered what they were thinking, but if their dark expressions were any indication, they were not happy to have been put in this position.

She glanced first at Grant, then Edward. They were both drop-dead gorgeous but entirely different. Grant was the taller of the two with brand shoulders, built like a lumberjack. His eyes were hazel, and his hair was dark brown and wavy with lighter highlights.

Edward, on the other hand, was tall and thinner with straight dark brown hair on the longish side that partially covered his deep blue eyes. In her opinion, he had movie star looks.

She picked up the slack. "How long are you staying?"

Edward casually placed his arm around her shoulders and smiled down at her. "As long as you need me."

She stole a peek at Grant sideways. If the scowl on his face was any indication, he was annoyed—or worse.

"So are we still on for coffee?" Grant eyed her.

What was she supposed to say? She clutched Max's leash tighter and tried to shake off Edward's arm. He just held on tighter. This situation was going downhill faster than a sled on a snowy mountain.

"Edward, why don't you go check in and join us afterward in the bar? We were about to get coffee," she added nonchalantly.

Edward frowned. "That can wait. I want to know what's going on. Your dad insisted I get here ASAP. He said you'd fill me in. Is there some place we can talk? And by the way, where did you get Max?" he asked, finally petting the whining dog.

What was with Edward? His behavior bordered on obnoxious. She'd never seen him act this way before. And now she'd no doubt made it worse by suggesting he join her and Grant.

Daisy raised an eyebrow. "Nothing is going to change in the next few minutes. Go check in, and I'll fill you in on everything when you come to the bar." She had no idea how that would work out. Most likely it wouldn't.

Daisy's eyes flitted back and forth from Grant to Edward and back again. It was obvious they weren't going to want to chitchat as a threesome. She didn't know how to resolve this soon to be disaster.

Grant's glance darted from her to Edward's arm around her shoulder. She finally wiggled free and watched as Grant glanced at his watch. "It's later than I thought," he said curtly. "I need to get to the clinic."

Daisy tried to stop him by putting her hand on his arm. "You're sure?" She gazed into his eyes. "You said you'd stick around while Tucker questioned me."

Grant removed her hand. "Edward is here. You'll be fine."

She wasn't fine. She felt like she couldn't breathe. On impulse, she hugged him. "Thanks for coming so quickly today. I was really worried about Max."

"I know," he said. "Glad I could be helpful."

"Call me later," she implored him with what she hoped was a pleading expression in her eyes. "I'll fill you in on Tucker's grilling."

"If I can." He nodded at Edward and walked off without a backward glance.

Daisy turned toward Edward, feeling a bit frustrated. "Now please go check-in. I'll meet you at the reception desk in a few minutes. I need to let Max walk around for a bit."

He stood, staring at her with his lips twitching as if something was on his mind, but then he merely said, "Fine. See you in a few." He walked off to pop open his trunk.

Edward might have figured she'd already walked Max, having seen her coming from the doggie park, but it was the best excuse she could come up with to have a few minutes alone.

So for the second time, she headed to the doggie park, and while Max sniffed the grass like there was something wonderful buried in it, she considered her situation. Edward was here for her. Now what? If her instincts were right, Grant assumed she and Edward had something going on, and possibly Edward thought she had something going on with Grant.

What a mess when she really had neither.

What would a passionate kiss with Edward be like? Certainly the few hugs and air kisses they'd shared had given her no idea. At least Grant's kiss in the carriage had left her wanting more.

She let out a deep sigh.

Between her job, Allan's job offer, Max, Betsy's death, Edward, and Grant her life couldn't get more complicated. Or could it?

Eighteen

Daisy found Edward at the reception desk talking to Samantha after a short stint in the park with Max.

"I see you met Samantha, the Inn's owner." Daisy took a cookie for Max from the jar on the counter.

"Max, sit," Daisy told him. He might not walk well on a leash, but he sat when cookies were up for grabs.

"Yes, I'm getting a history lesson on the Inn. Did you know the original owners of this mansion were rum runners? They converted it to an inn to cover their illegal activities of bottling bay rum in the basement during Prohibition."

Sandi waved her hand at Daisy. "Ms. Flowers, I hate to interrupt, but the detective got here about ten minutes ago. I told him you went to walk Max. I sent him off to the bar, like you told me."

"Thanks. Come on, Edward. Sandi can keep your overnight bag." She looked at Samantha. "I guess we might see you later."

"Are you nervous?" Edward asked as they walked down the hallway toward the bar.

"Not really. I have nothing to hide. I never should have gotten near that knife. But I'm okay. Besides, Tucker is a homegrown guy who's dating my sister."

Edward grasped her hand and stopped her. "Enough about Tucker. Tell me about Grant. He seemed annoyed that I showed up."

Daisy frowned. Edward didn't care about her having touched the knife? Instead he was interested in Grant.

"I told you he's a veterinarian. He's the one who found me with Betsy, the murder victim. His identical twin brother is engaged to Meghan."

"The Meghan you always talk about and tell me her fiancé is awesome and a dreamboat too?"

Daisy felt her face getting red. She refused to look at Edward. "Well, yes, they look alike but..."

Edward halted and turned to face her. "Do you like him?"

Daisy looked down at the floor. Why not be honest? "I might, but come on, Tucker's waiting."

"Hello, Tucker. Sorry to keep you waiting." Daisy walked up to one of the booths against the far wall. "I hope it's okay for my friend and coworker Edward Plant to listen in. He's the investigator at the law firm where I work."

Tucker checked out Edward, his expression inscrutable. "All right. Have a seat. Let's get started."

"Edward, you slide in first so Max can sit by me."

Tucker had the same spiral notebook and pen he'd used Saturday night already opened on the table. "I need to go through the night of the murder with you again. Some of my questions may be repetitive."

Did he think she had been holding back last time?

He turned to a page with lots of scribbles and picked up his pen. "First, tell me how you knew Betsy. From what I understand, she hasn't lived in Houndsville long."

Daisy paused to consider her response. "I didn't really know her. I was never properly introduced to her. I knew about her from other people."

"What other people?"

"First from Meghan, then Millie and Grant."

"From what I heard, you had a conversation with her at the gala that was unpleasant."

"I wouldn't call it a conversation. Betsy, to my way of seeing it, wanted to embarrass me."

"And how did she attempt to do that?"

Daisy felt Edward's eyes on her. She avoided looking at him. "There were a lot of people standing around who heard her accuse me of chasing after Grant."

Perhaps Tucker saw she was uncomfortable, but for whatever reason, his next question had nothing to do with the previous one. "When you walked Max, did you see anyone else walking around?"

Daisy closed her eyes and tried to picture the scene after the carriage ride when she walked Max.

"It was dark. I saw some couples hanging around the front door of the Inn. They could have just been leaving the gala and walking to their cars. I don't remember seeing anyone around the back side of the Inn."

"Did you recognize any of the people you saw?"

She shook her head. "No. But honestly, I don't know many people around here."

"When you saw someone on the bench, what did you think?"

"You already asked me this. I thought maybe they needed help."

"Why?"

Daisy closed her eyes again and tried to picture herself looking toward the bench. "They were slumped over. I thought maybe they were drunk and had fallen asleep."

He flipped to a new page in his notebook. "Did you know that it was Betsy Clarkson?"

"Not until I got close and saw her shoes."

She started to chuckle and caught herself. This conversation was meant to be serious. She'd better explain. "Tucker, I love shoes, and I had seen Betsy earlier at the gala. Her shoes were Manolo Blahniks. They cost around eleven hundred dollars. No one could forget them. I would kill...oops...I mean, I would love to have a pair of them."

Edward snickered.

"Why did you touch the knife?"

"I had no idea what it was. It wasn't sticking out, and I was trying to figure out what was going on."

"I have to ask. Did you murder Betsy Clarkson?"

"Of course not. I told you, I barely knew her."

"You just told me she humiliated you at the gala. You could have seen her outside and confronted her." Tucker pointed his index finger at her. "You could have murdered Betsy in a moment of passion."

"Come on, Tucker. Where would I have gotten the knife? How ridiculous. You must really be hard up if you think I murdered Betsy."

Daisy's head started pounding. Tucker's accusation had gotten her head so screwed up. Her stomach clenched. She felt sick.

"One last question," Tucker said, leaning forward to get in her space. "Were you aware that Grant left the gala to go take care of a client at the clinic?"

Daisy frowned. "Yes, I overheard him telling his sister, but what difference would that make?" The second she asked the question, she realized Grant's departure from the gala around the time of Betsy's murder made him a major suspect. In Tucker's mind, Grant could have left the gala, murdered Betsy, and then returned to the party. Maybe Tucker's accusing her of the murder was to throw her so she would say something bad about Grant.

No way. She refused to believe Grant had anything to do with the murder, no matter how much he hated Betsy.

Edward stared at her. Was he thinking Grant might have murdered Betsy, that Daisy had been hanging out with a murderer?

Such a mess. It seemed anyone who knew Betsy, including even Nicholas, Meghan, and Meghan's parents, all hated Betsy and could be considered suspects. How would Tucker ever find who killed her? So many questions and no answers.

Tucker jotted something in his notebook and shut it. "That's it for now. I might have some additional follow-up questions for you in the next few days."

"Are you saying I still can't leave? Can't you just talk to me on the phone? You know I need to get back to work."

"I'll let you know. I'll try to work something out." He stood up, shook Edward's hand, and walked off.

"Well," Edward said, frowning. "I'll tell your dad you have to stay here. He won't like that. Tucker seems to be in over his head. He's grasping at straws when he accuses you." He paused. "Now, your new boyfriend—that's a different matter. Maybe he killed her."

"Come on, you don't believe I'd hang out with someone like that. And what are you saying about Grant being my new boy-friend?" She laughed. "I didn't know I had an old one."

Edward smiled. "I thought it was me. Didn't you tell me you were going to marry me so you could be Daisy Plant?"

Daisy froze. The day they'd met would remain an embarrass-ing moment in her mind forever. She had been so infatuated with Edward that she had acted like a besotted teenager, but even now he made her feel something. She just wasn't sure what. Better to change the topic.

"You could have stopped me from almost admitting I killed Betsy for her shoes."

"No way! That was hilarious—and the highlight of the inter-view. You really are obsessed with shoes. Every time, and I mean every time, we go to Starbucks you ogle the shoes in that fancy shoe store. If I remember correctly, there's been times when you left me standing there waiting for you while you went to try on something you've seen in the window."

She huffed. "At least my obsession is only shoes, yours are fast cars."

"Touché."

"Now that I'm done with Tucker," Daisy said, "I can show you a bit of Houndsville while we take Max for a walk and stop by my mom's. It's near Stella's Shoes where I just might buy a pair of shoes to use to hit you in the head."

Edward grinned. "Ha, ha. You think you're funny."

"Yes, I do. Come on." She looped her free hand around his arm. "What do you say we take him and you to the dog bakery?"

"Take me to a dog bakery?"

"Yeah, it's great. You'll love it. And they do have people drinks. On a chilly day like today, a mocha latte would be perfect."

They headed out the main door and started walking. "All right. It's time to tell me how you ended up with Max."

Once again, she explained about Lisa. If something like this happened again, she swore she'd send out an email to all friends and family. She'd had to tell this story too many times.

They strolled along the street until Daisy pointed out a store-front. "Look, there's Stella's Shoes. Shame I'm not in the mood to shop."

"Not in the mood for shoes? What's going on?"

"It's been a long couple of days. It's not every day a person finds a dead body." She shivered. "Come on, I want you to meet my mom. Her shop's the one with the flower pots outside."

Edward opened the door for her and Max. Her mom was sitting on one of the stools at the front counter, looking frustrated while trying to cut the stems off some roses. Sidney was watching from the sidelines. He came over and wagged his tail at Max while Daisy reached down to pet him.

"Hi, Mom. I brought my friend Edward to meet you. He's the firm's investigator, and Dad thought it would be a good idea for him to come in case I need help. With Tucker questioning me again this morning, his timing was perfect."

"What? Tucker questioned you again? That's ridiculous."

"I think he believes I know more than I'm telling him. But say hello to Edward."

"Hello, Edward. I'm sorry for my bad manners. This whole murder thing has me in knots. Nice to finally meet you, and thanks for coming to Daisy's aid."

"That was a pleasure. Now Daisy's taking me to the dog bakery. I understand from her I'll love it. Want to join us?" he asked.

"Sorry, I'd like to, but I can't. I have several orders to get ready for pick-up."

"Would you like me to stay and help. I can see you're having trouble."

"I'm okay. It's just taking me longer with this cast, but it's all doable."

"Since you can't go, we can take Sidney with us. Edward can walk him. That way, Sidney will get out for a walk and a treat."

"Sure. He'd love that."

Nineteen

They left the main thoroughfare and sauntered down the winding brick pathway to the bakery. Daisy led the way with Max by her side. Sidney, whose short little legs had to pump fast to keep up, followed behind with Edward.

Daisy halted before they got up to the steps. "I remember coming here a lot. The homemade ice cream was delicious, but the old farmhouse was in such disrepair. Millie has done a great job of restoring it."

They walked up the few steps and opened the door. Bells jangled.

Daisy stopped inside the door. Edward bumped into her. "Wow."

"Pretty neat, huh?" She led him farther into the library.

Edward's reaction was hilarious. He almost stumbled over a humongous wolfhound spreadeagled on the floor. His eyes opened wide when another dog started howling.

"That's Woody. When he wants a cookie, he starts a ruckus."

"Well, you're right, this place is certainly unique."

"Come on. Watch where you're walking, and don't trip on another dog. We'll get drinks and pupcakes for Max and Sidney."

Edward laughed. "A pupcake?"

"Yup, a cupcake for dogs," Daisy answered as she led Edward toward the Collie Counter where Todd was busy helping a young person with her golden retriever.

"Hi, Daisy. What's up?" Todd asked when he saw her.

"Where's Millie and the rest of the crew? I want them to meet Edward."

"Carolyn isn't here, but MaryEllen and Millie are in the kitchen. I'll get them."

Todd turned around and slid open the pocket door in the wall behind him.

"Hey, can you come out here? You have company."

"We'll be right there," Millie hollered.

Within a minute MaryEllen came out of the kitchen carrying a tray with treats that looked like cupcakes. Luke stepped out beside her with Millie behind him.

"Hey, this is a surprise." Millie came over to hug Daisy. MaryEllen laid her tray on top of the display case.

Max started whining and pacing around.

"Max, sit," Daisy told him. "I'm sure Millie will give you a treat."

Millie nodded. "Of course, but first tell me who's the gorgeous guy with Sidney."

Daisy smiled. "Edward Plant. He's the investigator at my law firm. My dad sent him to make sure I don't get arrested."

"Don't kid about that," Millie said. "We all know you didn't murder Betsy, but you thought you might have touched the knife. Tucker would lose his job if he didn't question you."

Millie paused. "Hey! I just realized something." She glanced slyly from Daisy to Edward. "So if you're a Plant and she's a Flowers, I bet it was interesting when you two met."

Daisy's face grew increasingly warm. Dumb of her to have mentioned Edward's last name.

"Yes, it was a hoot. Daisy was very cute." Edward winked at her.

She glared back at him, daring him to mention what she said about being Daisy Plant someday.

"I told Edward you make a great latte. Could we each get one?" Daisy asked, purposely not answering Millie's question.

Millie shrugged. "Sure. I get it. You don't want to tell me about your first meeting. It must have been juicy, considering how red your face is."

She pointed around the room. "Go find a table. I'll bring everything over when it's ready."

Daisy steered Edward to one of the nearby tables. The dogs sat at their feet, Max with his head on her shoe. Daisy leaned toward Edward and murmured, "Listen, Millie can be relentless. No disclosures. You need to remember you're my friend."

Edward smirked. "Yes, ma'am, Ms. Flowers."

They sat and talked about Tucker and his questions until Millie brought over a tray with drinks, some biscotti, and cupcakes topped with strawberries. She laid the tray on the table.

"FYI, the cupcakes are for the dogs," Millie said. "Here we call them pupcakes."

Edward nodded. "Daisy told me that, but I didn't know dogs could have strawberries."

Millie grinned. "Surprised, huh? Fresh strawberries are very healthy for dogs. They're full of antioxidants and high in fiber and vitamin C."

"Look." Edward pointed toward the archway into the library. "Isn't that Grant heading this way?"

Daisy nodded. "Yes, it's him. I wonder why he's here now. He told us he had appointments at the clinic."

She took a deep breath. Now she'd have to deal with Edward and Grant being together again. She'd thought she was finished with that earlier.

Grant waved and headed their way, stopping beside his sister.

"Mil, can you talk to me for a minute? It's important."

"Sure. Have a seat. We can talk here, if that's okay."

"All right." Grant sat next to his sister.

Daisy stole a glance at Edward. She hoped he understood not to say anything about her conversation with Tucker.

"I'm pretty sure I found the supposed puppy mill Betsy told you about."

"What!" She leaned forward, paying close attention. "How?"

"Well, Tucker called and questioned me about the dustup at the Inn with Betsy the day before the gala. Seems someone told him about it. Anyway, it reminded me that's when I met Betsy's sister, Stephanie."

"I don't understand where you're going with this," Millie said, frowning.

"Then just keep quiet for a minute. I'll explain. The day before the gala, I found a puppy outside at the Inn. I took it inside to ask Sandi if she knew who it belonged to. She didn't, but Betsy appeared out of nowhere and tried to grab the puppy. Turned out the puppy was her sister's. It had slipped its leash as Betsy and Stephanie were walking to the spa."

Daisy interrupted. "I was there when this happened. That's the first time I ever saw Betsy. I didn't even know it was her until Grant called her by name. Her behavior toward Grant was disgusting."

Edward stared at her. Was he surprised she had stepped up to defend Grant?

Grant smiled at her. "She was a jerk to everyone. Anyway, that's what got me thinking about Stephanie having a young puppy. I wondered where she got it."

He paused. "So I called her this morning to ask. Turns out Betsy took her to some lady named Mrs. Breely. It's the same place where Betsy got Cleo."

Millie nabbed a piece of biscotti. "I'm still not following."

He leaned forward. "This could be the place Betsy was talking about."

"I don't see the connection. Why would Betsy want to make trouble for this person if it's where she and her sister got their dogs?"

"Right now, we have no idea. Maybe Betsy made up the puppy mill thing. Could be it was all a cunning plan to get you riled up," Grant said. "But something else Stephanie said made me think twice.

"Stephanie told me she bought the puppy to get it out of this lady's place. She said all the dogs looked to be in bad shape, and she didn't want something bad to happen to a little puppy whose life was just beginning."

Millie drummed her fingers on the table. "Why didn't she call the authorities if she was worried about the other dogs?"

"I don't know. Maybe it just never occurred to her."

"I have a way to solve this problem once and for all," Daisy piped up. "I could call this Mrs. Breely and tell her I'm looking to buy a collie puppy. Get her to let me come see her dogs."

Millie raised her hand to high five Daisy. "That's a great plan. Mrs. Breely would have no reason to suspect you were checking her out, and Grant and I could go with you. Of course we'd have to have a reason to go, but that's easy. You could say you don't have a car."

Edward shook his head. "Daisy, this is a bad idea. You need to get back to work."

"But Tucker said I had to stay."

"I think it can easily be arranged for you to leave. As you said, he can always reach you by phone."

Daisy sighed as she locked eyes with Grant. She hated to admit it, but Edward was right. It's just that she wanted to help Millie and Grant.

"Edward's right. I should be heading back to D.C. Besides, what if I do go and we see bad stuff? How would we get the dogs out of there?"

Grant shrugged. "I can't tell you what to do. You have to decide. It is true we might see bad stuff, and if we do we might need to call the authorities, but let's not worry about that yet."

"Okay," she stammered. "Let's do this." She glanced at Edward, only to see him frowning. To appease him, she said, "But it has to be in the next day or so. I have to go home."

"So call her now," Grant suggested. "If she asks how you got her name, use Stephanie's name."

"Do you have her number?" Daisy asked.

"Yup." He pulled a small paper from his pocket and handed it to her. She fished around in her handbag for her cell, found it, and tapped in the number.

She took a deep breath. She wanted to get this right.

A woman answered and said, "Hello."

"Hi there. Is this Mrs. Breely?" Daisy inquired politely.

"Yes, can I help you with something?"

"Yes, please." She tried to sound distressed. "My lovely collie just died, and I want another so badly. A friend told me you may have puppies for sale. If you do, I'd love to see them."

"Who is this friend who gave you my name?"

"Stephanie Carlson," Daisy said haltingly.

"Did you say Carlson? If so, I don't want anything to do with that family. I made a mistake ever letting them come here. That older one, Betsy, is trouble."

This was going downhill. She had to think quick. "Please! I'm not friends with them or anything. I just saw them walking a collie and asked where they'd gotten it."

"Then why'd you say they were friends of yours? Any friend of theirs is not welcome here."

"I'm sorry. I thought it would be good to say we're friends," Daisy piled on. "I'm desperate for a dog. I live in D.C. Sadly I don't know any breeders near my home."

Daisy pushed further. "Please. If you have any puppies, I'd love to come see them."

"I'll think about it," Mrs. Breely said. "Give me your number. I'll call if I want you to come."

Daisy bit her lip. This was not the outcome she had been hoping for. "Mrs. Breely, I have to get back to D.C. for work. I only have a few days to see your puppies."

Mrs. Breely paused. "You don't give up, do ya? I can't do anything until Thursday."

Daisy didn't even realize she'd been holding her breath. She nodded at Grant and repeated for him and Millie to hear. "So I can come see the puppies Thursday?"

Grant signaled her with all ten fingers. She got the message.

"Is ten o'clock okay?"

"All right. But give me your number in case I change my mind."

Daisy reluctantly gave Mrs. Breely her cell number and then tried to make it so Mrs. Breely wouldn't back out.

"Oh, thank you so much for letting me come. I really want a puppy, and I can't wait to see yours. Can you give me your address and directions to your home?"

Daisy put the phone on speaker so Millie and Grant would hear Mrs. Breely's directions.

"I'll see you Thursday, then." Now that she'd sealed the deal, Daisy ended the call.

She scrunched her brows. "Uh-oh! I just thought of something. I don't really plan to get a puppy, so what happens when we get there?"

Millie chewed her lip. "Just be disappointed in the puppies' colors. Tell her you wanted a sable if they're merles or tricolors."

Daisy shook her head.

What have I gotten myself into?

Twenty

Edward and Daisy left the bakery soon after she ended the call with Mrs. Breely. They headed back to the Inn, dropping off Sidney on the way.

"Once we get back, I'm going to respond to some emails and phone calls. My plan is to quit around dinnertime and meet you in the bar."

Daisy stuck out her bottom lip." Oh, I figured we'd hang out the rest of the day, but if you're planning to work, I will too."

"Don't pout." He looped his arm through hers. "I rushed here to be your knight in shining armor. Now I have some work to do."

She couldn't help it. She was bummed. She'd just assumed they'd spend the day together.

"Oh, all right. I'll call Meghan. See if she can give me a facial."

"Good idea. Then you'll be gorgeous when we meet for dinner," Edward teased.

"You mean, I'm not always beautiful? I thought I was." Daisy grinned.

He didn't seem to know how to answer her. Instead he turned toward her, gazed into her eyes, and kissed her lightly on the lips before saying, "See you later."

He walked off. She stood, stunned. She fingered her lips. First time he'd kissed her like this. What did it mean?

She took a deep breath. Someday she'd know, and then maybe she'd be able to figure out what she wanted. For now, she shook off those thoughts, fumbled around in her handbag until she found her cell, and tapped in the number for the spa. She was disheartened to find out Meghan was booked the rest of the day.

"Oh well, Max, it looks like it's just you and me. And I know just what I need to do."

She walked purposely to her suite and rifled around in several drawers until she found some stationery and a pen and got comfy on her bed with Max at her feet.

For the next hour or so, she agonized over a pros and cons list for Allan's job. When she finished, she wadded up the paper and threw it on the night table.

That was a waste of time. She still had no idea what she was going to do.

Did she want to give up her dream of following in her dad's footsteps? Would working for Allan be different than having him as a client? Would she like the job of being his director of development? And what about Edward? Would she ever get to see him?

On the plus side, she'd never have to deal with Corinne again, and the hours would be much more reasonable.

What a conundrum.

She buried her head under her pillow and closed her eyes, but she couldn't stop the thoughts running through her head.

For so many years, she'd believed her dad wanted her to follow in his footsteps. Had she been wrong? Had it been only her idea and never his? Was he sorry he'd brought her into his firm? If so, should she leave?

Way too many unanswered questions with no definitive answers.

She did know that if she accepted Allan's generous offer, she'd be moving to Houndsville, and that meant getting to spend time with Grant.

She liked that idea. It would give them a chance to get to know each other better, to see if they were good together.

Another plus would be living close to her best friend. Best of all, she could have a dog. She looked over at Max. Shame it couldn't be him.

Still no closer to a decision at five-thirty, she changed into black leggings and navy cashmere sweater. All ready, she leashed Max and headed to the bar to meet Edward.

An elderly couple stood at the base of the staircase. As Daisy walked down the steps, she heard the woman remark, "Look Curtis, a collie."

They waited for Daisy and oohed over Max.

"We had a collie when our kids were growing up," the woman said. "I miss that old fella."

Daisy watched them walk away hand in hand toward the front door. The woman glanced back at Max. She had tears in her eyes. Clearly she missed her dog. Daisy felt sad for them. She understood now that she'd become so attached to Max.

"You're a good boy," Daisy said as she headed in the opposite direction.

She stood surveying the bar from the doorway. Surprising for a Tuesday night, the bar stools were all occupied with additional people standing around. She assumed some of them must be locals.

She spotted Edward right away sitting at one of the small wood-paneled booths to the left of the fireplace. He looked up and smiled. Her heart skipped a beat. She made her way to the booth and scooted in across from him, positioning herself so Max had enough space to sit on her toes.

"Hi. You look beautiful. I assume you enjoyed your facial?"

"Stop teasing. I look the same. Meghan was booked."

He shook his head. "Well, I'm happy to see you after working for several hours." He sipped the martini in front of him.

A waitress appeared. "Can I get you started with something to drink?"

"Sure, I'll have a glass of sauvignon blanc," Daisy said.

Once the waitress left, Edward placed his hand on top of Daisy's.

"I called your dad and reported in with him. I told him Tucker might want to talk to you again, but I was sure we could persuade him to let you leave if you promise to stay in touch and be available by phone. He was glad to hear it. He's looking forward to you coming home. He mentioned he has a new case he'd like to review with you."

Daisy shook her head. "Wait. You know I'm planning to go see the puppies on Thursday."

Edward tapped his fingers on the table. "Yes, and you know my opinion about that."

"Look, I have my computer here with me, so if anything pressing comes up, I can handle it from here. And by now, the trial is almost over, so I'm not needed there."

"I told you most of your teammates didn't like what your dad did, especially when I told them you had come here to help your mom. But now you can leave, and you seem to be finding reasons to stay. Why?"

"It's only two days, and I promised Millie and Grant I'd go see Mrs. Breely with them."

"I get the feeling something else is going on here. Care to tell me? Are you staying here to see Grant?"

She wasn't ready to tell him about Allan's job offer. She shook her head. "No. I'm staying to help Millie."

Even to her, those words sounded weak. She refused to look at him. He knew her too well. He'd know she was holding something back.

The waitress brought her glass of wine and took their dinner orders, giving her a chance to figure out exactly what she wanted to tell him.

She took a sip. "Okay. Here's the truth, which you already know. My whole life, I've wanted to be a lawyer and follow in my dad's footsteps at his firm. Now, I'm not so sure."

He leaned toward her. "Daisy, you're a good lawyer. Don't throw in the towel yet. Give yourself some more time. I believe your dad will come around, and you'll be happier if that happens."

She wasn't sure that was the whole issue, but the one thing she didn't have right now was time. She had to give Allan his answer soon—in a few days.

"I told your dad he needs to be patient. The last few days have certainly been difficult." Edward squinted. "You seem preoccupied."

"Not really. Just hungry."

He shrugged as if he knew that wasn't totally true.

She was distracted. Edward's words had resonated. If her dad wanted to review a case with her, that was a good sign. Really good.

She'd sleep on it, but she believed she'd made her final decision about what she was going to tell Allan.

"So have you heard how the case is going?" Daisy asked.

"Your dad thinks it's going well. Oh good, here's our food."

"Can I get you anything else?" the waitress asked as she gave them their burgers and fries.

"We're good."

Daisy pretended to eat, nibbling her burger and sampling a few fries. Her stomach, as per usual lately, was in knots. She hated not telling Edward the whole truth. He was her friend and a major part of her life in D.C.

She yawned. "Sorry. I'm tired. The last few days have been extremely stressful. I'm going to go walk Max one last time and head to my room."

"Do you mind if I stay here?" Edward said. "It's still early. I'd like to get another drink at the bar."

Daisy shook her head. "That's fine."

She did care, but she wasn't about to admit it. She'd hoped Edward would want to go with her. After Saturday night, she wasn't fond of walking Max in the dark, even in the doggie park.

Edward stood up and waited for her to stand too. He put his arm around her shoulders and walked with her to the doorway.

"Don't wander too far. Sleep well, and I'll see you in the morning."

She walked out with Max and stood there for a minute, feeling a wave of sadness overtake her.

Why had he chosen to get a drink at the bar instead of taking a walk with her?

Here she was torn between him or Grant, and it wasn't clear if Edward had any interest in romancing her at all.

Twenty-one

Daisy cracked open an eyelid when she heard her phone ringing and peeked outside. It was still dark. She chuckled to herself. Who needed an alarm when someone was always calling to wake her?

"Edward, what's up? It's awfully early to be calling."

"I'm sorry. I've decided to get on the road. My mission here is done. I came to make sure you were okay. And I believe you're fine."

Daisy sighed. "We'll see."

"Meet me for breakfast? We can talk before I leave."

"Can you give me fifteen minutes?" Daisy asked, already sliding out of the bed.

"Yes. Meet me in the Oak Room," he said.

She rushed into the bathroom, brushed her teeth, washed her face, dusted her cheeks with blush, and put on lip gloss. Her hair was, as usual, a mess. She looked like Orphan Annie on a bad day. Only thing to do was to tie it up in a ponytail with a scrunchie. She grabbed the clothes she'd worn yesterday, and after a quickie stop in the doggie park, she and Max met up with Edward. He was reading *The Houndsville Times*.

"Any coverage of the murder in there today?" She slid into the seat across from him.

He held up the paper, showing her the front page where there was a photo of the Inn with a headline underneath. "Murder at the Fur-Baby Gala Still Unsolved."

Daisy shook her head. "They've had an article every day. I hope there's no mention of me again."

"Coffee, anyone?" the waitress asked, interrupting them.

"Yes, please." They both nodded. "And we can order now too," Edward said.

The waitress turned over their mugs and poured coffee before taking their orders.

"I'll have two orders of scrambled eggs and two orders of bacon," Daisy said.

"Didn't you have enough to eat yesterday?" Edward asked, winking at her.

"Max and I are sharing. Eggs and bacon will be a treat for him instead of dog food."

"In that case, I can put one order in a dog bowl." The waitress smiled. "We keep special bowls here for our furry guests."

Daisy reached down to pet Max. "Did you hear that? You get your own bowl. That's perfect. Thank you."

"Lucky dog." Edward petted Max and ordered a ham and cheese omelet. He asked if he could get it as soon as possible.

"I'll try, but the kitchen is backed up this morning," the waitress said apologetically before leaving to go to another table.

"It seems it's going to take some time to get our food. I'll go check out. Be back shortly."

Edward slid out of his seat, and Daisy watched him walk away. No matter what he did or didn't do, she couldn't deny her strong attraction to him. He screamed *sexy* with his longish hair, lean body, and tight butt. The young woman at the next table must have thought so too as Daisy saw her eyeing him.

While he was gone, she sipped her coffee and debated whether to read the paper. She finally picked it up and read the article about Betsy's murder. *Phew.* No mention of her name.

She went on to read another article and folded the paper when Edward reappeared at the booth. At the same time, the waitress set down their food.

Daisy put the dog bowl filled with eggs and bacon on the floor for Max. He dug in as if he hadn't eaten in days.

Meanwhile, she merely looked at her food.

Edward took a bite of his omelet. He studied her. "Why aren't you eating? Are you sad I have to leave so soon?"

She chuckled, smiling back. She did love his teasing.

"I would have stayed if I didn't have an appointment with a new client this afternoon."

"That's okay. Remember, I'll be back Friday. I'll see you then. By the way, I called HR and told them I need a few personal days."

She wanted to say more. To ask him why he hadn't walked with her last night or even why he hadn't kissed her more passionately. She refrained. Maybe she didn't want to know.

"So if you're not eating, and Max is done, walk out with me."

She nodded and picked up Max's leash. They walked side by side to the front door.

"I'll see you soon." He leaned in, brushing his lips against hers.

It must have affected him. He wrapped his arms around her and kissed her again more deeply.

Geez. He's leaving, and he's finally showing his romantic side.

She stood watching as he got into his car and waved from his open window, driving down the lane and out of sight.

She had no inkling as to what his plans were toward her, but she had decided to take his advice about work and to stick with it for now. It was time to call Allan and tell him she'd made up her mind to turn down his job offer.

Yes, she was going back to D.C., but not without regrets.

MaryEllen was already knee-deep in rolling dough when Millie hollered, "I'm coming in," as she slid open the kitchen door.

"Hey, you remembered to announce yourself," MaryEllen said, smiling.

"Lucky for me, I was thinking clearly, otherwise I might have been banned for life from here."

Millie glanced around. "Looks like you could use some help. I'll finish making the Luke's Hideaways if you want to start on something else."

"That'd be great." She handed Millie some cheese cubes. "Here, stuff this in the hideaways."

Todd and Carolyn breezed into the kitchen a few minutes later.

"Geez, it's cold outside." Carolyn rubbed her bare hands together. "I need coffee. Anyone else want a cup?"

"I do," Todd said, taking off his jacket.

"Me too," MaryEllen said.

"Me three." Millie eyed the nearby tray. "Do you think we could also have some of the biscotti?"

"One piece for each of you. We need enough for the customers."

Carolyn grabbed four mugs from the storage shelf underneath the steel table. "All right. Coffee's coming."

In the meantime, MaryEllen plated four pieces of biscotti.

Todd pulled out one of the stools and sat. "Mil, I'm curious. How is the murder investigation going?"

"I have no idea, but honestly, Tucker has so many suspects, it might take him awhile."

"Like who?"

"Well, for example there's Meghan and her parents and Nicholas. We know they didn't hurt Betsy, but they certainly disliked her, and I imagine Tucker has to check them out. And then there might be some people who hated Betsy for reasons we don't know, but I have my own plan."

MaryEllen frowned. "Oh, no. Here you go again, putting yourself in danger."

"I don't think so. I'm just planning to talk to a few people."

Todd frowned. "Like who?"

"Well, for one, Vince Cordoza. He's the photographer for *Leisurely Living Magazine*. Betsy called him a sleazeball. I want to know why. Then I'd like to talk to Annabel and Christopher. I heard Betsy arguing with Christopher and then later I heard Annabel and Christopher arguing about Betsy. I bet Annabel's holding back. I think she knows more than she's telling."

"Come on, Millie." Carolyn scowled. "With your history, what makes you think she'll tell you anything?"

"I'm prepared to threaten her. I bet even if Tucker has talked to her, she didn't tell him about how Betsy screwed with her too."

All three partners glared at her. MaryEllen shook her head. "We've told you before to leave this to the authorities."

"You'd better be careful. A murderer is still out there somewhere," Todd added.

Millie stood and paced back and forth. "You're all correct." She sighed. "The problem is, I can't sit and do nothing. Donations have dried up. People aren't sure if the foundation is involved somehow. I even got a few calls from donors who do automatic monthly donations, and they want to pause them. This is an unmitigated disaster."

Disregarding her partners' objections, three hours later, Millie left the bakery during a lull and cut through the park to Annabel's Coffee and Tea Emporium.

She'd told Carolyn she had to run an errand for Carl. She hoped her partners weren't aware of her true destination, although they knew her so well they had probably figured there was no way to stop her.

She passed a few people along the way and stopped to pet a cute Corgi, but mostly her thoughts were on the murder investigation. She couldn't help wondering if she'd be able to nail down the murderer.

She stepped into Annabel's. In the past year, Annabel had remodeled her store. She had divided her one large space into two smaller rooms. A display case filled with pastries and breads sat to the right of the door and several high-topped tables sat toward the back. Right now, several people were standing at the counter waiting to place their orders.

The second room off to the left was what Millie imagined a tea room from the past would look like. The room was painted a soft shade of yellow with chintz patterned draperies and tables covered in pristine white cloths surrounded by mismatched wood chairs upholstered in the same chintz as the windows.

The tables were set with white china and starched flowery napkins folded uniquely. A small vase filled with fresh flowers sat in the center of each table.

She had to admit Annabel had a flair for creating a warm and inviting place. Certainly the opposite of her personality.

She was sure if she and Annabel were friends, she would frequent the place often. As that was hardly the case, she only went there once in a while when she expected Annabel was not working. It was a good meeting place to sit and chat.

Today, Annabel stood behind her counter, boxing up some pastries. Millie stood off to the side and waited until the customer had her box in hand and walked off.

"Hello, Annabel. Can we talk?"

Annabel glared at her. "Whatever for?"

Millie murmured, "It's about Betsy. Can we find a quiet spot?"

"Millie Whitfield, just say whatever you have to say and get out of here."

One man tapping his foot at the counter huffed. "I've been waiting to be helped. If you're going to argue with someone, I'll leave."

"No, no, Mr. Larkins. She can wait. What can I help you with?"

Millie forced herself to wait while Annabel helped Mr. Larkin and the other few waiting customers.

Finally all the people left. Before anyone else could walk up to place an order, Millie blurted out, "I overheard you and Christopher arguing at the gala. It was obvious you were extremely angry with Betsy."

Annabel gasped. "You spied on me?"

Millie shrugged. "I did. I was surprised, to say the least. I thought you and Betsy were buddies. Seems I was wrong, very wrong."

Annabel stamped her foot. "I thought she was my friend, that she cared about me. No one else does. We had an agreement. I needed help financially with my renovations, and she'd promised to give me some money. Instead, she accused me of lying about my financials and reneged, but not until after the work was done. She royally screwed me."

Whether that was enough reason to murder Betsy was debatable, but everyone knew Annabel had a temper. She could have killed her in a fit of rage, but to accuse her would get Millie nowhere.

She'd play nice. "Everyone had run-ins with Betsy. She was a horrible person. Look how terribly she treated you."

"Don't play nicey-nice with me." Annabel shook her finger in Millie's face. "You started this whole thing by stealing the farmhouse from me. It should have been mine. I could have diversified. I'd be okay now if I had both businesses."

Nice wasn't working. Millie couldn't contain her exasperation. "Annabel, we've been through this before. I did not steal anything. You weren't able to come up with the money to buy out Christopher. Besides, having both places doesn't mean you'd be okay."

Annabel scowled. "You're a schemer, Millie Whitfield. Why are you really here?" She tapped her foot. "I bet it's to accuse me of murdering Betsy."

Millie shook her head. Annabel had figured her out. Of course it wasn't all that difficult. But one thing surprised her. She'd never admit it, but she felt bad for Annabel. She kept hooking up with losers and getting trampled.

"All right, Annabel, thanks."

As Millie turned to go, Annabel grabbed her arm. "You're looking at me when you have other people who had reason to kill Betsy. What about Christopher? If you heard our conversation, then you know he wasn't too happy with Betsy either. And then there's Vince Cordoza. There was something going on between him and Betsy. Both of those men could have had something to do with her murder."

Millie stopped in her tracks, her mind reeling. So Annabel thought Vince might be a suspect too. What could Betsy have done to Vince that was so bad he murdered her?

She'd already thought about questioning Christopher, but now she had a reason to question Vince too. He might have left Houndsville. And Annabel had never said she didn't murder Betsy, so she could have been trying to divert Millie toward someone else. And of course she should report all this to Tucker.

Twenty-two

Daisy tapped Grant on his shoulder. "Slow down. We're close, and it's hard to see any addresses with the rain pelting the windows."

He slowed to a creep.

Almost immediately, Daisy hollered.

"Stop! Look to your right." She pointed to an address sign hidden by some scraggly bushes and opened her window to see better.

"We're here. This is the right number...twenty-five hundred. Turn right."

"Finally," Millie said. "I can't wait to find out if Betsy was telling the truth about this being a puppy mill."

Grant turned onto the narrow driveway. The van's tires crunched over the ruts until they approached a dilapidated house with chipped paint, shutters hanging askew. An old pick-up truck was parked facing the house.

Grant pulled in next to it. "This doesn't look good. If Mrs. Breely lives like this, I can't imagine how the dogs are faring."

Millie shook her head. "It's almost impossible to believe, but so far it appears Betsy might have been telling me the truth."

Daisy frowned. "Let's hope it's not as bad as it looks. She glanced at her watch. "We're right on time. You two wait here."

Grant turned toward her. "If for some reason she doesn't allow Millie and me to come in with you, look around and try to remember as much as you can. When she shows you the puppies, act devastated that none of them look exactly like your sweet old dog. Then get out quickly."

Daisy nodded and raised the hood on her jacket before slipping out of the van and heading up the cracked brick pathway to the front door.

Grant had a point. The house might have been nice awhile back, but now several of the black shutters on the windows were barely hanging on, and the gray cedar siding needed cleaning. The dull front door was in need of fresh red paint.

She didn't see a doorbell, just a brass knocker, which she used while she looked around, waiting for someone to answer. There was a barn and a metal fenced in area off to the right. No dogs in sight. At least they weren't outside in the rain.

The door slowly opened. An elderly woman stood in front of Daisy. "Ms. Flowers?"

"Yes, ma'am." Daisy had visualized a younger person. In actuality, Mrs. Breely was elderly with steel-gray hair and watery blue eyes. Her flowery dress hung loosely on her thin frame.

"You wait here. I'll grab my jacket, and we'll head on out to the barn. The dogs are in the barn 'cause of the rain."

"That sounds perfect." Daisy nodded. "I do want to ask if it's okay for my friend and her brother to come see the dogs too? I'm visiting with them, and they drove me here. It wouldn't be nice to leave them in the van the whole time."

"If you brought someone here to make trouble for me, you should leave."

"No, ma'am. I would never do that. I really want a puppy." Daisy held her breath, hoping this was going to work out okay.

"All right, then. Tell 'em to come with us. I'll meet you outside."

Daisy turned around and waved at Millie and Grant, who quickly joined her.

Mrs. Breely returned, wearing a threadbare jacket. At least she had boots, even if they looked old and worn. Nothing about this situation made Daisy feel confident the dogs were okay.

"Mrs. Breely, these are my friends, Millie Whitfield and her brother Grant Stamford."

Mrs. Breely gave them a once over. "Call me Alice." She smiled wanly, showing off some very bad teeth. "You all, come follow me."

Daisy sighed in relief. So far, so good. Mrs. Breely was being friendly.

Daisy treaded carefully through the slippery and muddy gravel, glad she'd worn sneakers.

Mrs. Breely led them over to the barn and slid open large double doors, the stench overwhelming Daisy. She looked at Grant and Millie, and their noses were also scrunched up. How could Mrs. Breely not notice?

Inside, crates were jammed and stacked along a back wall. Daisy quickly counted about a dozen and a half. At first glance, most appeared to be filled with collies.

Daisy swallowed hard and bit her lip to keep from saying something inappropriate. Again, she peeked at Grant and Millie, their expressions hard to decipher. She wished she could ask Millie if this was what a puppy mill looked like.

Mrs. Breely tapped her on her shoulder. "I still got three pups from that same litter as the one you saw with that Carlson lady. Over there in that big crate." She pointed to her right.

Daisy wanted to see the pups, but she was here for information. She wanted to find out more about this place and what was going on here. She took a deep breath. "Mrs. Breely, I'm curious. How do you know Betsy Carlson?"

Daisy purposely didn't say anything about Betsy being dead.

"She got her collie from me several years ago. Then last year, I tried to be helpful, letting her mate her dog to one of mine. It turned out bad, and she blamed me when it was her fault. She should have known her own dog's genetics." She shook her head.

"Then about a month ago, out of the blue, she calls me, wanting to bring her sister here for a puppy. I told her no way."

Mrs. Breely ambled over toward the crates. She stopped, continuing to talk.

It appeared Alice wanted to confide in someone. Daisy grabbed Millie's hand, making sure she and Grant were close enough to overhear.

"See, it's like this. That bitch blamed me and my husband when her puppies were born blind and deaf. She said if we didn't give her money, she'd report us to the authorities for running a puppy mill, and they'd take our dogs away from us."

She scoffed. "We knew it weren't true, but we were scared of her. She had money and was mean enough to do it. After that, my husband Freddy got sick. These dogs meant everything to him. He paid her some money, but then she wanted more. He told her she'd have to wait, and he had no more to give her."

Mrs. Breely sniffled. "He worried himself to death because of her."

Daisy sucked in a breath. It was clear Mrs. Breely didn't consider her operation a puppy mill, but there were certainly too many dogs. Betsy had realized that too and had been blackmailing Alice and her husband. She stole a glance at Millie and Grant. She expected Millie to butt in, but she remained silent.

Mrs. Breely went on. "Several days after I told her not to come here, she showed up with her sister, unannounced. She threatened me again. This time, she said she'd report me to the authorities if I didn't give her a pup. I guess by now, she knew I had no money to give her. I had no choice. Did you see the pup? Is she okay?"

"Yes, Alice, when I saw the puppy, it was fine. Her sister named it Peanut.""Oh, that's good. Would have gone and stolen it back somehow if you told me different."

"Mrs. Breely, do you know how many dogs you have here?" Grant asked.

"Of course I do, young man. Seventeen. Used to be more when Freddy was alive. There's also several cats. They help control the mice population."

"That's a lot of dogs," Grant said. "Do you have someone to help you care for them?"

"Nah. I do it. I got a son, but he's gone now too."

"You have a son, and he died too?" Grant exclaimed.

Daisy was horrified but tried not to show it.

Alice shook her head. "I didn't say that. Last I heard, he's living in Ohio or some parts near there. He told me he had to get away. Staying around here kept reminding him what that Carlson bitch did to his dad, but he told me he'd come back if I needed him."

Grant spoke kindly. "Mrs. Breely, are you sure you're capable of caring for these animals by yourself?"

"I love my dogs and cats too. Don't you worry, young man. I take good care of 'em. I'll admit it's been hard since Freddy passed this last year. And now with me feeling poorly myself, well..."

Grant gently placed his hand on her arm. "If you don't feel well, you might need help. It looks like some of them could use vet care."

"Hey, if you're wanting to make trouble, you should leave. I love every one of these dogs." She waved her hands around the room and turned toward Daisy. "If you're here to see the pups, you'd better get a look. I ain't got all day for you."

Grant had overstepped.

Daisy wasn't ready to get thrown out. She wasn't here to get a puppy, but now that she was here, she wanted to see them.

"All right, let's see the puppies." She walked over to where Mrs. Breely had pointed them out and peeked inside the crate. They were sleeping, curled up together and hard to see, but in the crate next to them was a full grown collie with barely enough room. She froze. She took a double take. He or she looked like a smaller Max, and she felt his eyes on her, watching her. Her stomach clenched up.

"This dog looks like my Laddie did," Daisy said, quickly making up a name for her pretend deceased collie. "Same big expressive eyes."

She gulped. Her heart raced. She had an immediate overwhelming need to get him out of this awful crate. It was too small. "Can I take him out?"

Mrs. Breely shook her head. "Why? I thought you wanted to see the puppies."

"Please, Mrs. Breely." She could hear herself begging.

"Okay, then. Go ahead. Open the crate."

As Daisy bent to slide the lever, a large silver-brown striped cat suddenly appeared out of nowhere and rubbed against her legs. It was the largest cat she'd ever seen. "Wow! Who are you?"

"That's Chester," Mrs. Breely said proudly. "He's a Maine Coon, and he's waiting for you to open the crate. Teddy is his favorite dog here. They sleep together sometimes."

"Teddy, want to come out?" Daisy asked as she shifted the locking device to the right to open the crate. He stepped out slowly, sat gingerly on his haunches, and stared up at her.

Her stomach flip-flopped. She moved, trance-like, and knelt on the floor, unaware it was not particularly clean, and ran her fingers through his fur, feeling his bones.

He stuck his nose under her hand.

Her heart tightened, making it difficult to breathe. She bit down on her lip. She was about to say something she hoped she wouldn't regret. She took a deep breath. She blurted out, "I've changed my mind. I'll take Teddy."

Daisy could feel everyone's eyes on her. She couldn't talk, and she refused to look at Grant or Millie.

She briefly closed her eyes. Right now, her insides felt all twisted up. She felt compelled to not only get Teddy out of here, but all the dogs.

Grant walked over to her and grabbed her hand in his larger one. What was he thinking? She hoped she hadn't shocked him, that he'd support her decision. It meant more to her than she realized.

She didn't have long to wait. He whispered in her ear, "That was very special."

She had goosebumps on her arms. He was all in with her.

Meanwhile, Alice looked confused. "He ain't no puppy, but I guess you could have him. He's four, and he's a good boy. He'd be sad to leave his sister behind though." Mrs. Breely pointed to a tricolored collie in the crate next to him. "That's Maddy."

Mrs. Breely opened Maddy's crate and another dog, skinnier and with a matted coat, came and sat next to Teddy.

"I'd never guess they were related." Daisy petted Maddy. "They don't look at all alike."

"That's cause the mother was a sable and the dad a tricolor."

Mrs. Breely smiled. "Seems they like you. Maybe you could take both. They like each other, and I'd hate to see 'em split up."

Daisy tried to gather her thoughts. What should she do?

Mrs. Breely looked at her as if waiting for her to respond.

She believed wholeheartedly it was a good decision to take Teddy. Now she wobbled. Would Maddy be okay without Teddy, and he without her?

She exhaled and briefly shut her eyes. She had to decide without the benefit of time to think it through.

She looked beseechingly at Grant, her knees shaky.

"Listen, Daisy." He grabbed her hand and squeezed it. "You are trying to do the right thing here, but to be honest, it's not a good idea to break up a bonded pair. Two big dogs is a lot to take on. Maybe you should think about a puppy instead."

Daisy looked from Teddy to Maddy and then to Grant. He was only trying to help by giving her an out if she was unsure.

The words to tell Mrs. Breely she couldn't take both stuck in her throat. Instead out popped, "I'll figure it out. Teddy and Maddy will stay together."

She had no idea how she'd manage, but her heart told her this was the only conceivable answer.

Really, how much harder could it be to have two dogs? She'd have to keep telling herself that it would work out better with two. They could keep each other company while she was at work.

Millie reached into her tote. "Oh, this is awesome! You'll be so happy."

She pulled out first one leash then another. "Here, I just happened to have these with me." She hooked one to Teddy's collar and one to Maddy's.

Millie handed her both leashes, and Daisy shook her head. This was for real. She'd just agreed to rescue two dogs. Two dogs! Her heart soared and then plummeted. She still had to take Max back to D.C. How was she going to manage with three dogs?

Grant must have read her mind. "Listen Daisy, I'll take care of Teddy and Maddy for you until you are ready to take them to D.C."

He patted her back before whispering in her ear, "Give me a minute. Let me see if I can get more dogs out of here."

He turned his attention back to Mrs. Breely.

"Mrs. Breely, I'd like to take a few of these dogs for vet care."

Alice waved her finger back and forth in front of Grant's face. "Oh, I couldn't do that. My Freddy would be mad at me if I let someone remove the dogs."

"I thought you said he died last year," Millie sputtered.

Alice frowned. "Oh, he did, but he's with me every day." She patted her chest. "These dogs were his pride and joy. They're the last thing I have left of him."

Daisy winced. What a sad situation.

"Well, how about I come back one day with a vet, and we examine the dogs here?" Grant suggested.

Daisy drew her brows together. Why didn't Grant offer to examine them now? He must be afraid Alice would react badly if she found out he was a veterinarian.

"Oh no, dear. My dogs are well cared for."

Grant tried again. "Mrs. Breely, let me put this another way. Freddy wouldn't want anything to happen to his beloved dogs, if you become unable to care for them. You are alone out here. I'm offering my help."

"That's enough, young man. When I'm ready, I'll let you know what you can do." She added almost as an afterthought, "My son, Danny, can step in to help."

"You told us he lives in Ohio," Grant said, raising his brow.

"He left because he was real angry at that Betsy woman who threatened his dad. He was afraid if he stuck around, he might hurt her. If I need him bad enough, he'll come. He was just here last weekend, checking up on me."

Grant looked clearly frustrated. "All right, Mrs. Breely. I'm offering to help, and I'm nearby. Call me if you want." He turned to Daisy. "Settle up with Mrs. Breely, and let's get out of here."

Luckily Daisy always carried a check or two with her. She paid for the two dogs and led them outside. Millie and Grant followed.

Grant loaded Teddy and Maddy into the van. Daisy petted and talked to them. "You two are going to be so happy. No more cramped crates for you."

Grant closed the door, grabbing Daisy's hand before she went to get in the front seat. "Daisy, I'm a great believer that dogs know when their lives change for the better. Don't worry. You'll be great with them. Just give them lots of love, and they will adore you."

The return car ride was tortuous for Millie. Her head pounded. She hated leaving so many dogs behind. Mrs. Breely obviously could not care for them properly. As soon as she had time, she'd be calling a rescue group to see what authorities needed to be contacted to get the other dogs out.

Now that she had that settled in her head, she broke the silence. "Hey you two, Mrs. Breely may not be running a puppy mill operation, but she does have too many dogs. We'll have to figure out how to get them out of there, but something else is bothering me. All along, I've suspected either Christopher or Annabel murdered Betsy. Then Annabel told me to look at Vince. Now the list is growing longer. It's possible Alice or her son were the ones."

She waited for what seemed like forever for a response.

"She didn't seem to know Betsy was dead," Daisy answered first.

Grant shook his head, keeping his eyes on the road. "That's what I thought too, although she could have pretended not to know. To see if we said anything."

"Remember, she wasn't at the gala," Daisy said.

"Hmm," Millie replied. "The fact that we didn't see her doesn't mean she wasn't there on the property somewhere. She obviously hated Betsy."

Grant shrugged." We do know her husband paid off Betsy to leave them alone, and that she believed Betsy's actions killed her husband, which gives her a really good motive. Same for her son."

"Her son doesn't live here," Daisy murmured.

"Yes, but this is important. She told us he was here last weekend. That means he was here the night of the gala," Millie added.

"Okay, but how would they have gotten Betsy outside?" Grant asked.

"This all sounds like a stretch," Daisy said. "I say call Tucker. He needs to know all this."

The remainder of the drive back, Millie was so lost in her own head, she didn't realize they were back at the Inn until Grant stopped the van and turned around toward the back seat.

"Mil, sit here for a minute. I want to talk to Daisy."

She watched him exit the van and walk around to the other side to open Daisy's door.

Daisy turned to her. "Bye, Millie. I'll see you soon."

Grant opened the back side of the van so Daisy could see her dogs one more time before he took them with him.

"You two be good. We'll be together soon." She turned her back on them, wiped her moist eyes, then reached out for Grant's hand and walked a few feet from the van and Millie's prying eyes.

"Thanks for what you said to me back at Mrs. Breely's. I wish I could stay and talk. I need to get Max out of the room. He's been cooped up for a while. Can we talk later?"

Grant ran his hands up and down her arms. He didn't speak, merely bent his head and gently kissed her. Her world turned upside down.

"I'll expect to see you soon." He squeezed her hand before heading back to the van.

Grant's kiss, light and sweet, had her head in a cloud of doubt about her decision to return to D.C. And what about her feelings for Edward?

Twenty-three

Friday morning, Daisy's cell dinged. She'd set it to wake her early.

She reached out to turn it off and inadvertently almost pushed Max off the bed.

"Oops, sorry Max." She reached out to tickle his tummy and rub his paw before sliding out of bed and opening the draperies.

Her morning plan was to walk and feed Max and get on the road. She'd have to drop him at her apartment before heading to the office.

She wasn't worried about eating. She wasn't the least bit hungry, her stomach already in knots at the thought of what she was leaving behind.

Her cell pinged, not surprising since it seemed every morning someone was trying to reach her. This time, it was a text from Meghan.

Can we meet before you leave today?

Daisy winced. She really wanted to leave early, but at the same time she'd like to see her before she left. She texted back.

Can you come at seven? I need to be on the road early.

Meghan texted back a smiley emoji.

Daisy dressed, roused Max, and took him to the doggie park. After a stroll around the park, she walked back to her suite to get her suitcase and Max's tote and went to check out.

They were still early when they walked into the Oak Room and headed to one of the small tables for two. Max settled on her toes, his usual spot.

A waitress stopped by the table with a coffee carafe in her hands. "Coffee?"

Daisy nodded. "Yes, please."

"Pretty dog," the waitress commented as she poured coffee into her mug and left the carafe on the table. Daisy absently petted Max before picking up her cell to call her mom, who answered on the first ring.

"I'm calling to say goodbye for now. I'll be back soon to pick up Teddy and Maddy. And Mom, I'm glad you decided to become a foster failure. We both know Millie was counting on that."

They shared a laugh. "That's for sure," her mother said.

She spotted Meghan and waved. "Mom, I have to go. We'll talk soon."

"I'm here," Meghan said as she plopped down across from her and poured herself a cup of coffee from the carafe. "I feel bad we've had no real time to talk. Why not stay the weekend?"

Daisy shook her head." I'd like that, but I can't. My dad expects me back."

"I don't understand. What's so important you have to be back today?

"Edward told me my dad has a new case he wants to review with me."

Meghan nodded. "That's great. So he's not angry anymore?"

"Let's hope." Daisy tapped her fingers on the table. "Hey, I have something to tell you."

Meghan leaned forward. "Uh-oh, is it bad?"

Daisy shrugged. "Allan offered me a job."

Meghan's mouth fell open. "What! When? Why didn't you tell me?"

"Honestly, there wasn't time. He talked to me about it at the gala. I was planning to tell you, but then I had the misfortune of finding a dead body, and everything got screwy." She mumbled, "Doesn't matter anyway. I turned him down."

"Why?" Meghan smacked her hands on the table.

Daisy sighed deeply. "Try to understand. Two reasons. First, because Edward told me my dad wanted to review a case with me. I figured, like you, that meant he wasn't annoyed with me anymore. And then the second reason was even more important to me."

She wrapped her fingers tightly around her mug.

"If I left my dad's firm under the present circumstances, I'd feel like a quitter, and even worse, a failure. I couldn't do it." She shook her head. "And don't try to change my mind. I already called Allan. He was great. He told me he respected my decision, even though he was disappointed I wouldn't be joining his organization."

"But you're not a quitter. It's your dad's fault for making everything so difficult."

Daisy exhaled. "Meg, even if you're right, I can't do it. Not now. I came here to help my mom, and if I don't go back, it will look like I quit because of Corinne. I can't give her the satisfaction of believing that. I have to go back and show everyone I'm not a spoiled princess."

Meghan peeled Daisy's clenched hands from her mug and held on to them.

"Daisy, look at me. I'm your best friend, and I know better than anyone how long you've dreamed of working for your dad and seeing your name with his. But come on, you need to realize it's not working. Whether it's your dad's fault or yours doesn't matter. It's not making you happy. I'm sure if you called Allan back, he'd be thrilled to hear you've changed your mind. I can see how happy you'd be here. Grant, too."

Meghan released Daisy's hands and folded her arms across her chest. "I have one more thing on my mind." She paused. "This is hard for me to talk to you about. I think your decision to turn down Allan is not only about the job. Since your first day at your dad's firm, you've been infatuated with Edward, hoping to have a romantic relationship with him."

She stopped as if considering her next words.

"Daisy, it's clear he likes you, a lot, I believe, if his coming here immediately after the murder is any indication, but I get the feeling he's focused on something else. Maybe money, maybe business. I don't know, but he reminds me of your dad that way. A romance with you doesn't seem to be foremost in his mind."

Daisy shook her head. "You may be right about Edward, and Grant does seem to like me. It's all so confusing. Who would have ever thought I could like two guys so much? Anyway, I'm not ready to totally give up on Edward. But we'll talk more soon. I have to get on the road."

Twenty-four

Millie opened the door to the bakery. Her stomach growled. The scent of cinnamon in the air probably meant MaryEllen was baking biscotti. She hoped so. She'd love a piece or two.

She slid open the kitchen door. The first thing she saw was Hickory, MaryEllen and Bradley's collie. MaryEllen rarely brought him with her.

"Hi! How come you brought Hickory?"

"No choice. I know he really shouldn't be in the kitchen, but I overslept and didn't have time to walk him. It's Sunday, and Bradley left early to go fishing. I thought whoever got here first could take him outside for me."

"And I guess that's me," Millie said. "I'll take him now. It's supposed to start raining soon."

"Thanks." MaryEllen continued putting dough on the tray.

Millie leashed Hickory, and they left only to return in a few minutes. "Perfect timing. It's starting to drizzle." Millie hung up her raincoat and handbag on the nearby hook.

"Need help?" she asked MaryEllen.

"Sure." MaryEllen handed her a tray. "Mound the dough in the middle and sprinkle it with the cinnamon-sugar mixture.

Fifteen minutes later, Carolyn came flying into the kitchen, umbrella in hand. "I'm sorry. I know I'm dripping water, but Millie, you've got a problem."

"What do you mean?"

Before Carolyn could answer, the front door bells jangled.

"Uh-oh. Millie, I ran here as fast as I could. It's Annabel."

Millie rolled her eyes. "What is she doing here today?"

"Guess you'd better go find out before we open," Carolyn said.

Carolyn had forgotten to lock the door, and Annabel was standing inside with her hair plastered to her head, her clothes sopping wet. The drizzle had obviously changed into a driving rain.

"Can I get you a towel?" Even though Millie despised Annabel, she had trouble being unnecessarily mean. She didn't want to feel responsible if Annabel got sick.

Annabel waved off her offer. "I won't be here long." She glared at Millie. "I know it was you. After you saw me Wednesday, you couldn't wait to call Tucker and tell him I had a motive to kill Betsy."

Millie shrugged. "So what? You're right, I did tell him."

"I knew it!" Annabel screeched. "That's why Tucker hauled me in for questioning. You led him to believe I killed Betsy. How dare you?" She shook her fist in the air. "And I know why you did it. You want me to be accused of killing Betsy so word will get out, and I'll have to shut down."

Millie sighed. "I did not initiate the call. Tucker called and questioned me about something else. I only told him what I knew to be true."

Annabel ranted on." Don't even try to defend yourself. You hate me, and you hate that people like my tea room."

She stamped her foot, water dripping onto the floor in a growing puddle.

"You think you're so smart. Well, I got back at you," Annabel smirked. "I told Tucker that your precious younger brother killed

Betsy. Everyone knows he hated her. You see, I didn't want to listen to your crummy speech, and I walked out the front door to get away from hearing it. I stayed outside until I was sure you'd be done and was about to come back inside when I saw your baby brother leave the Inn in a hurry. Tucker sure was interested to hear that. Now, who's going to be his biggest suspect? You think you're so smart, but I got you back."

Millie stuck her finger right in Annabel's chest. "It's time for you to leave, Annabel. Now!"

Twenty-five

Daisy swiveled her chair to face outside, although there wasn't much to see with the rain pelting the window. It had rained ever since she'd left Houndsville on Friday, and much to her dismay, it was still raining this Monday morning. She never remembered it raining so much in one month. Luckily Max didn't really mind the rain, but she sure did enjoy walking him more in sunny weather.

Her cell pinged, distracting her.

It was Tucker. What could he want with her? She took a deep breath and swiped her finger across the screen.

"Hello, Tucker. Is there something you needed from me?"

"I have one question. Is this a good time?"

"For now. Ask away."

"What time did you and Grant go on your carriage ride?"

"Huh?" she replied, gripping the phone harder. Her mind whirled, the question catching her off-guard.

When she didn't answer right away, Tucker persisted.

"You're Hyacinth's sister, and I'm trying not to badger you. If you know, you need to tell me."

"It was some time after Millie's speech. I was having a good time, and I wasn't watching the clock. That's all I honestly remember. I don't want to speculate further."

"Are you sure you're not covering for someone? I will find out the truth, one way or another."

"I'm not. I assure you."

"Fine. Thank you for your time." He ended the call abruptly.

Before she had time to figure out the motive behind that strange call, her cell rang again.

"Hi, Lisa. What's up?" she asked tentatively, afraid of what she would hear next.

"Hi, Daisy. I have some good news. My mom's better. I'm coming home."

Daisy closed her eyes. *Okay*. She shouldn't have been surprised. Lisa had to come home to get Max eventually.

"When?" she managed to eke out.

"Wednesday. It'll be early evening by the time I get to my apartment."

"All right. We'll see you then."

She ended the call. Well, that gave her all day tomorrow with Max. It was totally irrational not to want to give him back when he had a good place to go, and she had two wonderful dogs waiting for her. It wasn't like she'd never see him again. He'd only be across the hallway. Still, she couldn't help but be sad. Tears started streaming down her face, and she couldn't seem to stop the flow. Maybe it was simply a culmination of all that had been happening lately, with too many things at once, but it felt like a spigot had opened, and she had no idea how to turn it off.

Someone knocked on her open door and stood in the doorway.

It was Corinne.

Crap. Why had she left her door ajar? Now her least favorite person could see her swiping away tears. Her stomach clenched up.

"Can I help you?" Daisy asked politely while gritting her teeth.

"Yes, I need Allan Gold's file on the Honeywell matter."

"Why?"

Corinne moved into the room and stood in front of her desk. "Just give it to me." She stuck her hand out.

Corinne's imperious tone grated on Daisy's nerves. She looked at her outstretched hand. It would feel so good to slap it away.

Instead, she flipped her chair around and went through some files on her credenza until she found what Corinne wanted.

She held on to it, hesitating to hand it over. "Why do you need this? I've been handling this matter for Allan."

"Not anymore," Corinne said smugly and grabbed the file. "You're out of the picture."

Daisy raised an eyebrow, seemingly unperturbed. "And why is that?"

"Allan offered me a job in his organization as his agent. I've accepted."

"No way. Why would he offer a job to someone horrible like you?" She clenched her hands together in anger.

Corinne put her hands on her hips and gloated over Daisy. "Because I'm a fabulous lawyer, and he knows it."

Now Daisy smiled broadly. She had the perfect retort. "Well, then Allan must think I'm better. He offered me the job first, and I turned him down."

"You're lying," Corinne sputtered. "You're nothing more than a spoiled brat whose daddy gave her a job."

Daisy flinched. Angered, she spat out, "That is not true, but think whatever you want. Just take the file and leave."

After Corinne left, she sat frozen in her seat. Naively she had hoped Allan's job offer would remain open and that he'd have trouble filling it.

Now the job would never be hers, and Corinne, her rival, would have the position. She went so far as to pick up her phone to call Allan and tell him he'd made a big mistake in hiring her. She might be a decent lawyer, but her people skills stunk. She didn't get along with anyone. Daisy stopped herself. He'd find out for himself soon enough.

She grinned from ear to ear. The expression on Corinne's face after finding out Daisy had been offered the job first was priceless. No way would she ever forget watching Corinne struggle to cover her shock at hearing that detail.

She shook her head. *Enough.* No more thinking about Corinne, she wasn't worth it.

If it hadn't been raining so hard, she would have stepped out to make a coffee run. She flipped her chair around to face the window. The few people on the street were hanging onto their umbrellas. Nasty weather. Best to stay inside.

She heard the distinct squeak of her door opening again. She certainly hoped it wasn't Corinne coming back for something else. She rotated her chair to see Edward barreling in and plopping down on the chair beside her desk.

Edward grinned as he leaned toward her.

"Have I got a good piece of gossip that you're going to love."

Daisy folded her hands in front of her, figuring she knew what he was about to say.

Triumphantly, he announced, "Corinne will be gone as of next week. She's leaving the firm!"

"I already know," Daisy said smugly. "She was just here to get one of Allan Gold's files. She positively gloated as she gave me the news."

"Why aren't you deliriously happy?"

"Maybe because Allan was not only my client, he was my favorite one."

Edward frowned. "I hadn't thought about how this means you're losing Allan's business. Surly he'll still give you some work."

"I'm sure he will. It's just that there's more to this story."

Edward's brows furrowed. "Like what?"

She tapped her fingers on her desk and took a deep breath. "I need to tell you something I've been keeping to myself. The night of the gala, Allan offered me the job that Corinne has now accepted. I seriously considered accepting, but then you told me my dad was waiting for me to come back. I took that as a positive sign and turned Allan down."

Edward fiddled with his hands.

"What I don't understand is that I came back early Friday, and I have yet to hear from my dad. He hasn't even texted. I thought for sure by now he'd have talked to me about that case he wanted to review with me."

"He's been extremely busy."

"Maybe, but it feels like something is wrong. I'm going to go talk to him and find out why he wanted me back but still hasn't talked to me."

Edward abruptly stood up and started pacing. He muttered, "I made it all up."

"What?" She wasn't sure she'd heard right. "Did you just say you made up that my dad had work for me?"

Edward stumbled over his next words, his expression uncharacteristically serious. "Yes. Seeing you and Grant together made me think I had to do something quick, or I'd lose you."

A lump the size of a grapefruit formed in her throat. "I'm trying to absorb this. You really made up a scenario to get me back here?"

"Yes." His brows were drawn together, his beautiful blue eyes darker than usual. He continued pacing back and forth in front of her desk with his arms rigidly by his side, like a soldier.

"So why not just tell me the truth? Why lie? We're supposed to be friends—and possibly more." She laid her feelings bare.

Edward shrugged, not looking at her.

She had no idea how to handle this conversation, which had suddenly turned very personal. If he liked her, why hadn't he just come out and told her?

It seemed like she'd flirted with him since the day they'd met, and he'd never reciprocated. Not really. Oh, sure they talked a lot, he teased her all the time, and they'd shared those few kisses in Houndsville, but he'd never taken it any further.

His silence unnerved her. Her stomach churned.

He sagged into the chair next to her desk. "Look Daisy, this is your dad's law firm. I have a great job here, and dating the boss's daughter is against house rules. It would surely get me in trouble and possibly fired. As much as I like you, I need this job. It's a great opportunity for me."

"Ouch!" There it was. Out in the open. His job came first. She knew she was being totally unreasonable about this. She only knew a little about his past. He had told her his family had been dirt poor. He'd been working since he was a kid to achieve a better life for himself. It was entirely logical for him to consider the ramifications of dating her.

The problem was hers. All hers, and it was tied up in her past with her parents. Just like her mother, she'd never come first—his job would.

She shook her head. She felt an overwhelming sadness. No way would she end up like her mom with a husband whose job took precedence over the rest of his life. Edward and her dad. Made from the same mold.

Whatever Daisy said now would be really important. It could affect her forever. She tried to choose her words carefully. She felt like she had no choice. "Edward, I don't want to lose what we have, but what you did was unconscionable. You should have been honest with me. You owed me that. I'd like you to leave my office."

Edward hung his head. "Daisy, can't we…"

She swallowed past the huge lump in her throat and pointed to the door.

"Please, just leave."

He started to say something. She shook her head and closed her eyes.

She heard the familiar sound of the door being closed.

She burst into tears. She'd just lost something irreplaceable. She realized now she'd expected Edward to be in her life forever. That someday she'd be Daisy Plant. What had she just done?

Would she ever see his mesmerizing blue eyes twinkling at her in that special way again?

She had to get out of the office. She grabbed her coat and slipped out her door and down to the garage. Thankfully no one stopped her. She drove home in a daze.

Her whole world felt like it was spiraling out of control, and she had no idea how to fix it.

Twenty-six

Millie flew into the bakery and collapsed on a stool at one of the high-top tables. Her three partners watched in concern as she rested her head on her laced fingers, her elbows on the table.

"Mil, what's wrong?" Carolyn stopped wiping down the tables.

"You're not going to believe this. It's never going to end. It's just the beginning of the week, and three more people called this morning to cancel their automatic monthly contributions to the foundation. One of them was Mr. Adams, an ardent supporter from the start. Why can't Tucker solve Betsy's murder already? I wonder if he's even talked to Mrs. Breely or her son."

Todd looked up from filling the coffee machine. "It hasn't been that long. I'm sure he'll figure it out soon."

"I'm not waiting any longer. I'm going to talk to Christopher."

"Why? What could he possibly have to do with Betsy's murder?" MaryEllen asked as she filled in the display case with woof-a-roos.

"Well, I told you he had a nasty conversation with Betsy at the gala that a group of us overheard. It sounded like they were having an affair, and she was dumping him. Then later I heard him arguing with Annabel. Annabel was complaining about Betsy, and he agreed Betsy never did anything if it didn't benefit her."

Carolyn shrugged. "Why would Christopher murder her if she dumped him? Most people would just get over something like that and move on."

Millie sighed. "Maybe's there's more to it."

"Look Millie, Betsy's murder has really gotten to you. You haven't brought Luke to the bakery for days now, and even your coat is buttoned up crooked." Carolyn pointed to Millie's lopsided buttons.

She looked down at her coat and rolled her eyes. For sure, she was a mess. "I know all of you are right, but it's too hard to watch my foundation fall apart."

"We all feel bad about that, but we keep telling you to leave it up to the authorities. They'll find the murderer," Todd added.

"That's a very good suggestion."

All three partners turned in sync toward the person standing in the doorway. "I didn't mean to catch you by surprise. Your front door was open."

What was Tucker doing here?" Oops, I must have left it open when I got here."

Tucker looked directly at her. "I hope you don't mind. I was trying to get here early before you open. I have a few questions for you."

"We can talk in the kitchen." Millie waved toward the door behind the counter. "We open soon. We'll have more privacy there."

Millie slid open the kitchen door and held out her hand for Tucker to proceed in front of her. She exchanged a worried glance with her partners. She had a feeling she knew why he was there.

She stood, leaning against the steel work table, hoping he wouldn't stay long. He looked grim as he stood next to her.

"My question concerns your brother Grant. Although after overhearing you, now you have me wondering about Christopher too. I briefly questioned him, but I'm guessing he wasn't totally honest with me if what you just said is true. But back to your brother."

Millie swallowed hard and bit down on her lower lip.

Tucker raised one eyebrow. "Did you know your brother Grant left the gala after your speech?"

Millie shrugged. "I know Annabel told you that. She's such a troublemaker."

"Yes, well she said the same thing about you. She believes you're trying to make me focus on her and not your brother. Your partners are correct. You need to leave the investigating to me."

He continued." So tell me, did you know your brother left the gala?"

"Yes. A client called him in a frenzy, and he went to meet them at the clinic."

She had no choice but to be honest. The truth would come out somehow.

"And do you remember what time that might have been?"

"Not really. It was like Annabel told you, after my speech. I'm not sure of the time. I had other stuff on my mind."

"And what might that have been?"

"I was trying to get more donations for my foundation, and I was still mulling over my fight with Betsy in the ladies' room."

"How come I'm just finding out about this?"

"It's not! When you first came to the Inn, I told you about the fight. You said you would question me later. I've been waiting."

"Darn, you're right. This is my first murder investigation, and I'm finding there are so many details to follow up on. Could you please tell me now what happened with Betsy?"

"Sure. Betsy refused to tell me the location of a supposed puppy mill. My friends and I found it on our own. It turns out it's not a puppy mill, just a woman operating a kennel with too many dogs. The important part is that Betsy blackmailed the owners, Mr. and Mrs. Breely, in exchange for keeping quiet about their business. The stress of it killed Mr. Breely. Mrs. Breely and her son both had a motive to kill Betsy."

Tucker nailed her with his eyes. "Look, don't try to divert me from your brother. He's a suspect, just like you and everyone else. I need to track his movements the night of the gala, and you haven't been very helpful about that. Let's talk about your run-in with Betsy. Someone besides me might think Betsy wouldn't tell you what you wanted to know, and in a rage you killed her."

"Oh, don't be ridiculous. You're in charge, and you know I didn't kill her."

"Please just answer my questions, Millie."

She was angry now. How dare he accuse her. "I'm surprised your girlfriend didn't tell you about the argument. Hyacinth was there in the bathroom, along with Meghan, Daisy, and Samantha."

Tucker sucked in a breath but otherwise kept a straight face. Millie couldn't tell if he was upset with Hyacinth or not.

"Don't be angry with Hyacinth. You're right. Betsy was taunting me with this puppy mill stuff. She said if I wanted information I'd have to come to her house the next day. I wanted that information badly, so why would I kill her before she told me what I wanted to know? Hyacinth knew that, so why tell you if it wasn't important?"

"Look, I'm sorry. I told you I may be in charge of this investigation, but I have to answer to other higher ups. Someone else might believe the opposite. That you killed her in a rage for not giving you the information you wanted." He looked downcast. "I know you didn't kill Betsy, but I'm getting pressure from the mayor to solve this case. He's not happy with the police department. I have to question you like you're a real suspect. And your conversation with Betsy could turn out to reveal a clue to solving her murder." He massaged his brow. "Was there anyone else in the bathroom when you quarreled with Betsy?"

"I don't know if anyone was in the stalls. I don't believe any of us used them. We all left shortly after Betsy because I heard the music signaling it was time for my speech."

"You know, it's possible Mrs. Breely was in one of the stalls and overheard Betsy talking about a puppy mill. That means Mrs. Breely could have figured out Betsy was talking about her. She might have thought she could handle the blackmailing, but intervention from the authorities would be more problematic. She'd have to act fast before Betsy told you her location. It could result in someone bringing authorities to her doorstep. She'd lose all her dogs. The gala could have been the perfect setup."

"I'm sorry, Tucker, but for your information, we've all talked about this, and none of us saw her at the gala."

"She's still a major suspect if your information is correct, and Betsy was blackmailing her and her son. If you remember anything else, no matter how trivial, you call me." He headed for the door and slid it open.

"I'll walk you out."

Millie walked him through the library. He stopped to look around. Most of the chairs and sofas were already filled up.

"This place is popular. Lots of people and dogs here."

Millie chuckled despite the seriousness of Tucker's visit. "That's the idea. It is a bakery for dogs and their owners."

"Makes me wish I had a dog," Tucker said.

Millie grinned. "That can be arranged. Lots of rescues available. Anyway, I hope you solve this murder soon. It's causing havoc with my foundation."

"I'll do my best. And remember your partners' advice. Don't go off on your own trying to find the murderer."

Millie escorted him to the door and watched as he walked up the brick path just in time to see MaryBeth come strolling down the path with Matisse, wearing an adorable hand-knitted sweater while Judy trailed behind with her three collies, Danica, her smooth collie, and Kona and Java, her rough ones.

She opened the door for them." Good morning, early birds. It's chilly outside, and we just finished brewing a fresh batch of espresso. Go enjoy."

Carolyn came up behind her and whispered in her ear, "How'd it go with Tucker?"

"Okay, I guess. He asked questions about Grant and then about my conversation with Betsy." She chewed her lip. "He told me he's getting pressure from the mayor to find the murderer. I told him about the Breelys. Other than that, I have no idea what's going on. It all makes me wonder if he's getting anywhere close."

"What a mess."

"You could say that again, which means I'm going to do exactly what I was told not to do. Keep investigating. First up, Christopher. He's certainly a suspect."

Twenty-seven

Before she left home the next morning, Millie stood and checked her appearance in the mudroom mirror. Her coat was buttoned correctly, her hat centered. *Okay*. She could proceed to the bakery.

MaryEllen had three piles of dough rolled out and was using three different sized bone-shaped cookie cutters to bake their daddy bear, mommy bear, and baby bear bone cookies.

"Good morning. You haven't made these cookies for a while."

"Nope, I haven't, but today I might even put sprinkles of them."

"Hi, we're here." Carolyn and Todd walked in together and hung up their jackets on the hooks they kept on the wall for just that purpose and put on their Best Doggone Bakery aprons.

Millie put on hers too. "So now that the gang's all here, I have an announcement. I thought about it all night, and I've got a plan to get Christopher to meet with me."

Carolyn rolled her eyes.

Todd piped up," I guess no matter what we say, you're going ahead so you'd better tell us quickly. I need to brew coffee for our early birds."

"Go ahead. I've got to go upstairs to find an old box of photos."

"What are you talking about?" MaryEllen asked as she ran her electric mixer.

"You'll see. Give me a minute."

Millie headed up the steps to the second floor.

Years ago, Christopher's grandparents had lived in this farmhouse. During some rough times, they had started selling a few flavors of homemade ice cream to help make a decent living. Their ice cream had become so popular they eventually turned their first floor living space into an eat-in ice cream shop and used the second floor as their living quarters.

Once Millie had obtained the farmhouse, she'd left the second floor pretty much untouched. She used part of the space as a small office, and the rest was used for extra storage.

From time to time, she thought about using the space for selling dog gear or other dog-related items, or even using it as a grooming area.

Her partners were less enthusiastic about her ideas. They wanted to keep everything status quo.

She found what she was looking for in the office—a cardboard box left behind.

"What's in the box?" MaryEllen asked when Millie walked back into the kitchen.

"Old photos." She dropped the carton on the steel table. "Christopher must have inadvertently left it here. It has loads of old photos of his parents and grandparents, all taken here at the farmhouse.

"What do old photos have to do with anything?" Carolyn asked, knitting her brows.

"They're how I'll get to Christopher. The lure, in detective speak."

"Funny. Now you're channeling Nancy Drew?" Todd laughed.

"Well, while Tucker is spinning wheels looking at Grant, maybe I'll be able to solve Betsy's murder. To begin, I need Christopher to agree to meet with me."

"And how do you plan to do that? You have no idea where he is," Carolyn said.

"That's true, but I still have his cell number in my contacts. I'm going to try calling now. He might have stuck around Houndsville after the gala."

She rummaged around in her handbag until she found her cell. She scrolled through her contacts and tapped his number.

He answered on the second ring. "Hello, Millie. What's up?" Millie signaled her partners with a thumbs up.

"Well, I saw you at the gala, and I wanted to talk to you, but I never got around to it. Are you still in town? I came across an old cardboard box of photos you might want."

"I wondered where that box had gotten to. I didn't think to call you. I figured I had thrown it out by mistake. I'm glad you have it. Those photos were special to our family. Lots of memories."

"I do have them. Want to meet up so I can give them to you?"

"Sure. When and where?"

"The bakery quiets down in the early afternoon. How about tomorrow at one at Annabel's?"

"I thought you and Annabel hated each other."

"Well, things aren't good, but Carl absolutely adores her chocolate top cookies. For him, I'll deal with her. Anyway, that's really the most convenient place for me if I'm working at the bakery."

"Okay. I'll meet you there," Christopher said.

She ended the call and looked at her three partners. "All set."

"It's time to open. I'll go unlock the door." Carolyn walked out. Todd scurried off to brew coffee, and MaryEllen stopped cutting out cookies to take her last tray of Luke's Hideaways to fill up the display case.

Millie was left alone. She took a seat at the steel table and fingered the box in front of her.

Okay. Now I just need to figure out how to question Christopher without letting him know I believe he might have murdered Betsy.

Twenty-eight

Daisy stirred. *What the heck!* It felt like someone had lain a Mini Cooper on her breasts, crushing her. She slid open one eye. *Nope.* She chuckled. It was Max, with his head across her chest. She smiled and petted him. In less than two weeks, he had become her cuddle buddy.

She sighed. Wednesday, the fated day, had arrived.

"Come on, Max. I'm going to make a yummy breakfast. I want your last memory of me to be a good one."

She scrambled some eggs, added precooked bacon bits, and toasted a bagel they could share.

After they'd finished, she rifled through her closet for her jeans, a warm sweater, and boots, and slipped on a hat and gloves. She wanted to walk Max one last time.

She murmured sweet words to him as they strolled along.

"You've been so much fun and such good company. I'll miss you."

She just wanted to hug him to pieces. She didn't give a whit that it was cold outside. She bent down to snuggle with him until he looked at her as if to say, Come on, let's walk some more. She headed home. Her apartment would not feel the same tomorrow.

Work was pretty awful. She stayed in her office, out of sight. She didn't want to run into Edward, and she didn't expect to hear from her dad. She tried to get some work done, but her mind kept going in circles about everything. Eventually she decided to leave so she could have a little bit of time with Max before Lisa came to get him.

One last time, she sat on her sofa with him snuggled next to her, staring at her door, wishing Lisa would never come.

The dreaded knock came too soon. She stalled for a minute before getting up and opening her door. Lisa burst past her and ran over to Max. She ruffled his fur before stopping to look at Daisy.

"I can't thank you enough for taking care of him. I owe you."

Daisy shook her head. "You don't owe me anything. It worked out really well. I'll miss him."

She couldn't get past the gigantic lump in her throat to say much. She wanted to tell Lisa about Teddy and Maddy, but right now that wasn't doable. She clenched her hands, struggling to hold back tears.

They left, and she felt lost and alone.

She leaned against the closed door, and the tears rolled down her face. She had Teddy and Maddy waiting for her, but she'd never forget Max. He was her very first dog, even if it had only been for a short time.

She headed into her bedroom. Maybe there'd be something good on TV, something funny to grab her attention. She hated that lately she'd been spending too much time feeling sorry for herself. Where was the easygoing, fun person she used to be?

Her life had been in turmoil from the first day she'd come to work for her dad and had become even more complicated after she'd gone to help her mom and Betsy was murdered.

She briefly wondered if Tucker was getting closer to solving the homicide.

By the time bedtime rolled around, she realized she had some hard choices to make. Just the prospect of going to the office the next day was making her stomach knot up. Not good.

Her life was not going in the right direction. It would be up to her to make it better. No one else could.

She sat on her bed and considered her options. Why was she staying in D.C.? To work in an environment she found toxic, or for a dad who didn't seem to care enough to help her? And most devastating of all, she had lost Edward, the man she'd imagined herself marrying someday.

She reached a nerve wracking decision, her stomach churning at the thought, and sent a text message to her dad.

Can you find time to talk to me tomorrow?

A return message came from her dad a few minutes later.

Yes. Tomorrow at nine.

She sighed. His usual terse answer. Where was the dad she remembered as a kid? She needed that dad to talk to her.

To finally get some answers.

Twenty-nine

When there was a lull at the bakery, Millie ran upstairs to her office to use her computer.

She groaned. "Oh, no." Another email from a donor who was pausing their monthly gift to the foundation, pending the outcome of the investigation.

Millie chewed her lip, a habit she'd been trying to stop. Until recently, she'd almost kicked it.

It was all about the foundation. She was becoming increasingly anxious. If people kept delaying or stopping their donations, the foundation wouldn't be able to help with any new rescues. All the more reason to try to solve Betsy's murder.

Millie glanced at her watch. Time to go. She grabbed her handbag and the box of photos and started walking to Annabel's to meet Christopher.

Usually she enjoyed walking through the park, especially with Luke. There was always something to see no matter the season. Today she had a mission, and she rushed to Annabel's, only pausing to view a cute portrait of a bull terrier in the window at Harper's Art Gallery.

She took a deep breath and went to open Annabel's door.

An elderly gentleman using a cane came up right behind her and held it open for her. She thanked him and walked inside.

The tea room didn't open until eleven. Millie spotted an empty high-top table in the rear of the main room near the small kitchen. So far, so good. She grabbed a tray, walked over to the display case, picked out a few pastries, got Carl's cookies boxed up to take home, ordered two cups of coffee, and sat at the table. She slid the box of photos on the floor under her handbag where hopefully Christopher wouldn't spot them right away.

If she was going to get any information from Christopher, she'd need him to sit and talk to her.

She walked back to the table to wait.

She glanced at her watch. One-ten and no Christopher. Had he decided not to show up? She shrugged. She thought about leaving when she spotted him heading to her table.

He waved and walked up to her." Hello, Millie. Sorry I'm late. You can give me my photos, and I'll be off."

Uh-oh. He didn't want to stay. "But I bought coffee and pastries for us. Come on, sit for a minute." She patted the stool next to her. "You can catch me up on what you're doing."

Christopher tapped his foot. "Since when are you interested in what I'm doing? I'm in a hurry. Just hand over the box." He held out his hand.

She mumbled. "Please sit. To be honest, I wanted to talk to you."

"Fine." He rolled his eyes and sat. "What's going on? Come on, Millie. What do you have to talk to me about?"

She twisted her hands together under the table. "Betsy."

"That's it. I'm out of here." Christopher stood up abruptly.

"I saw you with her at the gala. You were arguing. That makes you a suspect in her murder."

He plopped back down. "It's true, we fought. I met Betsy briefly when you wanted to buy the farmhouse. Annabel brought her by to see the property when she realized she was getting outbid by you.

She wanted Betsy to give her some financial help. It was already too late. You had a contract."

He drummed his fingers on the coffee cup. "Anyway, Betsy and I hooked up months later. She thought I had lots of money." He took one of the scones and nibbled on it. "I found out eventually, same as Annabel, that Betsy only did what was good for her. She really was a rotten human being."

Millie was concentrating so hard on what questions to ask that she never noticed Annabel until she bellowed, "Millie Whitfield, what are you doing here?" Then she came closer to the table, and with her hands on her hips, she leered at Christopher. "Whatever possessed you to sit with this horrible person?"

"Aw, Annabel, leave it alone," Christopher replied. "Millie has some old photos for me, and I want them."

"And what does she want in return? For you to rat me out. You had better be careful what you say. I know all about you and Betsy and even how you threatened her. The detective in charge would love to know too."

Christopher's face lost all color.

Annabel snickered and started to say more when a customer hollered, "Annabel, are you getting those cookies for me or not? I'm in a hurry."

She scurried off but not before she leaned into Christopher and mumbled under her breath, "Be very careful. You make trouble for me, and I'll retaliate."

Millie sat back and studied Christopher's face. He squirmed in his seat. "I told you all I know. Betsy dumped me when she figured I wasn't rich enough for her tastes. Sure, I was mad and may have threatened her. I dumped a lot of money on her. As for Annabel, she's scared that if she's fingered as a suspect, word will spread around town, and people won't want to come here." Christopher added, "Listen, Millie, I do think Betsy had another guy in the wings. You should try to find out who that might be. But I'm done here. Give me my photos."

He stood up, held out his hand, and tapped his foot.

Millie would have liked to ask Christopher why he thought Betsy had another guy, but she knew he was done with her. She had gotten all he was willing to tell her.

With that, Millie bent down to pick up the box and handed it to Christopher. He started to walk away but turned back to say, "One other thing. Don't underestimate Annabel. She hates you. She'll do anything to ruin your life."

Thirty

Daisy stood in the doorway to her dad's inner sanctum. He was sitting at his desk, hands folded in front of him.

She smiled." Hi, Dad. Want to go to the coffee bar around the corner? I'd love a latte."

"No, Daisy, we'll be fine here."

She walked over to his desk and sat in the chair across from him, clasping her hands together in her lap and sitting up straight, trying not to look vulnerable.

"Would you like water?" her dad asked.

"Sure." Better to keep her responses to the minimum so her voice didn't quiver.

Her dad reached into a side drawer and took out two coasters, placing one in front of her and one on his desk blotter, before he stood and walked over to an antique mahogany cabinet which she knew held a minibar, including a small refrigerator. He removed two cut crystal glasses, which he filled with ice cubes and water, and brought them over to his desk.

She sipped the water. "I hear the trial went well. Congratulations." She figured she'd start the conversation on a positive note.

"Yes, it ended well for us. How about you? Do you have an update on the murder investigation?"

"Tucker called the other day and asked me a few follow-up questions. They had to do with Grant Stamford. Other than that, I have no idea what's going on. He didn't even hint about whether there might be an arrest soon."

"Didn't you mention Hyacinth is dating Tucker? Have you talked to her?"

"Yes, she knows nothing. She told me Tucker won't discuss the investigation with her."

Her dad grunted. "Gotta give him credit. As an officer of the law, he's doing what's right."

Silence ensued. She fidgeted.

"Okay, Dad." She took a deep breath and exhaled slowly. "We both know I'm not here to talk about the murder, so I'll get right to the point."

She took a deep breath before continuing. "Maybe I should be giving myself more time working for you, but right now I get the feeling you aren't happy having me work here."

Her dad looked directly at her. Did she note a bit of sadness in his eyes? "Tell me, why do you believe that?"

Uh-oh. Was he taking offense at her comment?

"Come on, Dad. It's clear to me and those around us that you're dealing with me differently than the other first-years."

Her dad sipped his water and met her glance with his own bold stare. "And what if that's because I didn't want anyone to think you deserved special treatment just because you're my daughter?"

She leaned forward. "Dad, I get it, and maybe if you had conveyed your thoughts to me, I could have dealt with it better."

Her dad paused. "All right, Daisy. Let's have an honest conversation."

He sat back and folded his arms across his chest.

"I've been trying to figure out how to tell you what I think of your job performance. I admit I've been hesitant to do that. I can see we need to discuss it."

He proceeded to talk to her in a soft voice, surprising her.

"Look, Daisy. You're smart. You're a fine lawyer, but…"

Here he paused again.

Her stomach rolled. *Here it comes.* She tried to prepare herself.

"I don't believe the job here is a good fit for you. This firm does mostly trial work. The stakes are high, and to be honest, you aren't cut out for the stress of this environment."

Her stomach plummeted. This was worse than she had thought. She eked out, "What do you mean?"

"Well, for one thing, you don't think I've noticed you're not eating at any of our meetings, even when I order from that sandwich shop nearby you've loved since you were a kid? Come on Daisy, what's going on? It looks to me like you've lost quite a bit of weight too."

Daisy knew if her dad was being honest, she owed him the same. She leaned backward in her seat and gripped the arms of the chair.

"You're right, this job is stressing me out, and my stomach is a mess." She paused to take a sip of water before continuing "Maybe I'm not cut out for standing in front of a judge, but I could learn." She emphasized, "I am only a first year."

"Daisy, a lawyer who does well here is highly competitive, aggressive, and cutthroat. On the one hand, I'm happy to say you are not like that. Your personality and this job are not a good mix. Although you display a fine understanding of the law, you're kind-hearted and more of a team player. Can you see that?"

She looked her dad squarely in the eyes. "I guess, but why didn't you speak to me about this? Why did it take me coming to you? I've been trying so hard to please you."

Her dad took a deep breath and let it out slowly. "I didn't want to crush your dreams. Don't you think I know you've always wanted to follow in my footsteps? Do you think I'd forgotten when you used to sit in the conference room and draw? Do you remember what you drew over and over?"

"Yes," she said slowly. "A man with his arm around a little girl, and they're standing in front of a door."

Her dad interrupted her. "That wasn't all. That door had flowers all over it. You'd tell me that stood for me and you together."

Daisy was floored to see his eyes looking misty. She sat straighter, listening intently.

"I could see from the start this job wasn't right for you, but how could I tell you? My sweet and smart daughter was too nice for this job. I hoped being hard on you, you'd give up. I should have known better. You worked even harder to please me. Here I was trying to make it so difficult for you you'd want to leave, and you buttoned down and worked longer and harder."

Daisy could feel tears forming in her eyes. "Dad, you should have told me. I'm stubborn and wouldn't have wanted to hear it, but eventually it would have sunk in."

"I know. I let you down, and for that I'm truly sorry."

This long speech by her dad was hardly what she had expected. Maybe he did love her after all. She waited to hear what else he had to say.

"Look, I know the divorce was devastating for you and your sister. It couldn't be helped. Your mom and I have totally different goals and desires. I'm sorry, but I had to leave, and it wasn't because I didn't love you. I do. And I always will."

Daisy sat speechless. She had never expected her dad to talk to her like this. She was having trouble finding any words to express herself.

She finally did." I love you too, Dad, and I always will."

"This is probably not a good time to ask, but since you came to me, does that mean you have a plan looking forward?"

"I'm really not sure. I thought I had a backup job waiting for me, but that's gone now."

"What are you talking about?" he asked.

"Don't be angry. Allan Gold offered me a job in his organization as director of development. It would have been based in Houndsville. I turned him down."

"I'm not angry. Why didn't you come talk to me then? I want you to be happy. Actually I thought about asking Allan to give you a job. He enjoyed working with you, and you two seemed to hit it off. He has enough corporate work to keep you busy."

"Easy answer. A few days after the murder when Edward came to Houndsville, he told me you were looking forward to my return. That you had a case you wanted to review with me. I heard that, and of course I was going to come back if I could work with you."

Her father visibly cringed. "I'm sorry Edward did that. I have a feeling it was Edward who wanted you back here. Yes?" Her dad smiled. "Is there something going on there? Edward is a good man."

Daisy shook her head. "If you're asking if I like Edward, the answer is yes. I do, and I think he likes me. But there's nothing going on. Edward would never jeopardize his job here by dating me. So regardless of his feelings, it's not going anywhere." Daisy sighed. "The problem arose in Houndsville. I met up with Grant Stamford. I knew him in high school. I had a crush on him back then. When Edward arrived in Houndsville, I was with Grant. Grant was the person who found me at the murder site, and since then, he's been by my side."

Daisy sipped her water.

"Edward must have sensed the vibes between us and reacted badly. He told me what he did to get me back here. We both know that was a lie." She reached out for her dad's hands and squeezed them. "I don't mean that to sound bad. We both know you didn't need me back here. It's just that I'm having trouble forgiving him."

"I can understand why Edward did that, but give him a chance. In my opinion, he's worth forgiving."

"We'll see." Daisy wasn't quite ready to do that yet. Maybe in time.

"Why not call Allan and tell him you've reconsidered? I'm sure the job is still available. If you want me to, I can call him for you and explain the misunderstanding."

"Thanks, Dad. I appreciate the offer, but someone else accepted the job."

Daisy watched her dad's brows lower in an expression of confusion and then his eyes widened.

"Don't tell me that's where Corinne is going?"

"Yup. And she couldn't wait to tell me. In the end, Dad, you should be glad. Everyone here hates her. She makes anyone who has to work with her miserable, and it makes for a lousy work environment. There are other people here who are better lawyers and easier to get along with, but still, as you put it, competitive and cutthroat."

They shared a smile.

"So what are you going to do now? You're welcome to stay here until you find something. We can try to find some other work for you besides litigation."

"Thanks Dad, I'll think about it. It'll be difficult to be around Edward though."

He squeezed her hands.

She knew for sure things were good between them now.

"Keep me posted, and let me know if you want my help in any way."

"I certainly will. This was good. We cleared the air."

He stood." Daisy, come here and give me a hug."

Daisy couldn't think of anything she would rather do. She hugged him and murmured, "I love you, Dad."

Thirty-one

It was a brisk fall afternoon, and the bakery had been bustling all day. Millie couldn't remember a day that had been so busy. All her favorite customers had come in with their dogs. First Peter and Woody, then Judy with her three collies, Danica, Kona, and Java. MaryBeth with Matisse. Terry with her crew, Anne with Prince and Cosmo, and a newcomer Robert with Georgie, and that was just to name a few who were in and out during the day.

By the time Millie closed and locked the door for the day, the four of them collapsed in a heap on the sofa in the library.

MaryEllen shook her head. "Wow, what a crazy busy day. There are hardly any treats left."

"I'm exhausted." Carolyn took off her shoes and rubbed her feet. "That new customer with her Jack Russell Terrier named Happy sure made for a challenging day. He was determined to meet and greet everyone and show off all his tricks."

Millie chuckled. "You have to admit his somersaults were amazing. But listen up."

Millie sat forward. "I really need your input. Emails keep coming, donors keep dropping off, and as you know, the foundation is hurting. We have no choice. We have to figure out who murdered Betsy."

MaryEllen raised her index finger, wiggling it in Millie's face. "How did "we" get drawn into this investigation? And how many times does someone have to tell you to let the police handle it?"

"I can't stop," Millie said, frowning. "Until this murder is solved, nothing will get better. It's not only about saving the foundation anymore. Tucker keeps coming back to Grant as his main suspect. My brother made it known he despised Betsy after she tried to euthanize Cleo's puppies, and now he has an even bigger problem."

"Which is?" Carolyn asked.

"The night of the gala, he left to go see Stephanie Carlson at the clinic. She called him and said she had an emergency with her new puppy. The way Tucker sees it, his disappearance from the gala for a while gave him the opportunity to kill Betsy."

"You mean Betsy's sister called him?"

"Yup."

"So why can't she verify Grant was at the clinic with her? Seems simple enough," MaryEllen said.

"I asked Grant that question too. He says he doesn't understand it either. He keeps telling me Stephanie is a scatterbrain and probably wasn't clear about the time frame she was with him. She makes him look bad."

"What about following the money?" Todd suggested.

"What does that even mean?" Millie looked at Todd quizzically.

Todd shrugged. "I read somewhere if you want to find a murderer, you should follow the money."

Millie sighed. "Betsy did appear to have a lot of money, so I guess we could try to find out where it was all coming from. I just don't know how to do that."

Millie looked around at her partners and pleaded, "How about I get a piece of paper and you can help me make a list of likely suspects?"

All three partners shared a glance at each other and then nodded.

"Let's clean up first," Todd said.

MaryEllen stood up." Let's do it. You guys clean up out here in the library and the Collie Counter, and I'll start baking. Then when you're done, you can help me bake while Millie writes her list."

Everyone spread out to do their usual tasks. Millie vacuumed and straightened, Carolyn cleaned up the dirty plates and mugs and put them in the dishwasher, and Todd cleaned the coffee machines.

"All done," Millie said with her hands on the vacuum. "Come on, let's go help MaryEllen."

Millie made sure to announce her entrance to the kitchen, although MaryEllen had purchased bells that jangled whenever anyone walked through the door.

"You know, you don't have to holler you're coming in. We have bells now." MaryEllen looked up as she was about to put a cookie tray filled with woof-a-roos into the oven.

"I know." Millie smiled. "Old habits are hard to break."

MaryEllen shook her head and laughed. "Yeah, a habit I could never get you to follow." She looked at Carolyn. "Can you bake the pupcakes? Todd, it would be great if you could clean and cut the strawberries."

While Carolyn and Todd helped MaryEllen, Millie found a pad of paper and a pen in one of the storage drawers under the steel table and sat on one of the stools.

"Okay, listen up. We'll have two columns. Names of people we've eliminated and the names of people we still consider suspects.

The first column is the eliminated people. I'm writing down Nicholas, Meghan, her parents, Grant, me, and Daisy."

Carolyn inquired, "Okay, that sounds reasonable. So where does Christopher fit in? And what about Annabel?"

"I'm confused. Didn't you say Annabel and Betsy were friends?" Todd looked up from hulling the strawberries.

Millie chewed the tip of the pen. She figured that was better than her lip. "We've talked about that. So let's review."

"Annabel believed Betsy was her friend and would help her by giving her money for her renovations. Betsy reneged, and Annabel realized Betsy was not—and had never been—her friend. And even more, like us, she realized Betsy was a rotten person who only thought about herself. We all know Annabel has a temper and Betsy was good at taunting people. Betsy could have made Annabel so crazy mad she killed her in a fit of rage.

"As for Christopher, he emphatically asserted that Betsy thought he was wealthy and used him. He did get really mad at her at the gala, but I don't remember him threatening her. Annabel insisted he did, although she could have made that up to make him angry. She hated Christopher talking with me."

Millie put down her pen, rested her elbow upright on the table, and ran her fingers along her lip. "One last thing about Christopher Before he left, he implied Betsy might have been seeing another guy. I have no idea who that might have been. That kind of jives with Annabel telling me to check out Vince. She thought there was something fishy going on between him and Betsy. Maybe that's who Christopher was talking about. It's worth investigating."

"So write Annabel, Christopher, and Vince on your suspect list. Who's next?" Carolyn asked.

"Patrick Jetson. It was rumored he had an affair with Betsy, but that was a while ago. He'll never talk to me. He and Carl had a huge set-to over a property years ago."

"That seems like a long shot," Carolyn said. "So moving on. What about Mrs. Breely and her son? Didn't you say they hated Betsy? I thought they were your top suspects."

Millie picked up the pen and started nibbling on the end.

"Well, yes. According to Mrs. Breely, they gave Betsy money to keep her from calling the authorities to report they were operating a puppy mill. Mrs. Breely said they were afraid of her even though they were not in the puppy mill business."

Millie got up and started pacing around the table as she talked.

"All of this made Mr. Breely sick, and he died. The son blames Betsy, and for that matter so does Alice, giving both of them a motive. The problem is we never saw Mrs. Breely at the gala, and we don't know if her son was there. We don't know what he looks like."

MaryEllen opened the oven to take out the baked pupcakes.

"That doesn't necessarily mean anything. She could have driven up, killed Betsy, and left."

Millie shook her head. "Grant and Daisy and I talked about this after leaving the Breelys. Alice is old and frail. The only way this could have gone down is if she had help. We do know her son who lives out of town came to visit her the weekend of the gala."

Carolyn jumped in. "He could have driven here, and they could have planned the murder together."

"There's still a problem," MaryEllen piped in. If they weren't at the gala, how would they know Betsy would be outside?"

Millie continued to gnaw on her pen. "We talked about that too and then dropped it. We figured that was a stretch."

Todd wiped his hands on a dish towel. "I don't think so. I think you're on to something. Mrs. Breely's son hated Betsy so much, he wanted her gone. He found out Betsy made Mrs. Breely give her sister a dog. That was the last straw for him."

"Okay, keep going. This sounds real," Millie said.

"All right, so her son offers Betsy money to leave his mother alone. He tells her he'll bring it over the weekend since he plans to visit his mother. They plan to meet outside at the gala. Instead of money, Betsy gets a knife in her heart."

"Yikes." MaryEllen dropped a spatula with a pupcake on the floor. "That definitely makes sense to me. In this scenario, Mrs. Breely knows nothing. He plans this alone. No one would know he was at the gala, and with all the people at the Inn that night, there'd be so many people for the police to question they'd never think of him. Millie, I think you have your murderer."

Thirty-two

Daisy walked back to her office in a daze. The conversation with her dad had been a revelation, a shock for sure. In a good way. Now what should she do? She had some client assignments she could do, but she wasn't sure she could do even a decent job because her mind was elsewhere. She shrugged.

Granted, it was early, but she decided to leave and drive home. She really wanted to call Meghan to give her an update. It would be better to do that in the privacy of her home.

Meghan answered on the first ring. "Flowers, about time you called. What's going on?"

"Lots. Some good, some not. I'll start with the good stuff. I had a long talk with my dad. It went well."

"Does that mean you're staying in D.C?"

"Well, there's more. Lots more, but to answer your question, not necessarily. I could if I wanted to, but he was honest with me and told me he doesn't believe I'm cut out for trial work, which is just about all he does."

"Why?"

"Several reasons. Among them, I'm not cutthroat or aggressive enough. And he thinks I'm stressed. He noticed I wasn't eating."

"I thought you'd lost weight, but I didn't realize it was a problem. I'm sorry I didn't mention it, but this is the answer you needed. Call Allan and accept his job offer."

"I would, but he offered the job to Corinne. She accepted."

Meghan gasped. "When did that happen? You just turned him down."

"When he offered me the job, he told me he originally had someone else in mind. Obviously that was Corinne."

"No way! That stinks."

"Yup."

"So what now?"

"There's more. Edward and I had a fight."

"I'm so sorry, but why? I know that's something you never wanted to have happen."

Daisy gripped the phone. "It turns out my dad never said he had a case he wanted to review with me. Edward made that up."

"You mean he lied?"

"Right again. It seems he was the one who wanted me back here. He didn't like seeing me with Grant."

"That's rich. He didn't like you being with Grant, but he's made no real moves to be with you himself."

"He admitted he's afraid to jeopardize his job."

"Daisy, you know what that means. Right?"

She sighed. "Yes, as long as we're both here, we're never going to get together."

"I'm sorry, Flowers. I know how much you like him. I have a suggestion. Come to Houndsville this weekend. You need to come get

Teddy and Maddy anyway, but don't go back to D.C. right away. Stick around here for a bit. See if you might like to live here. You can even stay in our condo. We moved to the new house over the weekend."

"Wow! Thanks. That sounds great. I'll figure out when to leave and let you know when I'm coming."

"Perfect. I have to go. Grace is calling me. We're reading *Mollie's Tail* for the umpteenth time. She loves that book."

Thirty-three

"I'll come down Saturday," Daisy announced breathlessly when she called Meghan the next day.

"Hooray!" Meghan hollered. "I was worried you might change your mind. Is everything okay?"

"I guess." Daisy sighed. "It's scary. I'm leaving behind the only job I thought I'd ever want. Plus, I'm leaving behind the guy I expected to marry someday."

"Yeah, well maybe that's for the best. Besides, I have a feeling there's another guy waiting to see you. I'll leave a key under the mat."

"Great," Daisy said. "See you tomorrow."

All her plans in place, she flipped her chair around to look out her window for the last time at what she thought of as her maple tree.

She enjoyed staring at that tree when it was full of leaves and even when the leaves starting turning colors, but now it was just a bunch of bare branches. Sort of how she felt sitting in this office. Not vibrant and full of life, but rather cold and lifeless.

It was time for her to leave, she knew that for sure, but before she left, she had one last thing to do.

Apprehensive, she sighed deeply. Time to talk to Edward.

She couldn't bear to leave D.C. without trying to clear up the mess between them.

She heaved herself out of her chair, closed her door, and headed down the long hallway toward his office. It was a long walk, and today it seemed endless. All she could hope for was to have the right words that would make things better. She knocked softly on his door and opened it.

He was seated at his desk. He looked up. Daisy couldn't make out what he was thinking, his usual smile for her absent.

"Hello, Daisy. I'm surprised to see you."

"Hi," she mumbled back. He was wearing the tie with the daisies on it she had bought him a while back to remind him of her. Even though he didn't smile, his deep blue eyes, always so expressive, made her heart skip a beat.

"Can we talk?" she asked tentatively, clasping her hands in front of her.

Edward hesitated. *Darn.* Had she made a mistake coming to see him?

He shrugged. "Why? *You told me we were done.*"

She cringed. That was harsh.

She walked toward his desk. No inkling of his customary twinkling smile she always looked forward to seeing. No invitation to sit. She sat anyway.

"There's something I want to tell you before you hear it from anyone else."

"So tell me." He played around with some papers on his desk, seemingly uninterested.

She couldn't help but remember they'd not only been best buddies, he'd been her closest confidant until he had let what he thought was happening with her and Grant get in the way.

She folded her hands tightly in her lap. *Try and keep it light.*

"I'm off to Houndsville for a few weeks. I'm thinking of moving there."

"That's nice. I guess your dad knows and is okay with this."

She'd expected the cool voice, but it still hurt deeply. She thought about grabbing his hand but decided she would be further devastated if he pushed it away.

"Yes, I had a long talk with him. He's good with my decision." She didn't bother to tell him more about her conversation with her dad.

"So why tell me? As you said, we're done."

"Oh Edward, come on. You and I both know what you did to me was reprehensible. You led me to believe my dad wanted me back here, which was not true. Up until that moment, I thought you and I had something special going on. Regardless, I still needed to say goodbye. I can't forget the past that easily."

For a nanosecond, Daisy thought she caught a flicker of sadness on Edward's face.

There was silence on his end for a minute. "I hope it works out for you."

"So, I guess that's it." She stood up to leave but kept her eyes focused on his. "I'll miss you, Edward. We had some good times together. Give it some time and then maybe come visit." She smiled at him. "If you'd like to, that is."

He didn't answer, but he did get up from his desk and walk around to give her a brief hug, keeping his arms on her shoulders.

"Daisy." He spoke while staring into her eyes. "I'll miss you and our chats every morning. I know you were just kidding when you said you hoped you'd be a Plant someday, but it was always possible it might come true."

What! Her heart stopped beating and felt as if it shattered into a million pieces. She gulped hard and turned around. She didn't want him to see the tears forming in her eyes. She stumbled her way out the door.

Hours later, she opened the door to her apartment. Sad from her conversation with Edward, it was one more disappointment when Max was not there to greet her. He'd been gone for several days, and she still missed him running to greet her, tail wagging.

It was time to leave D. C. Everything here had come to a crash ending. She'd have to come back to pack up, if she decided to stay in Houndsville, but in the meantime, she loaded enough clothes and various other items into her several suitcases to last a few weeks.

She'd spoken to her mom, who'd offered to have her stay with her, but she'd declined. With Teddy and Maddy joining her, she'd have more room at Meghan's condo, and her mom had plenty to keep her busy with the shop and Sidney. She still laughed when she thought of her mom as a foster failure.

Next she called Lisa to tell her she was going to Houndsville for an unknown period of time. She should have knocked on her door and told her personally, only she couldn't bear to say goodbye to Max. It was just too hard.

She also alerted Hyacinth that she was coming to Houndsville for an indefinite stay. Hyacinth confided that Tucker was hoping they'd have a suspect for Betsy's murder in jail soon. Now she couldn't wait to see Meghan and Millie and get an update.

Last call was to Grant. He answered on the first ring and seemed happy to hear her voice. "If you're calling about Teddy and Maddy, they're fine. They've had all their shots and both tested negative for heartworms, so they're good to go home with you."

She smiled inwardly." That's great. I was hoping to hear that. I'm coming tomorrow."

"Are you just coming to pick up the dogs?"

She didn't want to tell him her plans over the phone. Instead she decided to be a little flirtatious. "Well, yes of course that's why I'm coming, but first I thought I might pick you up and take you to dinner."

She sucked in a deep breath. Would he want to be with her?

He chuckled as if he knew she was holding her breath. "I'll be waiting."

Thirty-four

"Repeat that," Millie said, answering her cell while she was straightening up at the bakery after it had closed. MaryEllen was running the vacuum, and the noise was deafening.

Meghan repeated, "Daisy is coming here, and she's staying for a few weeks at least."

"I thought I heard wrong. What about her job?"

"She hasn't been happy for a while, and her dad is supporting whatever she wants to do. Right now, I don't think she has any idea."

Millie's brain started whirling. She'd have to come up with a plan to keep Daisy in Houndsville, to give Grant and Daisy time together. Millie could only think of one thing that stood in the way.

"What about her and Edward?" Millie asked. "They seemed tight."

"They had a disagreement. She's devastated."

"Oh, no! What happened?"

"I guess she won't mind me telling you. Seems Edward didn't like seeing her hanging out with Grant. He made up some story about her dad needing her back in D.C. She confronted him, and he admitted he lied. Now they're barely speaking."

Millie hated to admit this suited her plans. "So do you think they're done?"

"Hard to say. She's been infatuated with Edward from the moment she first laid eyes on him, and I believe he likes her a lot.

I just don't think he'd allow love to get in his way where his career is concerned.

Millie took a deep breath. "And what about Grant?"

Meghan chuckled. "We all know you'd like them to get together. He's been paying a lot of attention to her, and I'm sure she's been enjoying that. All in all, I think she's totally confused over the two of them."

"I can help with that," Millie said.

"Millie, be careful. It could all backfire on you."

"I bet you'd love for Grant to hook up with Daisy too."

"Of course I would, but only if it makes Daisy happy."

"Okay, then let's make her happy with my brother. Where is she staying?"

"At our condo."

"That's perfect! She could buy it now that you've moved out."

"Oh, my goodness, stop," Meghan spat out. "You're jumping way ahead of yourself. She doesn't even have any job prospects here."

"We'll see. I'll talk to you later." Millie ended the call, grinning from ear to ear. Now when she wasn't trying to solve Betsy's murder, she could work on getting her brother settled down with Daisy.

Thirty-five

"Hi! I'm here driving down the inlet to your condo." Daisy caught a glimpse of Allan's development, making her think she'd given up a great job offer. She sighed. Oh well, she'd find something to do.

"Fantastic! You know where to find the key. Get settled and come meet us for dinner at the Inn. We're going early so Grace can come, and she insisted we bring Buddy and Bear to meet you."

"I'm supposed to meet Grant and get my dogs."

"So tell him to join us."

"All right. I'll call him now." She was about to call him when her phone rang. It was Grant.

"I'm sorry. Change of plans. Harry needs me to fill in for him tonight."

"Oh, I was looking forward to seeing Teddy and Maddy and going to dinner with you."

"Well, we'll do dinner soon, and you can get your dogs early tomorrow before I go to work."

She was disappointed but figured she had no choice. "Okay. Let me know what time I can get them."

Several hours later, all done unpacking, Daisy drove to the Inn and strolled into the lobby only to be met by a bouncing eight-year-old.

"Mommy and Daddy said I could wait here for you and bring you to our table." Grace grabbed her hand and pulled her along. "Come on. I can't wait for you to meet Buddy. He's a big boy now."

It sure seemed like Grace was in a big hurry, but Daisy figured she was being a typical eight-year-old, that was until she got closer to their table and saw not only Nicholas but Grant with Teddy and Maddy lying at his feet.

"Surprise!" Grace shouted and jumped up and down. "Look who's here to see you. Did we surprise you?"

"Yes, you sure did surprise me, and in a good way." Daisy bent down to hug Grace and looked around the table.

Meghan grinned at her. "We all conspired to fool you. Even Grant played along."

She stood awkwardly, wondering what to do first. Kiss Grant, pet Teddy and Maddy, or meet Buddy?

Grace settled it for her when she took her hand and pulled her over to Buddy. "Pet him first."

Buddy was all white and very fluffy. He must have been groomed recently. Daisy knew Buddy was blind and deaf. She crouched down and spoke to him softly. "Buddy, you are so handsome."

Grace put her hands on her hips, trying to look all grown up. "He is perfect, and he's all mine. Do you remember when my mommy said I couldn't have a dog? She made a big boo-boo. She told me I could have whatever I wanted when we had to move here. I picked a dog. That's how I got Buddy. He's my best friend."

Meghan winked at Daisy. "Grace, let Daisy pet her own dogs. I'm sure she's excited to see them."

Daisy stood up and walked tentatively over to Grant. She smiled at him and put her hand on his arm. "Nice surprise. I thought you had to work."

He looked at her and grinned.

"Yeah, well, I had to make up some excuse to throw you off track. Grace was determined to surprise you, and she can be very persuasive."

"I'm so happy. I really wanted to see Teddy and Maddy today." Daisy crouched down to pet her own collies. "They look wonderful. You got them groomed, didn't you?" She looked at Grant, who smiled back at her.

"I wanted them to be perfect, like Buddy." Grant winked at Grace.

"Thank you. But where's Bear?"

"My dog absolutely hates the car," Nicholas said. "He's a couch potato, so we figured he'd be just as happy at home."

Daisy ran her fingers through Maddy's fur and then she threw her arms around Teddy and hugged him. For a moment, she stayed with her nose buried in his fur, soaking up the thrill of knowing these dogs were hers.

"They seem totally relaxed around you. I bet they remember you." Grant reached down to pet each of them too.

"I'll never forget agreeing to get them both. I think we fell in love instantly."

Grant stared pointedly at her and murmured close to her ear, "Sometimes it only takes a nanosecond to know you like someone."

She swallowed hard. Her heart pumped faster with his mesmerizing hazel eyes focused on her.

Nicholas chuckled. "It appears Grace was correct to have my brother here."

Daisy could feel her face heating up. Everyone here was obviously in the Grant camp, cheering him on. A warm feeling spread throughout her body.

She changed the subject. "Can we order? I'm starving. I haven't eaten in hours."

Grant stood up and pulled out the chair next to him for Daisy and waved his hand in the air for the nearby waitress.

"Mommy, can I tell the other secret now? It's hard to keep it to myself."

Meghan glanced at Nicholas, and he took her hand. "Sure, Grace. Go ahead."

Grace stood. She ran over and hugged Nicholas. "He's my daddy now. Mommy and him got married. I got to go too."

Daisy hollered, "What? You sneaky friend. You didn't say a word."

"Yeah, brother, you didn't tell me either."

Nicholas smiled. "I didn't even tell Meghan. It was my decision. We've been engaged long enough. I wanted to get married before we moved into our first house. I got the license last week and made an appointment at the courthouse to tie the knot after the forty-eight-hour waiting period."

"This is the best news ever, but no fancy wedding? And I don't get to be a maid of honor?" Daisy stood and walked over to hug her friend and then Nicholas.

"For sure we'll have a big party in the spring to make up for that." Meghan grinned and squeezed Nicholas's hand.

"Time for champagne. Let's celebrate!" Grant smiled.

"Do I get some?" Grace piped up.

"No, but you can have a Shirley Temple."

Dinner was a joyous affair. Everyone chomped on burgers and fries while Grace amused them with her puppy stories about Buddy and his blind and deaf brother, Treasure, who lived with Meghan's parents.

It wasn't long after chocolate sundaes that Grace's head started bobbing.

Meghan tapped Nicholas on his arm." Looks like it's time for us to leave."

Grant put his hand on Daisy's arm. "I've got Teddy and Maddy's food in my truck, so I'll drive you home and help you into the condo. Leave your SUV here. We'll figure out when to pick it up."

She nodded as her stomach clenched. She'd be alone with Grant for the first time since the carriage ride. She had no idea what to expect.

She watched Nicholas stand up and gently pick up Grace, who rested her head on his shoulder.

Meghan picked up Buddy's leash. "Have fun. I'll talk to you tomorrow. Oh, and if you need me, I'll bring you here to get your SUV."

Daisy and Grant decided to leave too and walked out to Grant's truck. Grant harnessed Teddy and Maddy in the backseat while Daisy climbed into the front passenger seat.

She was tired, but she never expected to fall asleep.

A few minutes later, Grant stroked her arm. "Come on, sleepy-head. I'll walk you to your door."

Daisy opened her eyes and yawned. "I am tired, but since you live here in this complex, could you show me where to walk the dogs?"

"Sure. That's a good idea."

Grant jumped down out of his truck and checked their leashes before allowing Teddy and Maddy to jump out.

"Here, you take Teddy's leash. I'll hold on to Maddy. The dog park is nearby."

They walked around the corner of the building. Grant pointed out a fenced area that had a few benches and a tunnel for the dogs to run through.

"This looks nice."

"Yes, it can be if the right dogs are here. Let's go in, walk around, and then head back. I'm working early tomorrow, but later in the day we'll connect, and you can get your SUV."

"If I need you. Otherwise Meghan offered."

They only spent a few minutes in the park.

Grant walked next to her. "I know how much you loved Max, but you will find room in your heart to love these two."

Daisy sighed. "I already love them, but giving Max back was terrible. I only had him for a few weeks, but it felt like forever."

"Well, Teddy's certainly a happy boy for a dog that was cooped up in a too-small crate. His tail never stops wagging. Maddy is attached to him and hangs close, but she does love her cuddles."

He put his free hand on her arm, stopping her. "I told you earlier, and I meant it. It doesn't have to take long to start to care for someone."

She stood still, her eyes roaming over his face, and when her eyes met his, he bent to kiss her. With just a brush of his lips against hers, she knew she wanted more.

"Come on. Let's go to the condo," Grant said, leading the way. They stopped at the truck to get the dog food and headed into the building.

Grant laid the food at the condo door, handed her both leashes, and then knelt down to pet the dogs. "You both listen to Daisy."

He stood up and gazed into her eyes. "I'm curious. How long are you planning to stay in Houndsville?"

"Honestly, I'm not sure." She shrugged.

It was late and Daisy was past tired. She couldn't talk about her situation right now.

"Would you like to have dinner with me one night soon? Just you and me."

"Sure, I'd like that." She smiled.

Grant placed his hands on either side of her face, his lips lingering on hers. Her cell dinged.

Rotten timing. She pulled back. "I'm so sorry. I'd better see who that is."

She rustled around in her handbag, pulled out her cell, and glanced at the screen. There was a text message from Edward.

Hope you arrived safely in Houndsville. Miss you already.

She sighed deeply.

"Is everything okay?" he asked, putting his hand on her arm.

"Yes, it's fine. It was nothing."

She stuck her cell back in her purse, not wanting to think too much about Edward's message and what it meant. All she knew for sure was his text had spoiled the moment with Grant.

She fumbled around in her pocket for the key to the condo.

"I'm really tired, and I still have to get both dogs settled in." She stood on tiptoes and planted a short sweet kiss on his cheek before unlocking the condo door and disappearing inside.

Thirty-six

The bright sunlight peeked through the window blinds. Daisy lay in bed thinking about the day ahead of her. It should be perfectly wonderful. After all, it was her first full day with her very own dogs.

She lifted her head. Teddy and Maddy were each lying in their beds gazing up at her. She hoped that soon they'd feel comfortable sleeping on the bed with her.

What were her plans for the day? She had to get in touch with Meghan so she could get her SUV, and if Meghan wasn't working, maybe they could go to the bakery. Meghan could bring Buddy and Bear, and she could bring her dogs. That idea got her excited, and she jumped out of bed and padded over to them.

"Hey, you guys. Let me get dressed, and we'll take a walk before I feed you."

Teddy stared at her with his huge brown eyes as she spoke to him, and Maddy actually licked her face. Already, these two were helping to fill the ache of not having Max.

An hour and a half later, Daisy and both dogs were outside waiting for Meghan. Their plan was to get her SUV and bring it back to the condo, and then they'd head to the bakery with all four dogs.

Both dogs seemed totally relaxed. She petted them while thinking she was glad she hadn't left Maddy behind. This transition was probably much easier for them knowing they had each other.

"Hey, you two wait to see where you get to go today."

Daisy spotted Millie in the library as she filed into the bakery with her two dogs, followed by Meghan with Buddy and Bear. She waved, and Millie rushed over with Luke. She bent down to pet all the dogs before saying hello to her or Meghan.

She finally stood up and acknowledged them. "Oh, I'm so glad to see you. Come on. Let's get pupcakes for all these furry guys and gals."

Daisy pointed to Luke, who stood behind Millie, running his paw up and down her leg. "What in the world is Luke doing?"

"He heard the word pupcake. He thinks he should have one too. I've had to stop bringing him here all the time. He's quite persistent, and between everyone giving him a bite here and there, he's gained weight."

Daisy laughed. "That's really funny. Does he ever stop?"

Millie looked down at him. "Yes, but only after he gets what he wants."

Daisy peered around. "Hey Meghan, isn't that Betsy's sister?" She pointed to one of the sofas where a young woman sat holding a puppy with another dog sitting on the floor in front of her.

Meghan looked toward where Daisy pointed. "I don't know. I've never met her, but I bet that's her. I recognize the dog on the floor. That's Cleo. She was Betsy's dog."

Millie smacked her forehead. "I had no idea. I've never seen her here, so I went to introduce myself earlier. She told me she'd heard a lot about this place. I showed her around. She never mentioned her name. I guess that could have been on purpose."

Daisy murmured, "Do you remember me telling you about the day I arrived at the Inn, and Betsy was screaming at Grant for holding a puppy he found outside? Well, that was her puppy from Mrs. Breely's. I heard her introduce herself to Grant. Her name's Stephanie."

Millie looked at Daisy. "Did you meet her that day?"

"No. Why? She may have seen me, but that's about it. I also remember seeing her at the gala with her sister."

Millie chewed her lip. "I'll introduce you and Meghan to her, then you can sit and talk to her. She might be able to tell you something about what happened at the gala. After all, you just said she was there with her sister."

"I can't imagine what I'd say to her," Daisy said.

Meghan shook her head. "I can't either."

"That's easy. Both of you have collies, and she does too. Daisy, you could walk up to her and say you recognize her from that day at the Inn. Meghan can mention how cute her puppy is. If you tell her that, she'll probably warm up to you."

Meghan frowned. "Millie, how will that lead her to talk about her sister? That's dumb. And what if she asks about where I got Buddy? It's kind of unusual to see a blind and deaf collie."

"I bet Betsy never told her sister about that," Millie said. "After all, she was taking them to be euthanized. Why would she ever tell Stephanie that?"

"Regardless, I'm not doing this. I'm taking Buddy and Bear to the Collie Counter."

"Come on, Daisy. It can't hurt. You never know, she might end up revealing something."

Daisy hesitated.

"Please," Millie begged.

Daisy exhaled. "Oh, all right." Millie grabbed Maddy's leash from her hand before she could change her mind and walked over to the sofa. Daisy followed with Teddy.

Daisy waited to see how Millie would handle this. She didn't wait long.

"Hi!" Millie smiled. "This is my friend, Daisy. She just rescued these two collies, and I thought you two might enjoy talking." Millie pointed to Teddy and Maddie.

Daisy didn't know what to say. Millie had put her in an awkward spot.

Millie took up the slack." Daisy, why don't you sit here while I get pupcakes for the dogs. Would either of you like something to drink?"

"A mocha latte would be nice," Daisy said.

Millie smiled." Ahh, my favorite too. Maybe I can make one for myself and join you." She looked at Stephanie and played like she didn't know her name. "Would you like to try one?"

"Sure. I'd like that very much, and my name is Stephanie," she answered shyly before scooting over to make room for Daisy to sit next to her.

Millie walked off. Now it was up to Daisy to try to get some information. She still had no idea how to do this.

Stephanie bent down to pet Daisy's dog. "So you recently rescued your two dogs. Are they from around here?"

"Yes. They're from a breeder not far from here. A little old lady. Where are yours from?"

Stephanie pointed to the all-white collie sitting on the floor. "Cleo was my sister's dog, and I got Peanut from the same breeder. The lady's name was Alice Breely."

"Wow! What a coincidence," Daisy exclaimed. "That's where I went too."

Daisy studied Stephanie. She wanted to find out something to help Millie, even if it was just a tidbit. "You know, you look familiar. I think I saw you at the Buckshead Inn. I remember it was the day before the gala."

Stephanie caressed Peanut. "I was there that day. Peanut slipped her leash, and Grant Stamford found her."

Daisy tapped her hand on her forehead. "You're right. I saw your sister then too, right? Isn't she the one who was murdered at the Inn?" Daisy put her hand over her mouth. "Oops! I guess I shouldn't have mentioned that."

Stephanie avoided looking at her. "Yes. Betsy was found dead outside the spa."

Daisy could feel her face heating up. "I'm sorry. That must have been awful for you."

For a minute there Daisy thought she'd been caught. Lucky for her, Stephanie either didn't read the Houndsville Times or didn't recognize her name. If she had, it would have been a disaster. She would have known Daisy had discovered the body.

Stephanie shrugged as she petted Peanut. "It was terrible."

Daisy tried to think of something else to say, but nothing entered her head. It was good timing when Millie walked over with a tray of three lattes and pupcakes for all the dogs. She placed the tray down on the table in front of the sofa and went to sit, but her cell buzzed.

She wiggled her phone out of her apron pocket and glanced at her screen before answering.

"Hi, Grant. What's up?"

Millie moved away from them, but Daisy could hear her say. "No way! That's not good. Call me as soon as you're done."

Millie ambled back. She perched on one of the chairs facing the sofa and sat. She pointed to the drinks. "They're all mocha lattes. Take one."

"What's going on? Is something wrong with Grant?" Daisy asked.

Millie hesitated. "It's Tucker. He wants to speak to Grant again. It scares me that he's focusing so much on him. This time he asked Grant to come to the police station, and I don't understand why."

Daisy sucked in her breath. Did Stephanie have any idea they were talking about her sister's murder? If so, she seemed totally disinterested and more focused on the dogs, petting all four.

Daisy ran her fingers through her hair. "I could call my sister and see if she knows anything."

Millie patted Daisy's hand. "Nice of you to offer, but I'm sure Hyacinth doesn't know anything. Tucker is very closemouthed. The only thing we can do to help Grant is to find the murderer."

Stephanie put down her latte. Daisy noticed her hands were shaking. "Are you okay?" Daisy asked.

"Not really." Stephanie sniffled and placed Peanut on the floor. "I figured out you were talking about my sister. That's difficult. I'm going to leave."

She put on her jacket, picked up Cleo's and Peanut's leashes, and headed toward the door.

Daisy waited until she was out of sight before she said to Millie, "She sure was in a hurry to get out of here."

"It was like she got spooked by us bringing up her sister's murder." Millie sipped her latte.

"I guess we upset her," Daisy lamented. "We shouldn't have discussed Betsy in front of her."

"Hey Daisy, you got your dogs!" Carolyn hollered as she walked past to deliver a tray of drinks and treats to a group of dogs and humans nearby.

Daisy gave her a thumbs up. "I did. Come over and meet them."

"I'm coming too," Todd said, walking over and bending down to play with the two collies.

Teddy wagged his tail incessantly while Todd petted him. Maddy was a little more aloof, although she did seem to take a liking to Todd when he rubbed her rump.

"Hey Millie, isn't this when Mr. Cordoza was supposed to be here?" Todd asked.

Millie glanced at her watch. "Oh, it's later than I thought. He'll be here soon."

"Who's Mr. Cordoza?" Daisy asked.

"That's Vince. Remember, he's the *Leisurely Living* photographer. I heard rumors about him, and I'm hoping letting him come here to take photos will allow me to question him. He's on my list of possible suspects for Betsy's murder."

Daisy raised an eyebrow. "Why is he a suspect, and how in the world did you convince him to come talk to you?"

Millie grinned. "Getting him here wasn't a problem. Once I promised him he could take photos of the bakery and our patrons, he was a happy guy. When he was here last week to cover the gala, he stopped by the bakery to photograph me since I was chairman of the planning committee. He saw what goes on here and sold his editor on doing a story on the bakery. He was happy to come back to take photos of some of our owners and their pets. She paused. "I'm not sure he had anything to do with Betsy's murder, but she called him a slimeball, and we heard she tried to get him fired. Seems suspicious, and I want to find out why."

"Are your customers okay with him taking photos of them?"

"I made sure to have customers here who I knew wouldn't object. If you look around, you'll see Woody and Peter. An Old English Sheepdog is always good for photos. Judy is here with Danica and Kona and Java. I asked her to dress them in their *The Cat in the Hat* outfits. MaryBeth is here with cutie pie Matisse, and Terri is here with Chally and Scatty. And of course the biggest ham of all is Luke, so we're ready."

The bells jangled and they all turned toward the doorway to see Vince walking in with a camera around his neck. "Hi, Vince." Millie waved. "I'm over here."

Daisy recognized him right away. He was the guy who had photographed her right after she'd found Betsy. She slumped down in the sofa. "Hey Millie, I prefer to avoid him."

"No problem. I'll keep him away from here."

Millie didn't wait for Vince to get to her. She walked to him. "Come on. I'll introduce you to my partners, show you around, and make sure you're aware of the few people who don't want you to photograph them."

They walked from room to room. Vince grinned. "This place is a hoot. I got some great photos. My editor will be thrilled."

"That's great." Millie smiled back. "Can I ask you something?"

"Depends. What about?"

"Betsy Carlson. Did you have a problem with her?"

He fidgeted with his camera, avoiding eye contact. "Maybe. What have you been told?"

"That she was possibly blackmailing you."

Vince frowned. "Who told you that?"

"Never mind. Is it true?" Millie asked.

Vince mumbled something under his breath, but she couldn't make it out. Oh well, it didn't really matter if he was willing to talk to her.

"I have nothing to hide. I'll tell you. She was a bitch. Somehow she found out I used to work for a porn magazine. She threatened to tell the people at *LLM* about it. I was afraid I'd lose my job if they found out, so I gave her a ton of money. Twice. Fortunately I was off the hook when she was murdered."

He slung his camera over his shoulder. "And I took precautions. The Monday after her murder, I contacted my editor, Jim. Told him about my past. I was afraid the cops would find out about Betsy blackmailing me, and I'd be hauled in for questioning. I've been working for *LLM* for two years now and not a hint of me doing anything wrong."

"What happened?" Millie asked.

"He persuaded me to talk to the cops after telling me he wasn't worried about what I did in a past life as long as I delivered for him now."

He continued. "He wanted the scoop on the murder. He told me he was sending a staff writer to Houndsville right away, and he told me to stay here. He wanted to see if I could get some more photos of the murder scene and some of the people involved."

Millie scowled. "So you've been spying on some of us. And did you speak to the cops?"

"I did. They told me to stick around Houndsville in case they had more questions for me, which I was doing anyway." He shrugged.

"Well, now that I've allowed you access to the bakery and you've gotten photos of me and my friends, you need to stop," Millie demanded. "We hated Betsy, but we didn't kill her."

"I got your message loud and clear. You've been fair with me. No more photos of you and your pals. But being a photographer, I see things other people don't. If I see anything amiss I'll call you."

"Thanks. I appreciate that." It appeared Vince was telling her the truth, and Millie was no closer to finding the murderer. Her top suspect was still Mrs. Breely's son, and she had no way to question him.

"One last thing," Vince said. "If it's okay, I'll snap a few more photos before I leave."

Millie nodded. "Just make sure to ask the patrons first if you can photograph them."

"No problem. My focus will be the dogs. This is a dog bakery, after all."

Thirty-seven

Daisy snuggled closer to the warm body next to her. She absently stuck her hand out to pet Max and found a soft belly. She shot up. Of course this wasn't Max. He never slept upside down. She chuckled, seeing four legs hanging in the air. It was Teddy. Okay, this was still good. Very good. He had jumped on the bed to be with her. She raised her head farther, leaning on her elbow. He looked positively lovable upside down with his legs in the air.

She peeked around the bedroom. Maddy was sleeping on one of the dog beds she'd put near the window. She kept hoping that one day soon, she'd join them.

She grabbed her cell from the bedside table and took a photo of Teddy. She texted it to Meghan.

A minute later, her cell dinged.

"Hi, Meghan. Cute photo, right?"

"Adorable. But listen, I called to tell you I have an opening at the spa at noon. Someone cancelled. Come get a facial. Afterward, we can hit the bar at the Inn for lunch."

"Wow! I'd love that. See you then."

Perfect. She had all morning to be with Teddy and Maddy. She fed them and took a long walk around the condo complex. They even spent some time at the doggie park. She still had time to spare before her facial, so she decided she'd leave them in the condo and do some shopping.

Stella's Shoes was her first choice. She certainly didn't need any shoes, but she might end up seeing something she liked. She did—white fur-lined snow boots. She had to have them.

Bridget's Bookstop was next on her list. The bookstore was like a relic from the past, piles of books everywhere in a homey atmosphere with a big old velvet sofa as the centerpiece. Bridget was sifting through some books on a cart.

"Hello, Daisy. What brings you here?" Bridget asked. "Is there a certain title you're looking for?"

Daisy shrugged. "Not really. Just something light. Maybe a contemporary romance."

"There's a new author, Kathy Strobos, whose books have been selling really well. I just read her last one and loved it." Bridget walked over to a table and picked up a copy of *A Scavenger Hunt For Hearts*. She handed it to Daisy.

"I'll take it."

Her mom's store was her last stop. Unfortunately her mom had a sign on her door: "Be back in one hour."

She felt guilty knowing her mom had no one to run the store if she had a delivery. She could offer to help out occasionally. Just not too often. She'd tried working for one parent, and that hadn't worked out so well.

With her purchases in hand, she headed off to the spa. She was excited to have a facial and then have lunch with Meghan.

Meghan greeted her with a hug.

"This will be fun. Go change into one of our plush robes and plan to relax while I perform my magic."

She couldn't wait. She went into the changing room, hung up her clothes, put on the thick white terrycloth robe, and went to turn off her phone but noticed she had a text message.

She frowned. She hadn't heard her cell ping. She tapped on messages. Lisa asked her to call right away. She looked at the time. Uh-oh! She'd texted several hours ago. She had better call.

She tapped on contacts to find her number. "Lisa, it's me. Sorry, I just saw your text. What's up?"

"Daisy, I am so sorry to call you. I know you're in Houndsville relaxing, but my mom had another stroke. I must get back to Boston immediately."

Daisy knew what this meant. Daisy clenched the phone and said, "You need me to take Max?"

"Is there any way you could? I know I'm asking a lot. My flight leaves in three hours. If you can't, I'm going to drop him at any boarding place I can find that has an opening."

Daisy closed her eyes, and all she could see was poor Max being left somewhere, not understanding what was happening to him.

Daisy took a deep breath, trying to control her emotions. Max deserved better than this. "Don't take him anywhere. I'm coming to get him. I can't leave right away, but I will figure this out. Leave your key under my mat. I'll get him, but this time I'm keeping him. You can't keep doing this."

Daisy's declaration was met with silence and then a huge sigh. "Okay. I really have no choice. I know you'll take good care of him. That you'll love him as he deserves." Lisa added, "I'm really sorry to add to your problems, but Max threw up a few times yesterday and then again this morning. I'm not sure why. I was planning to take him to the vet, but now I can't. You might want to take him to one in Houndsville."

Daisy slammed her phone on the bench in the changing room, opened the door, and hollered, "Meghan, I need you."

Meghan stuck her head in the doorway. "What, is the robe too big?"

"No! I have to leave," she said, practically ripping off the robe. "Lisa texted me. Her mom had another stroke. She's flying out to Boston in a couple of hours, and if I don't get Max, she's taking him to any boarder she can find."

She threw on her clothes and grabbed her handbag. "I don't have time to stop at home. I'm going to leave right from here for D.C. Do you think if I'm not back in a few hours you could take care of Teddy and Maddy?"

"I would, but I'm working late. I'll take care of it though. You go ahead. Somehow I'll make sure your dogs are in good hands."

Daisy hugged Meghan. "Thanks. I'll call you when I'm on my way back."

Daisy ran out to her SUV and headed to D.C.

In no time, she'd gone from having zero dogs to having three.

Max, I'm coming. I promise you we'll have a good life together. I even have two friends for you to meet.

Thirty-eight

Two hours later, Daisy had Max and his gear packed up, and they were on the road back to Houndsville.

Daisy called Grant from her SUV. "I have something to tell you."

"You left to pick up Max."

"What? How did you know?"

"Meghan enlisted me to take care of your dogs. They know me. Since I wasn't sure when they were out last, I went and took them out after she called. They'll be fine until you get back."

Daisy beamed. "My dogs. That sounds so good. Hey, I do have a favor to ask. Lisa told me Max threw up a few times yesterday and again this morning. Do you think you could check him out? Make sure he's okay?"

"I'm booked the rest of the afternoon, but the clinic closes at five. Come around five thirty. I'll check him out. I'm sure he'll be fine. We can take him and grab a bite to eat at the Inn. My sister has been bugging me to meet her and Carl for dinner. She'll be thrilled if we walk in together. Afterward, I'll take you home, and Max can meet his new family. It should be an interesting evening."

"Oh, so you want to tease your sister?" She laughed. "Make her think we're dating?"

"Well, we sort of are, right? You're fun to be with, and I love teasing Mil."

Daisy walked up to the clinic door with Max at five-thirty sharp. She rang the buzzer, and Grant opened the door for her. She looked around. "So we're the only ones here?"

"Yes, why?" he asked.

She walked right up to him, dropped Max's leash, flung her arms around his shoulders, and kissed him deeply.

"It's nice to see you too." He chuckled as they split apart and smiled with a lopsided grin that made her feel warm and fuzzy.

Max's bark broke them apart.

"Looks like Max is jealous," Grant murmured. "And you should be more careful. As I pointed out, we're all alone here."

She laughed. "You don't have time to play around. If we're meeting Carl and Millie for dinner, and we're not on time, your sister will be calling to see where we are."

"True enough." He pointed to one of the exam rooms. "Bring Max in here. I'll check him out. See if he has a fever and maybe give you some pills, then we'll leave. We'll be right on time."

Daisy led Max into the room just as the front door buzzer rang.

"Oh, crap. I forgot a client called right before you got here. She was in a panic. Her puppy got into a bag of chocolate raisins. I told her to hurry up and get here. Wait in here. I'll use one of the other exam rooms. I'll most likely have to make the dog vomit, but it doesn't usually take long."

"Okay. I'll be waiting." And in a flirtatious mood, she blew him a kiss.

Grant walked out, leaving the door ajar.

Daisy could hear the front door opening and Grant telling the person, "Hurry up, let's get Peanut to vomit. By the way, where is she? Did you leave her in the car?"

A prickle of fear rose on Daisy's back. Stephanie Carlson? It was her dog that had eaten chocolate raisins? Daisy had a bad feeling about this. She walked closer to the exam room door and snuck a peek, all the while holding on to Max's leash.

It was difficult to see as Stephanie had her back to the exam room, but it appeared Stephanie was walking toward the door. Daisy figured she was going to get Peanut, but then Stephanie locked the door.

"Hey, what are you doing?" Grant asked, sounding exasperated. "Where's Peanut? I need to get her to vomit."

"Forget that. She's fine. All that matters is sooner or later I know you're going to figure out it was me who killed my sister."

What? Daisy froze. Had she heard Stephanie correctly?

Grant's mouth dropped open. "Are you actually saying you killed your sister?"

Daisy clutched the edge of the door with one hand to steady herself as her heart hammered in her chest.

If Stephanie confessed to killing Betsy, that must mean she had a plan for Grant.

"If you're telling me that, you must be planning to kill me too," Grant said loud and clear. He knew something bad was about to happen to him. He'd said that so she'd hear.

He needed help and fast. *Think!* What could she do? *Focus.* All she could come up with was to get to her cell to call for help.

Her legs quivered and her hands shook, but somehow she held on to Max's leash and tiptoed over to the table where she had left her handbag.

She struggled with sweaty hands to wrap Max's leash around the metal exam table leg and laid her hand on his rump. He sat.

She couldn't catch her breath. She had been frightened when she'd found Betsy dead, but this was worse. Much worse. Something bad was about to happen to someone she loved.

Yikes! She loved Grant. She couldn't swallow. She had to save him.

Shuffling in her handbag, she lifted out her cell. She couldn't control her hands. And how would she insure Stephanie didn't hear her is she used her cell?

She glanced around. She needed to hurry. Time was crucial.

A second door, she was sure, led to a bathroom or an office. It was shut. Opening it might alert Stephanie. Not an option.

She stayed.

She heard Stephanie and Grant talking.

He was trying to buy her time.

So far, Stephanie had no idea she was there. That gave her an advantage.

Her body trembled. She slid onto the floor. Max watched her.

She stumbled through the contacts on her cell to find Tucker's name. She could text or call. If she called and he answered she had a better chance of getting help faster.

Her fingers slick with sweat, she tapped in his number and pressed enter.

Tucker answered.

She cupped her hand around the phone and whispered, "Help needed at the vet clinic! ASAP!" Her voice trembled so badly. Did he hear her? Did he understand?

She had to pray he did. She had no choice but to put her phone on vibrate.

She treaded back to the door to listen in. A whisper of a sound from her or Max could mean the end.

Stephanie's back was to her. Daisy watched and listened.

"What made you think I would figure out it was you who murdered your sister?" Grant drew out each word and spoke gently as if prodding her to confide in him.

Daisy kept muttering. "Keep it up, Grant. Keep her talking. I'm sure Tucker is coming."

Stephanie sneered. "Are you an idiot or something? Don't you remember the night of the gala? I called you and told you Peanut was hurt, and I was scared and needed you to check her out. I had just killed my despicable sister and I knew I might need an alibi."

Stephanie giggled.

Daisy cringed. She had to be crazy to giggle at a time like this. She didn't want to miss a word. She put her ear up against the door.

Stephanie talked as if she were in a trance. "I came up with the plan to call you and tell you Peanut was hurt. All I had to do was drive home, pick up Peanut, and bring her to you. I tried not to hurt her too badly. She's a good puppy, but the poor thing cried when I bent her leg."

"By the way, if she didn't eat raisins where is she now?"

That's right, Grant, keep her talking.

"She's home with Cleo. They'll be fine till I get back to them after I'm finished here."

Daisy's stomach plummeted. Stephanie was clearly batshit crazy.

Stephanie waved her hands in the air. "You're such a good veterinarian, you saw that nothing was wrong with Peanut. The problem is you noticed I had a stain on my shirt. You even gave me a cloth to clean it with."

"Of course, now I understand." Grant smacked his head with his hand. "You were afraid I'd figure out the blood wasn't Peanut's. You brought her to me for limping, a possible sprain. The blood was your sister's. And now, stupid me, I fell for the same trick again now."

He shook his head. "I still don't understand why you killed your sister. Sure, she was impossible and a terrible human being, as everyone knew, but why kill her?"

Daisy wrapped her arms around herself to stop the shaking and repeatedly mumbled, "Tucker is on the way." She didn't know how much longer Grant could stall Stephanie. The woman was nuts.

Stephanie's voice became softer and more incoherent. Daisy needed to listen. Grant's life depended on her.

"I guess it won't hurt to tell you why I killed her. You won't be around long enough to tell anyone else."

No! No! Daisy's legs wobbled. It was about to happen. Stephanie would kill Grant if she didn't do something.

What? How?

"So Stephanie, tell me why you killed her."

Stephanie shrugged. "Why not? My parents died one after the other ten years ago. My sister was the executor of the will and thirteen years older than me. She was in charge of my inheritance and me. I was a good kid, always trying to make things easy for her." Stephanie curled her lip. "How do you think she repaid me? I'll tell you.

"I turned twenty-one several months ago. I asked her to give me my inheritance, and she laughed in my face. She told me there was nothing left. That she'd spent it all taking care of me. What a joke! She'd used my money for her own pleasure. I always wondered how she could live such a fancy lifestyle."

The rage that poured out of Stephanie contorted her features. She continued to rant.

"My sister hated Millie. I knew she wouldn't want to hear her speech, so I persuaded her to go outside with me. I planned to threaten her with the knife to give me money, but then she berated me and called me an idiot. She told me I'd never get any money from her. She made me so mad, I stabbed her. I'm glad she's dead."

Daisy's field of vision was minimal, and she'd never seen a gun up close, but she was pretty sure the black thing she saw Stephanie pull out of her jacket pocket was exactly that. It was verified when Grant enunciated clearly.

"Come on, Stephanie. You don't really want to shoot me."

Daisy held herself up by sheer force of will. It was becoming increasingly clear she couldn't wait any longer for Tucker.

Stephanie was prepared to shoot Grant. Daisy would never be able to live if Stephanie killed him.

Grant was smart. He would keep trying to buy time.

What can I do?

She turned around to see if there might be an instrument lying around that could hurt Stephanie.

Nope. Only a computer and several cabinets, which were closed. She couldn't open them anyway. Like the door, they might squeak if opened.

She spotted a spray bottle next to the computer.

What was in it? She tiptoed closer. The label read "Exam table cleaner."

Did that mean it was an ammonia solution? Or something that would burn a person's eyes?

What if she could get close enough to Stephanie to spray it into her eyes and somehow grab the gun?

She gulped.

For now, it was all she had. She was going to go with it.

She knew she had to move fast. To catch Stephanie off guard. She took what she thought was the deepest breath she'd ever taken in her life.

She would have only one chance to get this right.

She stole a glance at Max, who was sitting quietly. It was like he knew to sit still.

It hit her in her stomach, hard. This might be the last time she saw him.

She tiptoed back over to him. She shouldn't take the time to hug him, but if she was going to die, she was going to tell him she loved him.

She buried her nose in his fur, whispered for him to stay, and told him, "I love you."

She had to be strong. Her life and Grant's demanded no less.

She picked up her handbag and the spray bottle, which slipped out of her sweaty hand and flew in the air.

She reached out and nabbed it before it hit the floor. She swiped at the sweat pouring off her forehead, but with time running out, she placed the bottle with its sprayer sticking out just inside her handbag in a position she prayed she'd be able to access quickly.

One last deep breath and she walked out of the exam room pretending no one was there but her and Grant. This had to be her best performance ever.

"Geez, I'm sorry Grant. You probably wondered why I was in the bathroom so long. My stomach is a mess. I'm going to head ho—oops." She laughed as she walked toward Stephanie, keeping out of her line of sight. "I didn't know anyone was here. I thought we were alone."

Stephanie flipped around, gun in her hand.

Daisy was ready. She already had her hand on the spray bottle. She pulled it from her handbag and zapped Stephanie in the eyes.

Stephanie shrieked. "What did you do?" and at the same time she waved the gun in the air.

It fired off a deafening sound, momentarily distracting Stephanie and giving Daisy an extra second to push her backward with all her strength.

Grant grabbed for the gun. The three of them ended up in a tangled heap on the floor. At that moment the front door splintered. Tucker jumped into the room, followed by two officers.

Someone yelled, "Freeze! Police!"

"Ugh!" Stephanie raised her head and then plopped it back on the floor.

Daisy rolled over and lay on her back next to Grant, catching her breath. He reached over and squeezed her hand. She lay motionless, eyes closed. After a minute, Grant pulled her into a sitting position with her back against his chest. "I've got you. We're safe."

She leaned into him, feeling his rapidly beating heart. "Oh, no! I left Max tied up in the exam room. He's probably scared to death."

Thirty-nine

"What the heck happened to you two?" Millie sat up straighter. "Did you get in a fight with someone? Hey, wait a minute, what's Max doing here?"

"We'll explain about Max later. Actually, we were in a fight for our lives." Grant hugged Daisy tighter to his side.

Millie frowned." What are you talking about?"

Carl put his hand over Millie's. "Mil, let them sit before you start quizzing them."

Grant pulled the chair out for Daisy, made sure she and Max were settled, and then sat next to her, holding on to her hand.

She squeezed his hand tight, just thankful he was alive and here with her. "Do you want to tell your sister what happened, or should I?"

Grant sighed. "You should. She can't be angry with you when she hears she missed out on catching Betsy's killer."

"What! Stop kidding around. Get serious."

"He is serious." Daisy glanced from Carl to Millie. "We were at the clinic with Max when—"

"Do you mean Teddy?" Millie interrupted, looking confused.

"No, it was Max," Daisy said. "But that's not important now. Again, I'll explain later."

She squeezed Grant's hand tighter.

"Anyway, we were at the clinic when Stephanie came in. Grant had forgotten to tell me she was coming. That turned out to be what probably saved our lives. She came there to kill Grant. She had it all planned out."

Millie's face drained of all its color. "What? Why?"

Daisy sighed. "Give me a chance. I'm getting there." She continued. "She convinced herself Grant would figure out she had murdered her sister. Lucky for us she wanted to explain herself before she killed him. She had no idea I was in an exam room, which gave me time to call Tucker.

Carl looked shocked. "She really is off her rocker."

"Yup," Grant replied.

"How did you end up getting so messed up?" Millie asked.

Daisy swallowed hard. Picturing Stephanie pointing a gun first at Grant and then at her had her trembling from head to toe. Grant dragged her chair closer to him and put his arm around her shoulders.

She wanted to get this over with. "Stephanie pulled out a gun to shoot Grant. I couldn't let that happen without a fight."

"Gun! Did you say she had a gun?" Millie shrieked.

"She did, and you should have seen Daisy." Grant's eyes shined at her. "It was quite the spectacle. She confronted Stephanie, and before she fired her gun Daisy spritzed her eyes with whatever cleaner they use for the exam tables. It blinded Stephanie just long enough so I was able to grab the gun."

Daisy nodded solemnly. "Grant wrestled it from Stephanie just as Tucker arrived on the scene. The good news is we won't have to worry about Stephanie anymore. She'll be in prison for a long time to come."

Grant ran his fingers through his hair. "I wish I hadn't been so stupid as to fall for her ruse—and I did, twice. The first time was when she told me Peanut was hurt. That time, she needed to establish an alibi. And tonight, I fell for her telling me Peanut ate some chocolate raisins. She knew I'd want to see Peanut right away."

Millie threw her hands in the air. "This is all so unbelievable. I hate to ask. Is Peanut all right?"

"As far as we know, she's fine. Saying she had eaten raisins was just another one of Stephanie's lies."

"But I still don't understand what made her think Grant would know she killed her sister."

"Can we get something to drink first?" Daisy said.

"Sorry, of course." Carl waved to a passing waitress. Daisy ordered a glass of sauvignon blanc, Grant ordered a Johnny Walker Black neat, Carl the same, and Millie wanted a spicy Bloody Mary.

Daisy stopped to lay her head on Grant's shoulder. "You explain the rest."

"Okay. Go back to the night of the gala. After Stephanie killed her sister, she knew she'd need an alibi. Remember, she's crazy, so for some unknown reason, her plan was to hurt Peanut and call me to check her out. If she ever got called in for questioning, she planned to say she was with me at the clinic.

"That night when she brought Peanut in, I noticed a red stain on her shirt and offered her a wet towel to clean it up. She was smart enough not to panic. No one knew Betsy was dead. In her head, she was safe."

He looked at Daisy. "Daisy and I talked about it on the way here. We wondered what changed all of a sudden to make her decide to kill me. We figured it was when she was at the bakery and she overheard you telling Daisy I had to go to the police station to talk to Tucker. At that point, she no longer felt safe. That darn blood stain was her undoing. She brought Peanut in for a supposed strain that turned out to be bogus, and if I remembered the stain on her shirt, I might realize it was her sister's and she had killed her using me as her alibi. It's a stretch, but in her crazed mind, it all fit. Her only way to save herself was to kill me too." He sighed. "She's unhinged."

Daisy lifted her head. Grant's eye was turning purple. "You would never have suspected her of hurting her dog and killing her sister. That was her mistake. You're a very caring and concerned person, and you were only trying to help her. That's only one reason why I lo…like you."

Her face grew increasingly warm as Millie gawked at her. Grant and Carl did too. Then Carl burst out laughing.

"Sorry guys, I shouldn't be laughing after what happened to you, but Millie will be happy to add you two to her list of matchmaking successes."

Daisy stole a glance at Millie, who was beaming.

She faked a yawn." Grant, you can explain about Max to your sister tomorrow. I desperately need a shower and some sleep. Can you drive us home?"

Grant glanced at Daisy as he drove to her condo. "You were awesome. How did you come up with the idea to spray her in the eyes?"

"It was pretty much the only thing in the room," Daisy answered. "But you were pretty amazing yourself, keeping Stephanie talking. That's what gave me time to call Tucker and come up with a plan."

She shivered. "I still have a hard time imagining her stabbing someone, no less her sister."

"I know. Listen, we're almost to the condo. When you get there, you should call your parents and your sister. News about this will travel fast, and they all need to hear from you. To know you're safe."

Daisy took a quick peek at her watch. "It's early enough. I will."

Grant pulled into a parking space. "Come on. I'll walk you to your condo."

He opened the passenger side door and held her hand as they walked into the building and rode the elevator up to the fifth floor.

They stood outside her door. She dropped Max's leash, reached up, and cupped Grant's head in her hands and kissed him gently. He gazed into her eyes, put his hands over hers, and kissed her passionately. She wasn't about to let go. She wanted more.

She slid the key in the lock and pushed open the door.

Teddy jumped up to greet her, and Maddy stood behind him. Max stood still.

"Oops, I can't believe I forgot Max needs to meet his new family."

Grant smiled and kissed her lightly. "You have a lot to handle here. I'm going to head home. Besides, Tucker has asked to see us early tomorrow to go over everything. We'll continue where we left off soon."

Forty

Grant and Daisy looked at each other and at the small brick building in front of them. Daisy took a deep breath. The worst was over. Betsy's murder had been solved, and Stephanie was in jail, yet she still felt jittery.

"Let's get this over with," Grant said, taking Daisy's hand and walking to the door of the police station. He held it open for her, and she proceeded to the front counter where an officer asked, "May I help you?"

"Yes, we're here to see Detective Hartley."

He nodded. "Tucker told me he expected two people this morning. I don't understand. There are two already here."

Daisy frowned. "Two others. Who could that be?" She looked at Grant.

He shrugged. "I have no idea."

"Guess we'll find out. I bet it's your sister and Carl. Maybe they thought we'd need some support."

The officer walked out from behind the counter. "Follow me. I'll take you to Detective Hartley. He can figure out what he wants." He ushered them down the hallway and to the right.

Officer Dudley, as his name tag identified him, rapped on a partially open door.

Tucker was seated behind his desk, and seated near the window in two chairs were her dad and Edward.

She looked awkwardly from one to the other. Her dad rushed over to hug her. "After you called about stopping a murderer, I needed to see for myself that you were okay."

She threw her arms around her dad, hugging him. "It means a lot that you're here."

Edward's eyes roamed over her from head to toe. "So does it mean a lot that I'm here too?" he asked in his usual mocking tone.

Her face grew warm under his scrutiny, especially with Grant standing next to her.

She looked at him wide-eyed. "Of course it does." And it did. She couldn't help herself. He'd always have a place in her heart.

If Grant hadn't been standing there she would have hugged Edward too, but the hurt expression on Grant's face stopped her.

How was she supposed to handle having these two guys focused on her? She swallowed past the big lump forming in her throat and stood there waiting for someone to say something—anything.

"Tucker, do you think we could get started? I'm needed at the clinic," Grant said, walking over and sitting in one of two chairs across from Tucker's desk.

Daisy frowned. He was going to the clinic after this? They'd had plans to go to brunch. Had that changed?

She couldn't blame him if it had, yet she felt sad. He wasn't the type to stand around while Edward tried to usurp all her attention.

"Yes, we can start." Tucker opened a file folder on his desk. "I asked you here so we could go over some details, and so I could answer any questions you may have. You deserve that."

Daisy walked over to sit next to Grant.

"Thank you," Grant said. "But first, can you tell me about Peanut and Cleo?"

Tucker nodded. "After I arrested Stephanie, she told me about the dogs being alone in her apartment. She was worried about them and wanted to make sure they'd be okay. I sent my officers to her apartment to pick them up."

"I'm glad to hear that," Grant said.

"My understanding is that the big collie was Betsy's. The puppy was Stephanie's. My officers, under my authority, brought them here. I could have sent them to the Humane Society or called Millie. I know she's involved with rescue, but I made an unprecedented decision."

He drummed his fingers on his desk. "I snuck them home with me."

Grant smiled. "I'm Peanut's vet. I can't imagine anyone else knows she even exists. As to Cleo, I have no idea who Betsy used as her vet, but knowing Betsy no one will miss her as a client. I just want the dogs to be safe."

Tucker linked his hands together. "Thanks. I've always wanted a dog. Looks like these two are staying with me."

"I'll be happy to be your vet," Grant added.

"I have other news. We spoke to Mrs. Breely and told her she had a choice. Either give her dogs to rescue, or we're going to prosecute her. She agreed to our proposal but not without great trepidation. She was clearly upset and insisted she loved her dogs."

"Poor woman," Grant said. "She doesn't understand that love alone is not enough. She's had a tough time since her husband died."

MUTTS MURDER AND MAYHEM

"Well, we came to an agreement. We've allowed her to keep two dogs and a humongous silver-brown, striped cat for herself with her promise she would get them either neutered or spayed."

Tucker looked straight at Grant. "I hope you don't mind, but I told her you would be her vet going forward and will see that her dogs are well cared for. I figured you'd like knowing they were okay."

"That's the perfect outcome for everyone," Grant agreed. "Mrs. Breely clearly loves her dogs. Getting old and having to give up your dogs can be devastating. I can understand that. This way everyone wins."

Grant looked at Daisy. "I told you we'd make sure all the dogs were taken care of."

Tucker glanced at his watch. "I have a meeting in ten minutes, so let's talk about Stephanie. I realize you know what I'm about to say, but I'm sure your dad and your friend would like to hear it all."

Daisy squeezed Grant's hand. She held it tight and refused to even glance at Edward. Whatever he was thinking, she would rather not know.

Tucker took a deep breath. "No surprise. Stephanie confessed to killing her sister. Her plan was to only threaten her with the knife, but it all went bad when Betsy called her a dumb idiot and laughed in her face. Enraged, she stabbed her in a moment of passion. Once Betsy was dead, in order to establish an alibi, Stephanie called Grant and told him Peanut was badly hurt, and she needed him to check her out for a sprain."

Tucker focused on Grant. "She talked about the day she met you for the first time at the Inn, how gentle you were with Peanut, how kind you were to her. I imagine she didn't have much of that in her life, so in her mind you were a good guy who would help her. Maybe even lie for her."

Daisy shivered as she listened to Tucker.

"She sobbed when she told us about harming Peanut and again when she told us about planning to kill you. No doubt, her sister turned her into a nutcase. This story is truly sad."

He continued. "To backtrack a bit, after Annabel Larson reported seeing you leave the Inn and insisted I haul you in for Betsy's murder, I questioned you again. I wasn't aware that you had left the gala to go to the clinic. You never mentioned it when I questioned you that first night. You had no reason to know it was important."

Tucker leaned forward. "After that, I called Stephanie in for questioning. I wanted to verify your story. I was still considering you my prime suspect, and I needed to establish a timeline where you had time to murder Betsy and still get to the clinic. She wasn't helpful at all. She said she didn't remember the time she saw you, she was too scared for her puppy. At that point, I should have wondered why she was so vague and considered her a suspect. My mistake, and almost a deadly one. I'm sorry for that."

"She truly is crazy," Daisy mumbled.

"Yes," Tucker said. "She made lots of mistakes, but her fatal one was trusting that yesterday Grant would be alone at the clinic."

He glanced at Daisy. "If not for your quick thinking, Grant most likely would have died."

She grabbed Grant's hand and tried to make light of her actions. "Glad I was there to help out." At this point, she just wanted Tucker to finish. To get his explanations done and over.

"You were brilliant." Tucker closed the file on his desk. "Now, are there any questions? If not, you're free to leave."

Grant stood and held out his hand for Daisy. He looped his arm around her shoulders and kissed the top of her head.

"I need to get to the clinic. I'll talk to you later."

"Come on, Daisy," her dad suggested. "Let's get lunch before Edward and I head back to D.C."

Later that night Daisy stood looking out the condo window at the inlet below. All three collies sat nearby.

A full moon and the light from the gaslights around the inlet cast a glow on the myriad boats moored to their docks. From here, she could see that Allan's development was still in its infancy, and for a fleeting moment, she wondered how she would have made out working for him.

As she took in the serene scene below, she thought about what had happened this day. It had been a whirlwind of emotions.

Her dad showing up had been wonderful. Edward's presence meant they were on the track to becoming friends once again.

As to lunch at the Inn, it was a mixed bag. On the one hand, Daisy had been glad to be with Edward and her dad although she had missed being with Grant. Her dad never pressured her to tell him what she had planned for her future.

She informed him she was staying in Houndsville. Her plan was to take her time to figure out what she wanted to do with her career. In the meantime, she would help out at her mom's shop. She told him she wasn't ready to give up on the law, but she did know she felt much better not being under pressure every day.

For his part, Edward was unusually quiet and just listened to her and her dad. It made her sad he wasn't his usual kidding self, but when it was time to say goodbye, he hugged her and told her she may be out of sight but not out of mind.

She felt the same, although she was quiet about it. She admitted to herself she still wanted him in her life.

Grant appeared to want to have a romantic relationship with her. She thought about the few brief kisses she had shared with him and knew she wanted more. She'd have to leave it at that for now.

She started off to her bedroom, but out of the corner of her eye, she caught sight of a familiar truck driving into the parking area. She held her breath, watching intently to see what happened next. To see if she was correct.

A tall dark-headed figure got out of the vehicle and looked up at her window. Grant couldn't see her, but she saw him clearly.

She thought about throwing on a coat and running out to meet him, but then she realized they might cross elevators. She looked down at her apparel—jammies with dogs on them. Oh, what the heck. Nothing she could do about it. It was the longest minute of her life, but she waited for the knock on her door. It came. She opened the door and jumped into his open arms.

Life was good, and there would be more to come.

Hug your dog, today and every day.

Acknowledgments

Wow! Another book on its way to press and thanks go to the people who helped me get there.

First off, what's a book without a title. Thanks go to MaryBeth Jones for coming up with a great one.

Thanks to my editors Emily Poole and Judy Roth.

A special thanks to Kathy Strobos, a wonderful author, who I'm lucky to have as my critique partner.

And most of all thanks to my husband, my love, who supports me in this endeavor. Without you, none of this would be possible.

Luke's Hideaway Cookies

4 extra large eggs

½ heaping cup of oats

½ cup coconut flour

1 teaspoon vanilla

1 teaspoon baking powder

¼ cup yogurt

- Beat the eggs and then mix with the vanilla and baking powder. Add the oats and flour and yogurt and beat until smooth.

- Chill the dough for one hour.

- I use a muffin pan with mini baking cups because I want to make the cookies small. You could use larger baking cups, but then your baking time would differ from mine.

- Take a spoonful of dough and roll it into a ball. Place the ball in the baking cup and press to make an indentation in the center of the cookie. I filled the hole with a small piece of a strawberry. You could use cheese, bacon, peanut butter or any other dog appropriate food cut into small pieces.

- Bake for 10 minutes at 375 degrees.

Also by Ellen Gilman:

Mollie's Tail

The Best Doggone Bakery

Fur-Ever in Her Heart

For more information visit my website
EllenGilman.com